"No, Brock! I'm not going with you. I'm not going to marry you."

"Why not?" he demanded.

"I don't like you!"

He caught her shoulders. Hard, too hard. "What does that have to do with it?" He scooped her up in his arms, turned to the door and carried her down the narrow hall.

She *would* marry him. It was the only way out of this, the only way he could see to get through it, for both of them. He carried her across the threshold, kicked the door shut behind him and carried her outside to the car.

"Put me down! Brock, damn you, put me down! I'm in my nightgown. I'm pregnant!"

She was fighting him, of course. He had expected it. But he was going to marry her whether she liked it or not....

Dear Reader,

Many of you love the miniseries that we do in Intimate Moments, and this month we've got three of them for you. First up is *Duncan's Lady*, by Emilie Richards. Duncan is the first of "The Men of Midnight," and his story will leave you hungering to meet the other two. Another first is *A Man Without Love*, one of the "Wounded Warriors" created by Beverly Bird. Beverly was one of the line's debut authors, and we're thrilled to have her back. Then there's a goodbye, because in *A Man Like Smith*, bestselling author Marilyn Pappano has come to the end of her "Southern Knights" trilogy. But what a fantastic farewell—and, of course, Marilyn herself will be back soon!

You won't want to miss the month's other offerings, either. In *His Best Friend's Wife*, Catherine Palmer has created a level of emotion and tension that will have you turning pages as fast as you can. In *Dillon's Reckoning*, award-winner Dee Holmes sends her hero and heroine on the trail of a missing baby, while Cathryn Clare's *Gunslinger's Child* features one of romance's most popular storylines, the "secret baby" plot.

Enjoy them all—and come back next month for more top-notch romantic reading…only from Silhouette Intimate Moments.

Yours,
Leslie Wainger
Senior Editor and Editorial Coordinator

Please address questions and book requests to:
Silhouette Reader Service
U.S.: 3010 Walden Ave., P.O. Box 1325, Buffalo, NY 14269
Canadian: P.O. Box 609, Fort Erie, Ont. L2A 5X3

HIS BEST FRIEND'S WIFE

CATHERINE PALMER

INTIMATE MOMENTS

Published by Silhouette Books

America's Publisher of Contemporary Romance

SILHOUETTE BOOKS

ISBN 0-373-07627-4

HIS BEST FRIEND'S WIFE

Copyright © 1995 by Catherine Palmer

Printed in U.S.A.

Books by Catherine Palmer

Silhouette Intimate Moments

CATHERINE PALMER

loves creating stories with locales and backgrounds that are as exotic and diverse as the ones she grew up in herself—and as the daughter of missionaries, she's been to quite a few places! One of the most exotic—Kenya, Africa—brings back fond memories of living on a 19,000 acre cattle ranch and thrilling to the sight of wonderful animals such as gazelles, lions and giraffes.

She now resides in Missouri, with her husband and their young sons, and between writing, being a member of the RWA and her interest in art, she is kept very busy. Though her first joys are her family and her writing, she also enjoys crafts, tennis and swimming.

For my three best friends—
Tim, Geoffrey and Andrei

Chapter 1

"I'm going to marry you, Mara."

"What?" The word didn't make a sound. "What...?"

He placed a finger on her lips. "Marry me, and I'll give Todd's baby a home, money, medical care—whatever you need. Both of you. I'll pay the bills, the insurance premiums, the creditors. I'll put the baby in my will. I'll do everything. Whatever you want."

"You're insane."

Balanced on a scale in her tiny bathroom, Mara gaped at the man beside her. Brock Barnett looked as he always had. Six feet, four inches tall. Two hundred pounds. Black hat. Black hair. Gray shirt. Wrangler jeans a little worn at the knees. Black boots. Nothing about him had changed.

He even acted the same. Moments ago, he had barged into her apartment demanding to know why she hadn't told him about her pregnancy. When she mentioned her trouble seeing over her stomach to weigh herself, he had propelled her into the bathroom and onto the scale.

"I went to the county clerk's office this morning to see about the license," he continued. "I've already been to the lab for my blood test. Now all we have to do is get yours, and we're set."

"But that's . . . that's—"

"I'll manage Todd's company until we find a buyer," he cut in. "I've already told the Bureau of Land Management. They said the restoration project has been on hold while they iron out the legal details of Todd's contract. I told the project director I'd find capable people to do the work."

"In Las Cruces, New Mexico?" she cut in, suddenly furious at his cocky self-confidence. "You think you can find somebody around here with the experience to run a historic restoration company?"

"Anything's possible." His brown eyes, like dark wet oak, searched her face.

"You're crazy. Get out of my bathroom."

"The moving company's set a date to box up your stuff. You can live in the west wing of the ranch house. There's a room for the baby, and you can use the Lincoln—I'm always in either the pickup or the Jag. We'll fence the swimming pool, and I thought we could turn the weight room into an indoor playground with a seesaw and one of those nifty little—"

"Brock!" Mara pushed his chest. It felt like a granite bluff. "Stop talking. You're rambling. You're scaring me."

"Scaring you?"

"I'm not going anywhere. This apartment is my home. This is where Todd and I . . . we . . ." She couldn't start crying. Not in front of this man. She had the horrible realization she might want him to hold her. "Just move, so I can get off this scale."

"I'm not going anywhere until you listen to me."

"You can't trap me in my own bathroom!"

"Looks like I did." He gave her a smile more tender than cocky. "Come on, Mara. Hear me out."

"I heard you, Brock. You're nuts."

He propped one booted foot on the edge of the bathtub beside a romance novel she had been reading, and then he lifted his eyes to Mara's face. "You'd give up the chance at a brand-new car?"

"Of course I would."

"How about a big house with two maids and a French chef?"

"Forget it. Look, I told you—"

"Free medical care?"

"I can take care of... I can get help." She searched for an escape, just as she had every day in the past months. Only blunt reality emerged—haunting her, nipping at her heels like a hungry wolf. Orphaned at six, she had been raised in foster homes until she turned eighteen. Now ten years older and a widow, she rejected the idea of welfare—but she tossed it out at Brock anyway. "The government. They have programs, you know."

"You'd give up life insurance? Health insurance? The best medical care money can buy for you and the baby?"

"Oh, Brock, don't be so..." She couldn't finish. What was he? Irrational, ridiculous? A taunting, tempting devil?

"How about a college fund? I can send your son to Harvard, Mara."

"Harv—" She caught herself and stared at him. Who could think of college? "But he's not even born yet. And how do you know it's a boy?"

"Boy or girl, that kid's going to grow up. He'll need things—clothes, toys, education, summer camp, a car. I'll make you the beneficiary of my estate. Both of you—you as my wife and the baby as my child."

She drew back and wrapped her arms around her middle. Everything unbearable that had happened in the past five months grew out of this man. "This baby will *never* be yours!"

He sucked in a breath at her vehemence. "Look, I am the baby's godfather. Todd wanted me to be."

"Who told you that?"

"Your friend, Sherry Stevens. We met at your wedding. I saw her again at Todd's funeral, and I've called a few times to check on you. She let it slip this morning that you were pregnant." His eyes went dark. "And she told me Todd wanted me to be the godfather. You'll honor that wish. I know you will."

Furious at her own best friend's betrayal, Mara lashed out. "You're trying to tempt me just so I'll release you from your guilt."

"Bull!" He lowered his head until his mouth was an inch from hers. "That is bull!"

"You think you can walk out of this with a clear conscience."

"Never." He fought the fist that formed in his throat. "If you think I can escape living with this for the rest of my life, you're the one who's crazy. Todd was my best friend."

"My husband!"

"I *know!*" His voice boomed off the tiled walls in the tiny bathroom.

For a moment Mara thought she saw the ropes that held him in control snap. He stared, breathing like a locomotive, eyes of heated bronze. And then he leashed the anger, visibly took it, folded it and stuffed it away. His brown eyes turned to wet oak again; his black lashes dropped like fallen fans across his cheeks.

"I know he was your husband," he whispered.

Mara bit her lower lip as she watched pain write messages across his face. For the first time in all of this, she felt the urge to reach out, to comfort, to console. But it was him! Him!

"Mara," he said, eyes on the bathtub. "I'm not trying to buy you off. I'm doing what I can to honor Todd and take care of the people he loved."

Her shoulders sagged as the breath left her chest. "Oh, Brock, I'll be all right."

"You'll be better than all right with me for a husband." He set his hands on his hips. Mara Rosemond looked as beautiful as he remembered. Soft, straight blond hair brushed her shoulders. Set above high cheekbones, her gray-green eyes tilted up at the corners. Pale pink lips had always curved easily into a smile. She wasn't smiling now. "Come on, let's go get that blood test."

"No."

"Yes, Mara."

"No!" She grabbed his sleeves and twisted them in her fingers. "No, Brock! I'm not going with you. I'm not going to marry you."

"Why not?" he demanded.

"Because it's...you're.. I don't want to marry you!"

"Yes, you do."

"I don't like you!"

He caught her shoulders. "What does that have to do with it?"

"It's your fault! Your fault!"

"Damn it, Mara, don't make me—"

"I hate you! I hate—"

He scooped her up in his arms, turned to the door and carried her down the narrow hall. "What?" she cried out. "What?"

He couldn't answer. Didn't care. She would marry him. It was the only way he could see to get through this, for both of them. He carried her across the threshold and kicked the door shut behind him.

"You didn't lock—" She twisted in his arms, her bare feet flying, kicking. "My stuff, my things—"

"I'll buy you new stuff."

"I don't want your money! Put me down. Brock, damn you, put me down! I'm in my nightgown. I'm pregnant!"

At the Jag, he cocked one leg and balanced her bottom on his knee as he jerked open the door. She fought him, of course. He had expected it. He set her on the low seat and grabbed the seat belt. As he fastened it around her swollen stomach, she hammered his back with her fists.

"Just a blood test, Mara!" he growled, snapping the buckle. "You can have the next two days to try to talk me out of the marriage."

By the time she could respond, he had slammed her door, opened his, climbed inside and started the engine. He managed to drown her words as he gunned the Jag out of the parking lot.

"Coming through!" With his shoulder, Brock pushed open the door to the clinic and carried Mara inside. "Head me toward the lab."

The waiting room erupted with cries of surprise, dropped magazines, a scramble of children. The receptionist gawked. A nurse threw open the door to the examination section of the clinic.

"Sir—you need to take your wife to ER at the hospital. The obstetrics unit can take care of her. We're not equipped—"

"You have a lab, don't you?" He frowned in bewilderment for a moment, his concentration taken up with Mara. In his arms, she felt like a block of ice, frozen, clenching her teeth, fists, knees. "I came here first thing this morning. Had a blood test in the back."

"Is this an emergency, sir?" The nurse attempted to keep her voice low. "Has her water broken?"

"Water? No, it's blood—"

"Blood? She shouldn't be miscarrying at this stage!" She touched Mara's arm. "Ma'am, can you tell me when you began to feel contractions and how often—"

"We need a blood test," Brock interrupted, his voice loud. "We want to get married."

The commotion in the room evaporated. The nurse's face drained of color. "Oh." She pursed her lips. "I see."

Brock squared his shoulders. "Just give us that little twenty-dollar blood test so we can sign the marriage license."

The nurse leaned toward Mara. "Ma'am, are you all right?"

Eyes shut, Mara couldn't respond. All the way across Las Cruces the clenching intensity had built—a spasm in her back, a hard band across her womb. Brock had been unaware, of course.

For the last two months she had been plagued by false labor. Though she took medication, each time a contraction began, she worried. What if her water broke? What if the baby came? It was too early!

Now she knew vaguely they were in a clinic somewhere. A nurse asked questions. Brock rambled as the contraction began to slink away like a naughty child. It left her legs, then released its hold on her abdomen. She let out a breath.

At the comforting motion of Brock's stride, a scent drifted around her head. Clean, starched denim and leather. She allowed her head to roll against his arm, sensing the contracted muscle against her cheek. This arm felt strong enough, more than strong enough.

"You're sure about this?" The lab technician eyed Brock.

"We're sure," he announced as he laid Mara on an examining table.

The technician looked at Mara for confirmation. "Are you feeling all right? A physician could speak with you, if you'd like, Miss Rosemond."

"*Mrs.* Rosemond," Mara corrected her softly. "I'm married."

"Oh, but I thought…you were going to…with him…"

"My husband died."

"I'm so sorry. We have counseling services here, Mrs. Rosemond."

"She doesn't need counseling," Brock cut in. "She needs a blood test."

"I'm concerned about her mental and physical condition, sir."

"She's been through hell, ma'am. What do you expect? Mara…" He laid his hand on her shoulder. "Mara, are you okay?"

"I'm waiting for the next one."

The lab technician caught her breath. "Contractions… She's in labor!"

"No, I'm not," Mara said calmly.

"Take her blood," Brock bellowed. "I've got to marry the woman before this baby gets here. Do it. Now."

The technician tied Mara's arm and flicked the tender skin inside her elbow. In a moment the needle stabbed into her vein. Mara squeezed her eyes shut. *Here we go again.* The place in her back began to knot.

"Done!" the technician announced, removing the needle. "You may sit up now, Mrs. Barnett . . . Rosemond."

Mara bit the inside of her cheek. The contraction hammered through her pelvis. She reached out and found a hand. She squeezed, dug her fingers into flesh. Breathe, breathe, breathe.

"Mara, Mara!" The voice at her ear sent a trickle of calm down her spine. "Easy now, Mara."

The hammering began to shrink into a gentle thud, the sound of her own heart. She could hear in snatches. "Eight months . . . widowed . . . fell off a cliff . . . marry me . . . blood . . . Barnett . . ."

Another voice. "When was the last? . . . stay with her . . . delivery . . ." A bright light flipped on overhead. "Mara, I'm going to check you now . . ."

She gripped the fingers she held, felt cool lips on her forehead, her hair. The constriction crept from her stomach into her back where it held on for a moment. Then it vanished.

"Mrs. Rosemond?" A face appeared in the space above her head. An old man with white eyebrows drifting off the sides of his face. "I'm Dr. Brasham. Delivered hundreds of babies. When was your last contraction?"

"The car," she managed.

"In the car!" Brock Barnett's face emerged, eyes flashing gold sparks.

"How long ago? Ten minutes, would you say?"

"Maybe . . . seven."

The doctor frowned. "Any contractions before the one in the car?"

"It's false labor . . . Braxton Hicks contractions. I'm taking ritodrine."

The doctor regarded her for a minute, his eyebrows like angel's wings. "I think perhaps . . . not this time. You're dilated to three."

"Three!" Her gasp brought her back to reality.

"Would you like to rest here at the clinic while I contact the hospital? I think you're going to have a baby—you and your . . . fiancé."

Chapter 2

Brock sat on a low stool beside the examining table, Mara's fingers clenching his. The doctor and two nurses hovered around her, taking her temperature and blood pressure, asking questions, checking everything. She was counting on him, and he knew it.

A strand of her hair draped over the table. He studied it, wondering at the natural curl that turned up the end of each yellow-gold thread. Above him, her stomach was canopied in a white sheet that rose like an alpine mountain in winter. Surely the mound beneath it wasn't all baby.

But it was. And that baby intended to be born.

As the certainty socked him full force, Brock's hands went damp. He hadn't planned this part. On learning about the pregnancy, he'd mentally outlined everything. He would cover Mara's insurance premium until after the baby came, then he would register her and the child on his own policy.

The Bureau of Land Management didn't like his plan to continue the restoration company. But the BLM had its hands full coordinating private land owners and state and federal agencies managing the seven forts. Protection and preservation was their priority. Restoration was a luxury made possible only through funding by private foundations. The cost of reopening bids and hiring an out-of-state firm would be prohibitive.

Brock had covered all the bases, even in his own house. His maids aired out the west wing and put fresh linens on the beds. The French chef planned menus. Brock bought a crib that now waited like an empty sentry box for pink fingers and tiny toes…a little rosebud mouth…a wisp of hair….

Lord have mercy! He hadn't thought about the actual baby. This had been a project to tackle and put in order. But there lay Mara with her round stomach, and her hand gripping his….

"Get this woman to the hospital!" he commanded the doctor. "Get a move on, here."

Dr. Brasham laid a hand on Brock's shoulder. "Babies are unpredictable, Mr. Barnett. Mara hasn't had a contraction for some time. True labor involves regular contractions that dilate the cervix. We'll leave you here for a half hour, and if your labor continues, Mara, we'll send you to the hospital to check in."

She nodded as the doctor and nurses left the room. From across the room, Brock watched her place both hands on her abdomen and run them gently around the dome of her baby. The gold wedding band Todd had given her shone in the soft light.

Brock studied her carefully. He didn't know the first thing about fatherhood or marriage. His parents divorced when he was ten, and his mother took his sister east. Brock grew up on his father's ranch with horses for company and oil pumpjacks setting the rhythm of his life. Carpentry fascinated him. Even now he worked in his shop every evening.

But you couldn't call horses, books, adzes and lathes a family. You couldn't call housekeepers and ranch hands a family. No, Brock didn't have a clue how to be part of a family.

Well, Mara could take care of the baby herself. It was her baby, after all. Hers and Todd's. Brock had nothing invested in the whole process except the responsibility to provide the child's basic financial needs. That, he could do.

"I want to go home," Mara said softly. Her voice brought Brock back to focus. "I'm tired."

She turned her head to see Brock around the side of her stomach. He was leaning against the bunny-and-carrot-strewn wall, his brawny arms folded across his chest, his Stetson pushed down on his brow and his usual swarthy tan faded. Well, what do you know? The man was shaken up.

Good. Mr. Fearless Confidence deserved a little anxiety. Someone needed to teach Brock Barnett he didn't control the world. Those broad shoulders visibly announced the man who bore them as a tough, stubborn bull. Mara had to smile. Leave it to a tiny, fragile, unborn baby to throw the old bull off-kilter.

"Oh, Brock, when the doctor does that episiotomy," she said, sprinkling a dose of concern into her sigh. "I don't know how I'll be able to endure the pain...the contractions...the pushing. The baby is already so big, but without the episiotomy I might tear, and then the stitches will be that much worse. And if my water breaks before I can—"

"Your friend Sherry'll get you through," he cut in. "You told me she took the classes with you."

"Classes can only do so much. I'll be so stretched with the baby's head pushing against that tender membrane—"

"You'll be fine. Sherry'll be right beside you."

"The doctor will take his scalpel—"

"Excuse me a minute." He bolted for the door. "Nurse?" he bellowed. "Isn't it about time you checked on..."

Brock's voice faded as he headed down the hall, but Mara could hear him issuing commands...anything to regain control. She smiled. Thank goodness when the time came she wouldn't have to rely on Brock.

Mara had been right about the false labor. By noon that day the doctor had confirmed her suspicions, and Brock drove her back to her apartment. At the front door she informed him to leave her alone, to refrain from calling Sherry and to forget his crazy idea of marriage.

Brock had regained his color, and with it his stubbornness. "You think over my offer before you turn me down,

Mara. I never claimed to know about babies, but I do know how to keep a bank account in the black. I can keep you off welfare and give that kid of yours a future."

"This baby is Todd's, and it has a future."

"Not the one I could provide. What would Todd want, Mara? You think about it."

He did leave her alone, but Mara felt his presence. His offer was tempting, and the reality of her situation dim. The following week brought Mara a flood of bills, a notice that the checking account was overdrawn and a cost estimate from the hospital for labor, delivery and postpartum care.

She knew she could never give up her insurance. Even a normal birth was financially impossible. Then the credit-card company wrote to warn her legal action would be taken if she didn't pay Todd's bill in full immediately. A lawsuit! If she couldn't afford to pay off the debt, how could she afford a lawyer?

Thursday evening, Sherry came over after her work at a downtown clothing boutique. Birdlike, with dark brown hair and a slightly cynical view of life, she perched on the edge of Mara's couch. Her sharp brown eyes missed nothing as Mara finally poured out the whole situation—her financial straits and Brock's offer.

"What would Todd want?" Sherry repeated. "Mara, he would want Brock's help for his wife and child. Todd put his own life in the hands of his best friend. Of course he would place his family there."

"Oh, right. Brock Barnett can take care of everything." Mara grabbed a tissue and stared at the pink wad through blurred eyes. "Sometimes I actually pick up the phone to accept his offer."

"Maybe you should."

"And rely on that man?"

"Brock is a responsible person, Mara. He runs his ranch. He has lots of money. Let him help you."

"He's responsible, all right. He's responsible for Todd's death!"

"You don't know that for sure."

"He asked Todd to go with him to Hueco Tanks, didn't he? They were the only two climbers up there that evening, so they were responsible for each other's safety. Todd fell, and Brock didn't. Why on earth should I trust that man with my child's future?"

"But to go on welfare? Would Todd want that?"

"Of course he wouldn't. I just don't see any other way out."

"Brock is a way out. He wants to take care of you, Mara."

"He wants to buy his way out of his guilt."

"So let him."

"And be stuck with him as my husband for the rest of my life?"

"Oh, Mara, you don't expect this arrangement to last forever, do you? It's for now, for the baby."

Mara dabbed the tissue in the corner of her eye. All week she'd felt emotional. She'd told herself she missed Todd, but in truth her husband seemed far away. His memory had been buried under stacks of bills, his voice stilled by ringing phones.

"A man like Brock Barnett," Sherry continued, "is too attractive to live celibate the rest of his life. You know women are after him, Mara. Look at that body! I mean...those eyes and that mouth. The shoulders. Some woman is going to snag him, and he'll want to get married for real. You just make sure you get everything legally situated to take care of yourself and the baby in the years to come. He'll use this marriage to buy off his guilt, and you can use it to take care of your needs."

"Both of us using each other? That's real healthy."

"You both need it right now. So why not?"

"Because I despise Brock Barnett."

"Then you shouldn't have any qualms about using his money."

Mara shook her head. "You're as crazy as he is, Sherry."

"I'm looking out for your interests." She paused for a moment. "They're going to take your truck, you know.

They'll claim all your assets. You won't even be able to stay in this apartment, Mara.''

"I know," she whispered.

"Do you want to be homeless? Do you want to live in a shelter? Do you want to have supper in a soup kitchen every day? Do you want your baby to grow up eating food bought with government stamps?"

"Gosh, Sherry, thanks for the uplifting sermon."

"Hey, what are friends for?" Sherry stood to go. As she picked up her purse, she regarded Mara. "Maybe I should keep my mouth shut, but you know me. You once told me you grew up on government welfare. I know you don't want to go back to that. So, do what you have to do to stay free."

As Sherry walked to the door, Mara tossed her tissue into the trash basket. "If I marry Brock Barnett, I won't be free," she said softly. "I'll be living on *his* welfare system . . . under his terms."

"But he owes you, Mara. The state doesn't." Sherry opened the door. "Let me know what you decide."

Brock shoved a log onto the fire and watched as sparks shot up into the stone chimney. The spicy scent of piñon smoke drifted into his cavernous living room. He took a deep breath. A wispy curl of ash danced out of the grate and pirouetted onto the black, gray and red Navajo rug where he knelt. He let out his breath, brushed his palms on his thighs and hunkered into a more comfortable position.

Two weeks and Mara hadn't called. The deal was off, and he should be damned glad. He wasn't used to having people around. He studied the orange flames licking against the blackened wall of the firebox. Todd's kid would grow up just fine without Brock Barnett around.

He stretched his legs out and eased down onto the old wool rug. Hands behind his head, he stared up at the vigas that crossed his ceiling. Yep, Mara was definitely gone. Oh, he might run into her some day. He'd catch a glimpse of blond hair. Then he'd see those gray-green eyes and pink lips. He'd know her right away. She'd be thin again, but not as angular. Motherhood would have made her breasts a little heavier, her hips a little rounder, her flesh even more soft and silken to the touch.

Brock tried to shut out the picture. He'd been seeing Mara in his thoughts too often. She was Todd's wife, by God. She didn't belong in his own fantasies. Squeezing his eyes shut, he reminded himself Mara was a mother, not some sexy, long-legged beauty. She wanted a warm teddy bear like Todd in her bed, not a tall, hard man with callused palms and sunburned lips. Mara had probably never had a sensual fantasy in her...

Brock opened his eyes. That book on the edge of her bathtub the day he'd gone to her apartment to confront her. The novel's cover showed a woman half-naked and a man clearly aroused... their lips a breath apart... their eyelids half shut in ecstasy.

What in hell was Mara reading a book like that for? She was a widow, Todd's widow. She was pregnant.

"I'll be damned," Brock muttered as he stood, giving the logs in the fire a kick. "Well, I'll be damned," he repeated. But it wasn't an expression of anger. He was intrigued.

Chapter 3

Mara rolled over in bed and squinted at the alarm clock. Six-thirty in the morning. Groaning, she groped for the covers. The bed was a mess, blankets on the floor, sheets pulled from the mattress.

She had been in labor all night. Braxton Hicks contractions again, she felt certain. Her water hadn't broken and the discomfort had come and gone without regularity. Now her bones ached, her stomach rolled, her legs trembled. She had debated calling the hospital, but she knew there was no point.

Her hand brushed across the familiar cool rectangle of her paperback novel, and she picked it up with a sigh of relief. Escape. The false labor had to be the result of the previous day's stress. First her landlord terminated her lease. Then her insurance company phoned to give her two days to pay before they canceled her policy. The bank already had claimed the pickup, and she'd been forced to turn in her credit card and close her savings account.

This morning she would have to take a taxi to the welfare office. Mara gritted her teeth as another pang swept through her. The last three contractions had been ten minutes apart.

She gripped the sheets as her abdomen tightened in an unbearable constriction. Welfare was the last thing in the world she wanted! Every time she thought about walking into that building in downtown Las Cruces, she cringed. Could she actually do it? Oh, Lord, she needed a way out.

When the compression of muscle and tissue finally began to subside, Mara opened her book. With a shudder, she stared at the black script on the creamy white page.

His fingertips slipped down her bare back, tracing the rise and fall of each tiny, rounded bone in her spine. She shivered with delight and anticipated the moment when his lips would . . .

Mara let the book fall onto her face. She couldn't imagine such a thing ever happening to her again. If she thought of men, she could see only Todd, the man she had always loved. Now Todd was dead, the apartment was lost, the money was all spent and . . .

Another contraction clenched her abdomen. From under the pages of her novel Mara peered at the clock. Ten minutes. Not today! Not now. She brushed the paperback aside. She needed to get busy. Take a shower. Fix a bowl of cereal. Pack those last boxes.

When the pressure subsided, she slid off the edge of her bed and stood on wobbly legs. As she made her way to the bathroom, she reminded herself the baby wasn't due for three weeks, and first babies were almost always late. Sherry had gone to Albuquerque for Thanksgiving, but she'd be back in time to coach Mara through labor.

In the bathroom, she pushed aside the shower curtain and turned on the water. As the tiny, blue-tiled room filled with steam, she allowed her one escape to filter into her thoughts. Brock Barnett. She was sure his offer still stood. A house to live in, food to eat, a car to drive, insurance . . .

She snapped up the chrome shower pull. Absolutely not! She would never rely on that man. As water spattered into the tub, Mara lifted her leg over the side. A dull ache poured into her back and tightened into a belt of steel around her belly. Fighting to catch her breath as the contraction hammered through her, she glanced out at the bedroom clock.

Nine minutes.

Brock grabbed the phone on the second ring. Who the hell would call him at this hour? "Barnett," he barked.

"Brock?"

He knew her voice immediately. "Mara? What's wrong?"

"I'm calling to let you know I've made a decision. I will marry you, and I'd like to get it over with this morning. Tomorrow's Thanksgiving, so I want to take care of it today. I've called the courthouse, and it's first come, first serve at the county clerk's office. We'll meet at nine."

Brock dropped into a chair by the door. He drew his hat from his head and set it on his knee. The kitchen suddenly seemed uncomfortably warm, and he ran a finger around the inside of his collar.

"Look, Brock," Mara said, "you made an offer, and I'm accepting it."

"Yeah... but nine this morning? That's an hour..."

"Look, either you marry me this morning, or you don't. Which is it?"

Brock studied the gray felt Stetson on his knee. "I'm in the habit of planning things out, Mara. What's the status on the baby?"

Her breath caught. "It's not... not due for three weeks. I have to be out of my apartment by noon, so bring your pickup to town when you come. You can load my boxes and take them to your house."

Brock smoothed the brim of his hat as he listened to the emptiness on the other end of the line. Mara had been forced out of her apartment, and she must have lost the truck. Only this much loss, this much fear had driven her to accept his offer. She must despise him more than he knew.

"I'll marry you at nine," he said simply.

As she hung up, he stood and settled his Stetson on his brow. He was going to marry Mara Rosemond, a woman who hated his guts. For some reason he didn't feel a bit sad.

* * *

Brock watched Mara plod down the sidewalk from the taxi to the courthouse. A tight bun at the nape of her neck made her cheekbones stand out against the hollows of her eyes. Her blue dress clung to her stomach, its hem sweeping up into a curve at her knees. Her black coat, clearly not maternity wear, covered nothing more than her arms and back.

"Did you bring the blood tests?" she asked as she climbed the stairs.

"Good morning to you, too, Mara." Brock took off his hat, but she brushed past him into the warmth of the building. "Is Sherry coming?" he asked, matching his stride to hers.

"She went to Albuquerque for the weekend." She pushed open the door to the county clerk's office and stepped inside. Brock handed over the blood test results and twenty-five dollars. He and Mara presented their driver's licenses, signed a form and were told to wait.

They sat on a long bench, and Mara glanced at her watch. Six minutes since the last contraction. She'd barely made it into the courthouse. She shut her eyes and leaned her head back against the wall just as the ache swept into her back. Hands inside her coat pockets, she squeezed the polyester linings.

"I reckon we'll have a turkey and trimmings at the ranch tomorrow," Brock said. "Pierre's the best cook you ever saw. My dad brought him over from France years ago, and I kept him on even though I don't eat enough to make him worth what I pay him."

Biting the inside of her cheek, Mara struggled for control. Brock's voice floated somewhere beside her. "One time I put everybody on a health kick, the whole staff. Pierre had himself one royal French hissy fit. So we're back to eating his sauces and fresh butter every day."

Mara took a deep breath as the contraction began to slip away. She glanced at her watch. She had at most six minutes to get through this. "Now," she croaked. "Let's do it now, Brock."

At her tone, he slipped his arm around her waist and lifted her to her feet. She leaned into his body, aware that he felt as warm and sturdy as a big oak tree in the summertime as he led her into the clerk's office.

As the clerk flipped through a book, she took off her glasses and studied the couple. "You are Mara Renee Waring Rosemond?"

Mara nodded, fairly sure of her name. The familiar dull ache had begun edging across her abdomen. It had been five minutes since the last contraction. As she listened to the clerk, she allowed her eyes to slide from her swollen stomach to Brock's flat one. The white cotton fabric smelled of starch, clean and freshly ironed. At his waist, a heavy silver buckle was studded with chunks of turquoise. The buckle fastened a leather belt that held up a pair of black jeans. Tight jeans.

"Mara?" The woman's voice barely penetrated.

Mara lifted her head and nodded, a monumental effort. Her voice sounded hoarse and distant. "Yes, I will. I do...of course."

Brock studied the woman at his side, unable to suppress the frown that crept around his mouth. Damn, he couldn't read the woman. She was a contradiction—turning his marriage offer down, then agreeing to it; telling him she hated him, then that she wanted to get married after all.

Now here she was, still wearing Todd's wedding ring, dressed more for a funeral than a wedding. "Yes," he said firmly as the clerk pressed him for a commitment. "I will." In spite of his irritation with Mara, he would do whatever it took to take care of Todd's widow and baby.

"Brock and Mara," the clerk said finally, "I pronounce you husband and wife. Brock, you may kiss your bride."

"What?"

"I said, you may kiss your new wife."

"Wife..." Goose bumps skittered like spilled marbles down Brock's spine. He was a husband. A married man. He looked down at Mara, her head heavy on his shoulder, and her hair smooth, cool, silky blond. She smelled like talcum powder. The edges of her coat had slipped apart, and her stomach molded against his side. He was taken off guard by how hard it was, how firm and solid with undeniable life.

He swallowed, pent up and confused. In some sensual way, the moment stirred him. Her breasts beckoned, her flesh invited his touch. She was his bride, and he had every right to kiss her.

Todd's wife.

No. In spite of another man's rings on her finger, she was Brock's wife now. Her gray-green eyes stared into his. Her lips were pale pink as he let his eyes trail across them. He could hardly breathe.

Yes, he wanted to kiss her, his bride. He would kiss her, whether she liked him or not, whether she was Todd's widow or not. He slipped one arm around her shoulders and cupped her head with his hand. Trembling, her lips parted slightly. He lowered his head.

"Brock," she whispered. "Take me to the hospital. I'm about to have this baby."

Chapter 4

Brock threw the pickup into gear and stomped on the gas. The truck spun out of the parking space into the early morning traffic. Mara curled into a ball on the seat.

"Get me to the hospital," she puffed, her face bright red. "Ohhh! Run the traffic lights, Brock. I mean it."

For the first time since he'd climbed down the cliff after Todd had fallen to his death, Brock knew true fear. He glanced from side to side, pushed the gas pedal to the floor and tore through a busy intersection. Cars honked and brakes screeched. "If Sherry's in Albuquerque," he demanded, "how the hell is she going to get here in time?"

"Quit your damned swearing and drive!" Mara snarled. "I phoned her at eight this morning, and she promised to leave right away."

"Eight! Albuquerque's a four-hour drive." Growling in frustration, Brock steered the truck through a red light. "Why didn't you tell me you were in labor?"

"It's none of your business."

"None of my b—" He cut himself off, gritting his teeth. He glanced at the woman beside him. Though it was a chilly morning, perspiration beaded her temples. Her eyes were squeezed shut, and her mouth formed a tight, white line. She had sprawled out on the seat, no belt around her middle, her legs spread and her feet propped on the floorboard.

Alarmed, Brock grabbed her arm. "Put your legs together! You're going to have the baby right here! What if the baby... falls out?"

"Don't be ridiculous," Mara snapped. "I'm not pushing yet."

"Pushing? Don't push, for crying out loud!"

"It's a stage. You can't help it."

"Great! You should have told me, Mara. A person doesn't get married when she's in labor. And she doesn't have a baby in a pickup. It's not logical. There's a right way and a wrong way to do things."

"Shut up, Brock!"

"There's the hospital. I can see the sign."

"Go to the emergency entrance. Ohhh, no!" Mara curled into a ball again, and Brock could barely hear her moans through the fabric of her coat. Her bun had come apart like a haystack in a storm. Wispy strands of blond hair scattered across her shoulders as she clutched air with two fists.

"Hang on, Mara," he said, forcing a calm to his voice.

"Get...me...morphine!"

"Morphine!" Brock threw open his door and lunged out of the pickup. He ran around the vehicle and practically tore her door off its hinges. He lifted her against his chest. The emergency room doors slid apart as he hurtled toward them like a fullback headed for the end zone. "It's a baby!" he bellowed. "We're having a baby!"

Two nurses at the reception desk dropped their charts. One ran for a wheelchair, the other pressed an alarm and dashed toward Brock. In seconds, he and Mara were surrounded by nurses. Questions flowed.

Brock tried his best with the answers as they bundled Mara into the wheelchair. "She's preregistered. Mara Barnett. My wife."

"Rosemond!" she groaned. "I'm registered as Rosemond."

"We just got married," he clarified.

"Then you'll have to start over." The nurse grabbed his arm. "Go right down that hall to the first window."

Brock's boots pounded on the slick floor. He skidded to a stop and hammered on the Plexiglas window. "Mara Rosemond's here!"

The registration clerk nodded and turned to her file cabinet. Brock glanced down the hall. Orderlies wheeled Mara along a corridor and out of sight. "What are they doing with her?" he demanded of the clerk.

"Your wife will need to be prepped for delivery if there's time. Don't worry, you'll get there for the birth."

"No, you don't understand. Sherry's coming here to—"

"Your insurance company?" the clerk cut in. In a daze, Brock rattled off what he knew. Before he could finish, the nurse appeared at his side again and ordered him to follow her right away.

"Where are we going?" Brock hollered as he ran down the hall.

"Labor and delivery." The nurse shoved him into the open elevator. "Mr. Barnett, your wife is dilated and in transition. You shouldn't have waited this long. I'd advise you to monitor things more closely next time."

"Next time?"

The nurse marched out of the elevator, Brock in tow. "Now, we insist on gowning you. Put these on." She tossed him a pile of blue paper clothing. For some reason, Brock found himself jerking on the flimsy gown and tugging the cap over his hair. The nurse tied the mask to his face while a second nurse held the booties as he stepped into them.

"You don't understand," he tried. "There's a woman named Sherry—"

"Follow me, Mr. Barnett." The nurse gripped his arm.

The doctor in the labor room looked as unrecognizable as Brock did. He was a pair of bright blue eyes, a pair of gloved hands and a voice that bespoke utter calm and confidence. "Your wife is doing beautifully."

"Not my doctor," Mara moaned from the bed beside him.

"Dr. Mecham has been notified, and he's on his way."

Brock stared in dismay at Mara's ashen face. She was lying on a gurney with a flimsy calico gown over her chest and thighs. A monitor showed the rise and fall of two lines of light. Mara's contractions. And the other line ... the baby's heartbeat!

A chill slid down Brock's spine as he reached for Mara's hand. "Can you see that?" he asked, leaning near her ear.

She turned her head, and a wan smile tilted her lips. "Oh, it's so ... Ohh! Here comes another one!"

Brock stiffened as Mara's monitor line shot up at a steep angle. Her face went rigid; her fingers clenched around his. A low moan started in the depths of her chest and grew louder as the contraction intensified.

"Do something," Brock commanded. "This woman is in agony here."

"Actually, she's doing very well. Breathe, Mara," the nurse said gently. "Not too fast. Slowly, slowly. Breathe through the contraction."

"To hell with breathing. Give her morphine," Brock ordered.

As the contraction consumed her, Mara became nothing but the sum of constricting tissue centered around her abdomen. She drifted above herself, staring at the suntanned fingers gripping her white hand, pressing Todd's gold rings into her flesh. Whose hands were they? One so frail ... and the other wound around and through it as though an oak tree's roots had slowly encompassed a marble statue. She loved those two hands.

But now someone was touching her shoulder, stroking her face. She couldn't bear the sensation! Her eyes, wild and shimmering, darted to the face above her. "Don't touch me!" she growled. "You ... you ... you ..."

The word became a part of her puffing. She stared at the man behind the blue mask. Who was he? She'd seen him before with those deep brown eyes. She knew him ... knew him well ... didn't like him.

"Brock, come and take a look at your baby's head," the doctor said.

"Brock!" Mara exploded. "I hate...hate...hate..."

"Don't worry," the nurse whispered gently to Brock. "This is common in the transition between the stages of contractions and pushing. She's not completely aware of what she's saying."

Brock allowed himself to be led to the end of the gurney. Mara did hate him, he remembered. It didn't matter that they were married, or that he'd wanted to kiss her...wanted to kiss her even now, and hold her.

"Can you see the baby's head?" The doctor directed Brock's vision.

Brock gazed at the tiny circle between Mara's thighs. Amid the pressure of stretched tissue, it was there. The very top of the baby's head. Suddenly, everything else evaporated.

"Mara!" Brock leapt to her side and grabbed her hand again. "I saw the baby! It's right there, the head!"

"Really?" Mara heard her own voice filled with tired elation. A baby! That's what this was all about, wasn't it? The contraction had faded a little, and she wondered who she'd been barking at. This man in the blue mask? But he was so wonderful...standing there with her, holding her hand, helping her through. "How much did you see?"

"A circle about the size of a dime. And hair. Blond hair!"

"My baby has hair. I feel so...ohhh..."

"It's another one," Brock announced as he focused on the monitor's rising line. "Help her, doc!"

"Why don't you help her, Brock?" The doctor laid a hand on his shoulder. "Help Mara maintain the rhythm of her breathing."

"I have to push," Mara puffed. The sensation came over her as though she had been caught in a rush of floodwater from a broken dam. And it felt wonderful to turn the contraction into something productive!

"Push!" she exulted.

"Not yet, Mara," Dr. Fielding cut in. "Try to hold back for me."

"Hold back?" Her voice was a squeak of dismay.

"We want to get you into delivery. Come on everyone."

As the nurses surrounded Mara. Brock stood by, frustrated he could do nothing. Mara's strength amazed him even as he was reminded of her anger. He knew she still blamed him, and nothing would erase that.

"Brock!" she cried out as the hospital staff lifted her onto another gurney. She flung her arm out toward him, her hand open wide. A tear squeezed out of the corner of her eye and slipped down her cheek. Brock held back a moment, aware she was calling to him—to anybody—out of her pain. Now she needed the support of a strong hand, but later she would resent that it had been Brock's.

"Brock," she groaned. The tear slipped onto her earlobe.

He hesitated, then leaned forward and dabbed it with his finger. "It's okay, Mara," he murmured. "You can push in a minute."

The words swirled around inside Mara's head as she fought the flood tide urging her forward. She had to push! There was absolutely no way to hold back. A warm hand brushed the side of her cheek. It was Brock's hand, and she was so thankful for it. She turned her face into his palm and pressed her lips to the hard, male flesh.

"We're going down the hall, now," he was whispering against her ear. "The doors are opening, and now we're in the delivery room."

"I'm scared. Please don't go away, Brock."

"I won't. I'll stay right with you, Mara. You can do this."

"Oh, Brock, I'm so...ohhh..."

The nurse flipped on a light above the gurney. "It's okay to push now, Mara," she said gently.

Mara hardly needed permission. Gripping the handholds at her sides, she summoned more strength than she had ever known she possessed. The core of her body seemed to glow as she strained toward it. The room around her vanished, all but the ultimate focused urge to push.

Brock glanced at the end of the gurney and saw that Mara's legs had been draped in a green sheet. A nurse wheeled a cart of silver bowls and instruments beside the doctor. The anesthesiologist wrapped a cuff around Mara's upper arm to read her blood pressure.

Brock took his place at her side again, holding her hand as she poured her energy into the effort. On the ranch, he'd witnessed birth a thousand times. But this was different, so human and filled with magic.

"Brock," she whispered through panting breaths. "Don't go away."

"Never, Mara."

"Stay with me."

"I'm right here."

He watched her face turn bright crimson and the skin over her knuckles go white. At this moment, she could have moved a mountain.

"Brock!" The doctor beckoned. "Come see!"

Reluctantly, Brock left Mara's side. At the foot of the gurney, his heart jerked to a halt. A small forehead emerged from Mara's body...a pair of tiny eyes...a miniature nose...two ears...a rosebud mouth.

"It's a—a baby...." He couldn't breathe, couldn't think.

The doctor cradled the precious life. Mara pushed again. A shoulder emerged, then another, so small and delicate they hardly seemed real. And she pushed again. The infant body slid into the world, a perfect jewel.

"It's a girl!" Brock shouted.

"A girl!" Mara's echoed voice wavered between laughter and tears. "Is she all right?"

The sudden piercing cry announced that Mara's newborn daughter was indeed fine. Brock's vision swam. He'd never seen anything in his life as beautiful as that small, creamy baby.

"She's a dandy," Dr. Fielding announced. The tiny baby's holler faded to a whimper as the doctor laid her on Mara's chest. Tears rolled down the new mother's cheeks at the sweet, soft pressure of her daughter's body against her own breasts. She touched tiny arms and tinier fingers.

"It's okay, precious," Mara whispered against the sobbing child's delicate cheek. "Mama's here now."

"She's bigger than we thought," the doctor said. "She'll be fine."

Mara tried to smile, but she couldn't work her way past the tears. She was holding her baby! A daughter... a baby girl... She wanted to share this, wanted someone special....

"Brock," she called.

"Mara." He was instantly at her side. "She's perfect, Mara."

"She is, isn't she?"

"So are you."

"Oh, Brock, I miss Todd."

"I know, Mara."

"I love her so much."

The nurse touched Brock's arm. "We need to warm up your daughter, now. And the doctor wants to finish with you, Mara."

The baby was whisked away, and Mara felt the greatest emptiness she'd ever known. "Where is she?"

"They've put her in a warming bed," Brock explained. He didn't want to leave Mara's side. "They're weighing her. Now they're putting bands on her ankle and wrist. They're stamping her foot with black ink."

"She's crying!"

"She doesn't want anyone messing with her. She's like her mama."

Mara laughed. Brock grinned beneath his mask. He'd never seen anyone so beautiful. He told himself it was just the intensity of the moment, but he couldn't deny a feeling he'd never known in his life. Somehow he had become attached to this woman. A thin silver thread connected them. It was a filament that might become tangled or frayed or stretched to the limit. But he didn't think it would break.

Mara let out a deep breath. "I'm a mother," she murmured. "My baby has a mother."

Brock studied the woman whose hand he clasped. *Your baby has a father, too,* he wanted to say. But he knew those were words Mara must say. And she hadn't said them. Not yet, anyway.

* * *

The recovery room was small, with only a single bed. In delivery, Mara had been stitched and pushed and manhandled more than Brock thought was necessary, but what did he know? Now in the narrow bed, she was shivering like a puppy in an ice storm.

"All right, Mara," the nurse said as she opened the door. "You can hold your daughter for a few minutes before we take her back."

Feeling extraneous, Brock stood to one side as the nurse laid the tiny blanketed bundle in Mara's arms. He could barely see the top of the baby's head, and that white cap covered all the skin. Mara cooed and clucked as her lips trembled with emotion.

In a moment, Dr. Fielding swept into the room accompanied by Mara's physician, Dr. Mecham, who had finally arrived. Brock shoved his hands into his pockets and thought about stepping outside to look for a snack machine as everyone laughed, offered congratulations, admired the baby. He edged toward the door.

"And you must be Mara's new husband!" Dr. Mecham, baby in his arms, swung around and gave Brock a warm smile. "This must have been quite an experience for you."

"It sure was." He glanced at the baby, hoping for a glimpse of her face. He could just see the tip of a small pink nose.

"Here, take a closer look." Dr. Mecham held out the bundle. "Haven't you held her yet?"

Brock took a step backward, his eyes darting to Mara. She was talking to a nurse. Brock looked at the physician again.

"Wouldn't you like to hold her?" Dr. Mecham asked.

His mouth as dry as concrete on a summer day, Brock stared at the blanketed bundle. "I better not," he murmured.

"I think you'd better. Might as well get used to it now."

The doctor set the baby against Brock's chest. As he gazed down at the miniature face, Brock slipped his hands around the blanket. The baby's weight, solid and undeniable, filled his arms. In the corner of his elbow, her round head nestled contentedly, her eyes shut tight and her pink lips making little ohs.

"What do you think?" Dr. Mecham asked.

For a moment, Brock couldn't speak as emotion flooded through him. He touched her tiny ear, stroked a finger across her petal-soft cheek, then kissed her forehead.

"She's a keeper," he whispered.

Chapter 5

Brock had never seen such perfection. Maybe the baby in his arms was a little bit pink and wrinkly, and maybe her eyelids puffed out and her head was slightly lopsided. So what? She was the prettiest, sweetest little girl he'd ever laid eyes on.

As Brock studied Mara's daughter, the strangest emotion tugged at his stomach and swelled his heart. He'd never been in love before, but he'd have sworn this must be the feeling. At this moment, he would do anything for the little baby he held. He'd lay down his life for her. By God, he'd kill to protect her.

"I believe Daddy approves," Dr. Fielding said.

Mara couldn't take her eyes off Brock. He was holding her baby as though she were a precious gem. His brown eyes had melted into pools of chocolate fudge, and the expression on his face spoke volumes. For the first time in his life, Brock looked . . . gentle.

How could that be?

Mara didn't want such tenderness from him. It made her feel somehow connected with the man. True, Brock was her husband—but in name only. And he wasn't the baby's father. He really had no right to look at her daughter that way.

But he had helped through the birth. He had laid his money and his reputation...even his future...on the line for this baby. He'd done it out of guilt. Mara had to remember that. Yet she had the sinking certainty she couldn't have gotten through the birth without him. She had wanted him. Needed him.

Did she want him now?

"Mom, are you planning to nurse this daughter of yours?" Dr. Fielding asked. "If so, we'll let the hospital's parent educator take over."

"Yes, I want to," Mara said.

"I'd better go." Brock held out the baby to any takers.

"No, it's okay," Mara said without thinking. "You can stay." And before she could amend her words, the doctors had left, the baby was lying in her arms, and Brock was seated on a chair in the corner while the education nurse untied the strings of Mara's gown.

"Now, you'll want to find a comfortable position," the woman said. "I recommend holding the baby at several different angles during each feeding to be sure your breasts are completely emptied of milk."

At the intimacy of the moment, Mara could feel a pink heat flush through her cheeks. She glanced over the nurse's shoulder to see Brock, elbows on his knees and chin propped on his fist, staring at the floor between his boots.

"Now, place the baby right here," the nurse explained, deftly tucking the little bundle into Mara's lap. "All babies have a natural sucking instinct, so the moment your breast touches the side of her face, she'll start to grope for your nipple."

Again, Mara glanced at Brock. Head down, he was still staring at some place on the floor between his boots. She focused on her baby. Tiny mouth pursed, the little one didn't seem to have the slightest interest in nursing. Mara knew she would have to forget about the tall man in the room and concentrate.

"How can I get her to open her mouth?" she asked.

"Stroke her cheek with your finger," the nurse said. "See? Look how she's rooting. Now just slip your nipple between her lips. There you go. Oh, she's interested all right. Look at that!"

Brock lifted his eyes for a second. A tingle washed down his spine. Mara's robe had spread open wide, baring her full breasts. The baby was nestled against one, and the other lay exposed, creamy and round, its tip drawn into a firm, pink cherry.

He quickly dropped his gaze to stare at the carpet snag between his boots. He couldn't think about Mara's breasts.

Bottles, that's what they were. Baby bottles. They held milk for her daughter. Nourishment. Sustenance.

So why did he feel uncomfortably hot and tight? He shifted on the chair. Definitely, he could not think about Mara's breasts. They belonged to her and the baby, and they were none of his business.

"This liquid is called colostrum," the nurse was telling Mara. "It's the first, most nourishing fluid in your breasts. The colostrum helps provide natural immunities for your baby."

"What about milk?"

Brock involuntarily looked up. Mara was gazing down at her baby. The new mother's blond hair was spread around her shoulders like a golden cape. Her eyelashes shadowed her cheeks, and her mouth had flushed to a soft pink. She was smiling.

His eyes wandered a little lower. Absolutely, he should not look at her breasts. The one he could clearly see was very large, much larger than he remembered—not that he'd ever seen Mara's bare breasts. He wondered if he'd ever even thought about them.

"Your milk will come in by tomorrow, I imagine," the nurse was telling her. "But you want your daughter to take as much of this colostrum as possible."

"Her sucking feels . . . all right."

"Today, it does. But tomorrow may be a different story. Most women experience quite a bit of soreness in the first days of nursing. I'm going to give you some special cream.

I recommend you rub this into your nipples and all around the breast area. Maybe your husband could do it for you?"

The nurse swung around to look at Brock, who jerked his eyes to the window. He spotted a tree that still had a few golden leaves clinging to it, and pretended to be completely lost in fascination.

"I don't think so," Mara whispered to the nurse.

"Whatever is most comfortable for you. If you feel any lumps or clots forming, place warm washcloths on your breasts and massage them like this."

Brock swallowed. He ought to go find a soft drink machine. Or a bar. The image of his hands rubbing cream into Mara's nipples had sent a shaft of white heat into his loins. At the thought of Mara massaging her own breasts, he fidgeted uncomfortably.

Baby bottles, he told himself. That's all they were. Mara was a mother, not a sensual fantasy. He couldn't think about her. Couldn't look at her. Couldn't want her.

"You and your daughter both did very well," the nurse was saying. "I'll come around later in the day to see if you need help again."

"Thank you." Mara pulled her gown together and tied the tiny strings.

"I'm going to take her back to the nursery now, Mara."

"I'd really like to keep her." Mara heard her own voice filled with longing as the woman lifted the baby out of her arms.

"She needs to be warmed up again. It won't be long before you're in your own room, and you can spend all the time you want with her."

As the nurse walked toward the door with the baby, Mara glanced at Brock. At this moment of loneliness, she couldn't help longing for Todd. Then oddly, she realized that Brock was good enough—he was all she had.

"Stay?" she asked him, suddenly exhausted again.

He nodded.

"By the way," the nurse asked. "What's your daughter's name, Mara?"

"Abigail," Mara said softly. "I'll call her Abby."

"That's a beautiful name."

As the door shut, Brock studied Mara. Her hands lay limply across the empty space where her baby had nestled. The wedding rings Todd had given her circled a pale finger. She looked tired and alone.

"Abby," she repeated, her eyes on the small window. "It means, 'her father was joy.'"

Brock nodded, understanding the sentiment even as he was reminded that the child was not truly his and never would be. Then Mara shut her eyes and let out a breath.

"Abigail," she whispered. "Abigail Barnett."

Brock smiled.

For the next three days the hospital became the whole world as Mara adjusted to motherhood while little Abby adjusted to her new living quarters. Neither transition was easy. Mara's milk did begin to flow, but it took Abby quite a while to figure out how to suckle effectively. In the meantime, Mara's nipples grew tender and sore, and her breasts alternately seemed to have too much or not enough milk.

The hospital room itself was pleasant enough, pale blue walls with a pastel border around the ceiling. A window looked out on the streets of Las Cruces, placid and cold for the Thanksgiving holiday. A clean bathroom provided a warm shower. A sofa catered to the guests who came to visit—neighbors from the apartment complex, Mara's former co-workers at the academy where she had taught, members of her Sunday school class. Bouquets of pink carnations and white roses jostled for space on the wall shelf, while boxes of tiny ruffled dresses gathered in a corner. Mara couldn't imagine her baby ever big enough to wear them.

Little Abby hated bath time and diaper changes, and Mara wasn't crazy about them, either. Her stitches and aching body made movement difficult, though she spent a good bit of time walking the floors of the neonatal unit. She showered and changed into a gown Brock brought in a suitcase, and once or twice she almost felt normal again. Then her breasts would begin to throb or her chair would require a doughnut-shaped cushion, and Mara remembered that she had changed forever.

Her entire life was new, different and, she had to admit, generally unpleasant. When Sherry had arrived breathless and apologetic an hour too late for the delivery, Mara was basking in the afterglow of Abby's birth. But two days later when the petite woman breezed into the room with a meal of leftover turkey, a spoonful of stuffing and a bowl of cranberry sauce, Mara stared at the paper plate as though it were the saddest thing she'd ever seen.

"I'm married to him," she said. "Brock Barnett."

Sherry set the plate on the rolling tray and perched on the edge of Mara's bed. Her dark brown eyes sparkled as she waved a pink-nailed hand in dismissal. "Not that I would know—since I've never strapped the bonds of matrimony and motherhood around my own neck—but I'd guess it's just your hormones talking, Mara. You know what they say about the baby blues? You feel sad for no reason at all."

"No reason! Sherry, I'm a widow who married a man I don't even like."

"You like Brock."

"How could I? Thanks to him, I don't have a husband."

"*He's* your husband," Sherry countered firmly, "and you do like him."

Mara groaned. "He's been so unbearably nice. He packed all my stuff and moved me out of the apartment. He brought me lotion and shampoo and a new box of talcum powder. Expensive, designer talcum powder, Sherry. He's bought Abby everything from diapers to booties to a velvet Christmas dress she'll probably be too big to wear by December. This morning it hit me that I was actually looking forward to the moment when he walked through the door. You're right. I don't hate him as much as I should. And I hate myself for that."

"Let it go, Mara."

"I'm trying. But when I look into Abby's eyes, all I can think about is Todd. He was so excited about the pregnancy. He couldn't wait to be a father. He talked about holding her and teaching her things, you know? Three months of my morning sickness . . . that's all he got.''

Sherry pulled tissue from the box by Mara's bed. "Here you go. You can't wish this sadness away, so you might as well feel it. I think it's part of grieving for Todd."

"I can't forgive Brock for what he did, and I can't let go of Todd. Not now.''

"Abby is Todd's daughter, Mara. Of course you can't let him go. You never will, and you never should.''

Mara stared at the door through which Brock had come and gone at least twenty times since Abby's birth. Half the time, he was wheeling the baby into the room in her bassinet. He rarely stayed while Mara nursed, and they barely spoke to each other. When they did talk, they discussed only the most mundane, factual things. But he was there, always there, as though he belonged.

"If I shouldn't let go of Todd," Mara said, fingering his wedding rings on her hand, "and if he'll always be Abby's father, how can I live with myself for marrying Brock Barnett?''

"Because you know why you did it.''

"I don't want to live at his house, Sherry.''

"Why not?''

"Because . . ." Mara conjured the image that had been bothering her all morning—Brock at the breakfast table, freshly showered and dressed in a denim shirt and jeans. She could almost smell the scent of his cologne. "Because I don't want to see him.''

"You won't see him. He's a rancher. He'll be out feeding cows, or whatever. You know, up at sunrise and to bed at dusk. Besides, you'll be taking care of Abby all the time.''

Mara pondered this for a moment. Sherry was probably right. Todd had told her Brock's ranch house was an enormous, sprawling adobe structure with two separate wings and a courtyard in between. She and Brock could probably live side by side without ever setting eyes on each other. Just as well.

"How long do you suppose he'll want to stay married?" she asked Sherry.

"Given Brock's track record, what do you think? I imagine he'll decide he's had enough of married life after a month or two, and he'll want to have a little fun again." Ever disdainful of the male gender, Sherry rolled her eyes. "I wouldn't worry about it. Just make sure he signs everything so Abby is legally protected the way he promised."

Mara tried to project the future Sherry had outlined. She and Abby would live alone in the big house until Brock's hormones came calling. Then they would move out, the marriage would be annulled and Mara would fend for herself, as she had before and could again.

"Brock married you out of a sense of obligation, Mara," Sherry reminded her. "He feels it's his duty to keep Todd's daughter out of the welfare system. That's all. As soon as he's figured out a way to settle you and Abby into some other satisfactory situation, you'll be rid of him. In the meantime, take advantage of his remorse."

"Oh, Sherry!" Mara had to laugh at her friend's cynicism. Though the model-thin brunette was pursued by flocks of ardent men, she had never dated one she trusted enough to love. At twenty-eight, she enjoyed her independence and viewed men merely as a means to an end.

"I'm not as mercenary as you," Mara told her.

Sherry shrugged. "Maybe not, but a big house, two maids, a swimming pool and a car of your own are nothing to sneeze at. You're getting a free ride on this man's guilt trip."

Mara touched the white silk bow on the new nightgown Brock had brought her. At the time he had given it to her, she had sensed a genuine generosity in his eyes. He had brought the pink-papered box into her room early on the morning after Abby's birth. After laying it on Mara's bed, he had waited in silence for her to open it.

"It's got little slits in the front at the top," he had explained as she drew the satiny confection from the tissue paper. Then he shoved his hands into his jeans pockets, and Mara would have sworn he blushed. "Well, it's a special nursing gown, so you can feed Abby better. The lady at the boutique told me it was just the thing."

Mara had softened at the thought of the tough cattle rancher searching through boutiques for just the right kind of gown to help with Abby's nursing. Now, she wondered if the gift had been merely another token to ease Brock's guilty conscience.

"I imagine he'll start to resent the situation after a while," she said. "Abby and me living in his house and all."

"As I've said before, Mara. So what? Let him resent it. He offered to do this, and now he's got to live with it."

Mara knew Sherry was trying to comfort her, but somehow she felt worse than ever. Could she live with a man who resented the very sight of her? Could she live with a man she could never forgive? Did she have any choice?

Only the sight of the nurse wheeling Abby's bassinet through the door lifted Mara's spirits. As the woman stopped the plastic-sided cart next to the bed, Sherry pulled back the edge of the blanket that covered Abby's face.

"Oh, Mara, I've never been the mommy type, but she's precious."

"She certainly is," the nurse concurred. "And she's a pretty good little sleeper, too."

As Mara read out the code on her wrist bracelet, the nurse checked the matching codes on Abby's arm and ankle tags. Then she lifted the baby out of the bassinet and laid her in Mara's arms.

"This kid is all that matters," Sherry said softly. "Focus on her, Mara. Abby is all you need."

Mara gazed down at the tiny pink face and tried to make herself believe Sherry was right.

"Your rooms are in the west wing," Brock said as he drove Mara and Abby across the metal cattle guard between the highway and the dirt road that led to his house. "There's a porch outside your bedroom door. It's a good place to watch the sun go down."

Mara studied the man beside her. His tan Stetson shaded his eyes from the late-afternoon light that gilded his straight nose and firm, unsmiling mouth. These were the first words he had spoken since they left the hospital, and she wondered if Sherry's prediction had come true already. He certainly didn't seem thrilled to be transporting Mara and her baby to his house.

So what? Mara told herself, repeating Sherry's refrain. She didn't have to please Brock Barnett. All that mattered was Abby. She glanced behind her at the infant carrier strapped into the back seat of the car. The sleek purr of Brock's Jaguar had lulled the baby to sleep the moment it pulled onto the street.

Abby and her needs. She was all that mattered in Mara's life.

"Is there a place at the house for Abby to sleep?" she asked. "The cradle…it isn't…well, Todd didn't finish it."

Brock worked the gears of his bronze Jag with a leather-gloved hand. "I bought a crib."

"You did?" She couldn't hide her surprise.

"There's a swing, too. It winds up. And one of those molded bathtubs. Yellow, I think."

"Oh." Mara tried to picture Brock walking through a department store selecting baby furniture.

"I reckon Abby won't need a high chair for a few months yet, but I got her one of those, too."

Mara stared at the endless miles of barbed wire fencing that slipped past her window. A high chair meant Brock expected to have Abby around when she was big enough to need one. Maybe he really did intend to make the arrangement last, at least for a while. Did *she* want it to last beyond the time it took to get back on her feet? Could she stand being there with him for one day, let alone weeks or months?

She allowed herself another look at the man. Dressed in a chamois-colored shirt that clung to his shoulders, a pair of faded jeans and brown leather boots, Brock's tall frame fairly announced male perfection. He was lean, fit and suntanned, and his black hair curled just a little beneath his hat. Again, Mara recalled the first time she had met him, and the way his deep voice had slid into the pit of her stomach. He truly was a sight that would stir any woman's soul. Any woman but this new, utterly maternal Mara.

She turned back to the window. Truth be known, she felt more like a punching bag than a woman. She had been poked, prodded, stitched and pricked until her whole body ached. Worse, she had been forced to admit her figure was a long way from its former shape. A long, long way.

Inside her blouse, her milk-swollen breasts stood out like a pair of overripe cantaloupes. She had tucked round absorbent pads into her bra cups, and she felt sure anyone who bothered to look closely would detect them. Not that any man would take a second glance at Mara. She had been appalled to discover that her stomach was almost exactly the size it had been before she gave birth. Only it was no longer hard and sleek with its cargo of baby. No, this stomach sagged like an old, half-full laundry bag. She had been assured she would firm up quickly, but she felt repulsive.

"It's too cold for the pool these days," Brock said, cutting into her self-deprecations. "But you can use the hot tub in your wing. Might help with those stitches."

Mara suddenly flushed. For the first time since Abby was born, she flashed on the moment of birth. Brock had been watching, hadn't he? He'd seen her body—seen the doctor cut her, seen how she was formed and shaped. He had seen her at her most raw and elemental moment. How embarrassing!

She leaned her cheek on the cool window and shut her eyes. So what! Sherry would say. So what if he saw you, and so what if you look like the Saggy Baggy elephant?

"Come summer, the pool is mighty nice," Brock said. "I swim laps, myself. You swim, Mara?"

She nodded, at that moment resolving she would never again be caught dead in a bathing suit.

"Abby might like the water, if we watch her close," he continued. "I learned to swim when I was just a pup. Rode horses, too, but Abby won't be ready for that for a few years. Still, it never hurts to start kids out young. I was roping by the time I was nine or ten."

Mara forced herself to listen. Again, Brock was talking about the distant future—and Abby was part of his plan. She had to focus on the present situation and turn off the inward microscope. It was just the baby blues talking, she told herself. She had never been one to allow negative thoughts to rule her life, and she wouldn't start now. If Brock wanted to chat as they drove the long road up to his house, she could join in the conversation. The least they could do was be civil to each other.

"Who taught you to swim?" she asked, seizing on the first thing that came to mind.

She saw his jaw tighten. After a long pause, he spoke two words. "My mother."

Mara let out a breath. Great. She had put her foot in her mouth on the first try. Todd had told her Brock's parents divorced when he was ten years old. His mother and sister had lived on the East Coast, while he had grown up with his father on the ranch.

"I learned how to swim at the city pool," she tried again. "There was a special program for foster children. We swam and did crafts, that kind of thing. It was fun."

Brock eyed Mara from under the brim of his hat. Her voice didn't mirror her words. Had she enjoyed her childhood? Her drive to escape her past told him she probably hadn't.

"Ever ride a horse?" he asked as he swung the Jag onto the gravel driveway of his house.

"Never."

"Too bad."

"I don't think so." Mara leaned forward, trying to keep her mouth from dropping open at the sight of the massive adobe home looming before them. "I don't know the first thing about horses."

"You'll learn, once you've been here a while. I'll take you out one of these days when you're feeling better. Nothing like a good long ride to take your mind off things."

He pulled the car around to the side of the house and pressed the button that lifted the first door of his three-car garage. As the vehicle slowed and came to a stop in the dim light, Abby woke with a start. The baby began to whimper, and Mara unlatched her seat belt.

"Oh, you're awake," she cooed as she leaned between the seats. "It's okay, Abby. Mommy's here."

As Brock set the brake, he allowed himself one last glance at Mara. Her hair, brushed shiny-smooth and gleaming, lay like scattered wheat across her shoulders. He leaned a little closer. Her hair smelled of flowers and herbs. Running his eyes down her body, he took in the swell of her breasts beneath her blouse, the sleek lines of her thighs in her black leggings, the length of her legs.

This was definitely the last time he would look at Mara this closely, Brock instructed himself. Every time he saw her, or caught her scent, or brushed against her, his own body reacted so strongly it shook him to the core. From the moment they stepped out of the car, he resolved he would keep his distance. He would stay in his side of the house, work his usual long hours and leave her completely alone.

"She's probably hungry," Mara said, turning to face him.

"Yeah."

For a moment, neither spoke. Brock let himself memorize her gray-green eyes and her pink lips. He would think about them later, when he was alone and safe. He would remember her strength as she pushed Abby from her body, and he would recall the sight of her tight nipples as she nursed her baby.

"Brock," she said, and he felt her breath on the skin of his face. "About the hospital and everything..."

"I didn't plan on being in there, you know."

"I know."

"The nurse just—"

"Thank you. I mean, I'm glad. You helped."

She gave him a quick smile and then turned away. In moments, she had opened her door and Abby's, and she was bending over to unbuckle the infant seat.

Brock reached for the handle of his own door. Okay, he thought, you're welcome. And now it's time to back off and face reality. Mara was a mother, not a hot date. She disliked, resented and blamed him for the terrible turn her life had taken. Most of all, Mara belonged to Abby and to Todd. And she always would.

Chapter 6

"I'm Rosa Maria Hernandez, and this is Ermaline Criddle, and, oh, my goodness! Would you look at this baby? How darling! How beautiful!"

Mara stood in the grand foyer as Brock's housekeeper and her assistant pressed close for a better look at the household's newest member. Rosa Maria, a small, round woman with bright black eyes and black curly hair, possessed the perkiest smile Mara had ever seen. She fairly bubbled with joy as she oohed and aahed over Abby.

Beside her, Ermaline gushed with equal ardor, but she couldn't have been more opposite. Tall, almost gaunt, she looked as though she hadn't eaten in a week. Her teeth were two sizes too big for her mouth, but her face was genuine and kind.

"She's a doll," Ermaline said. "Three days old? I tell you what, me and Frank, that's my husband, we've got four kids. Every one of them's been three days old before, too, but I'd swear I can't remember them ever being this small."

"They grow so fast!" Rosa Maria tapped Abby's cheek. "So fast! One day you can hold them in your arms, the next day they're getting a driver's license. Oh, my goodness, you better enjoy this one, Mrs...uh..."

"Mrs. Barnett," Brock announced as he walked into the hall and set Mara's suitcase on the floor.

"You can call me Mara. Really, that's...that's fine."

"Mrs. Barnett," Brock countered. "We try to keep things a little formal around here."

Ignoring him, Mara hugged Abby tightly as she tried to absorb the reality that this was Brock's world—and now had become their own. Two housekeepers? The house was huge, but who ever messed it up? And who was this older man? Tall white hat, white apron, white cravat knotted at his neck.

"Pierre Britton," he announced in a crisp voice, "at your service, *Madame*."

As the chef executed a neat bow, Mara glanced at Brock. He winked and gave a little shrug. "Just tell Pierre what you want to eat, and he'll fix it for you. As long as it's not hamburgers. Pierre doesn't do hamburgers."

"I am a chef, *Madame*, not a fry cook. I have trained with the finest in France."

"I'm looking forward to eating your cuisine," Mara said.

Pierre beamed. "The boy grew up with my food, and see how he is? Very healthy."

Mara couldn't help but smile at the image of Brock as a little boy. She turned to him just as he lifted her bags, but the sight of the roped muscles in his arms reminded her that the boy had long ago become a man.

"I'm healthy, all right," he said, "as long as I head for the bunkhouse once a week to chow down on beans and fried steaks with the hands."

"*Oui!*" Pierre exclaimed. "Terrible, the things our boy does."

"Man cannot live by *cordon bleu* alone."

"Steaks, half burned and half raw. Potatoes fried in fat. Beans laced with lard. *Oui,* terrible, terrible!"

Brock gave Mara a lazy grin as he brushed past her. "I love to rile him," he said in a low voice. "Come on. I'll show you the house."

"Tacos, he eats!" Pierre was exclaiming as Mara carried Abby across the warm terra-cotta tiled floor of the foyer. "Tamales, refried beans, nachos and *menudo!*"

"And what's wrong with *menudo?*" Rosa Maria snapped.

"Cow's stomach!"

"You feed him snails!"

"Your hot chilies will burn his intestines!"

"And your éclairs will give him a heart attack!"

Brock chuckled as he beckoned Mara into the spacious living room. "They've been fighting for twenty-five years. They're happiest when they're at each other's throats."

Pondering this pair who had so obviously been a big part of Brock's life, Mara carried her daughter into the place that was the heart of his home. Huge, rough-hewn beams lined the twelve-foot ceiling. Each viga was supported by an intricately carved corbel buried in the wall. Walls in the light rose color of traditional adobe had been smoothly plastered, even around niches that contained New Mexico artifacts.

Mara took in the fragile beauty of baskets woven by Mescalero Apaches, clay pots shaped, painted and fired by Indians of the Santa Clara and San Ildefonso pueblos, and kachinas carved and decorated by Hopis. Large, old Navajo wool rugs lay on the tile floor, their patterns evoking spirit gods and their colors of white, gray, black and brown reminiscent of the landscape.

"I keep a fire going even in summer," Brock said as he crossed by the colossal fireplace that was an unusual combination of stone and carved adobe. "Hope you don't mind."

"No," Mara whispered. With effort, she tried to adjust her image of furniture from her own snagged plaid sofas and garage-sale lamps to Brock's long, buttery leather couches, wool upholstered pillows, mission-style cabinets, silver-inlaid tables and wrought-iron lamps.

"This part of the house used to be all there was," Brock explained, leading Mara and the baby past windows that faced north toward the vast plains that stretched to the San

Andres Mountains. "This great room is more than a hundred years old. On the other side of it there, you can see the courtyard with the new swimming pool and the gardens. What are now the kitchen, dining room and library used to be bedrooms. My father bought this land from a descendant of the original Spanish land grant owner. We moved into the house when I was just a kid."

Mara followed Brock out of the great room and down a long hall lined with Native American and Hispanic art. "So, your father collected New Mexican artifacts?"

"These are mine. I pick up things wherever I go. I particularly like the native crafts—baskets, pottery, silver, weaving. I'll buy a painting if it's one I'm partial to."

Mara gaped at the collection of originals by Peter Hurd, Henriette Wyeth and Gordon Snidow. A large framed Peña hung on one long wall, a Gorman on another. The value of the paintings was inestimable, yet Brock treated his art-laden hall as casually as if it were a refrigerator hung with children's finger paintings.

"If I can find an authentic Hispanic religious artifact," he was saying as she readjusted Abby on her shoulder and hurried to catch up, "you know, a *retablo* or a *santo*—I'm as happy as a skunk eatin' cabbage."

Mara absorbed this new tidbit of information, and it only made her more curious. "Todd never told me you liked art."

"I don't know why not. I'd be hunting something every time we went off someplace together."

"So, did your father add the two wings onto the house?"

"I did."

"You?"

"Sure. Surprised?"

Mara couldn't deny it. She had always thought he lived solely on his father's coattails. Todd certainly hadn't told her Brock had added onto the old house. Her husband had told her his best friend liked history, but he hadn't mentioned anything about artifact and craft collections. She had thought Brock's interest in archaeology was merely another passing whim, like the others that filled his time—

parasailing, spelunking, hang gliding, white-water rafting and, of course, rock climbing.

"I took over the ranch about six years ago, after my father died," he was saying. "He founded Barnett Petroleum and turned his attention to the oil leases he owned over in the southeastern part of the state. He let this place go to hell. I was pretty burned about it. When the bottom dropped out of oil, Dad dropped out of life. Tipped the bottle, you know?"

Mara knew about that. She'd lived in more than one foster home where drinking had been a problem.

"When I was in college," he continued, "I'd come home on the weekends and try to put things back in order around the ranch. Dad died about the time I graduated, so I moved in and took over."

"You got out of the oil business?"

"I found a management group in Artesia to take care of things for me. I look in on the operation regularly just to keep my hand in the pie. The oil pays for itself and a little more. Well, a lot more, but I've put the money in stocks and other investments. I let my pals in New York play around with it."

Mara focused on the tiny bundle in her arms. Stocks and bonds, expensive art, valuable religious relics, oil and cattle—it all seemed so foreign. She had never had much money, and what she had she certainly never played around with. When she lifted her eyes to Brock, she knew he could read the expression on her face.

"Some of the money goes to causes I support," he said. "Charities, foundations."

"I remember Todd saying something to me about that," she told him, without mentioning the disagreement that had led to those words. Mara had disparaged Brock's reckless, foolhardy adventuring and his carelessness with money while Todd, as always, had risen to his best friend's defense.

"Anyway," Brock continued as he led Mara down the hall, "my goal has always been to get this place back on its feet. Last year the ranch turned a profit for the first time in thirty years.''

It was the only note of genuine pride Mara had ever heard in Brock's voice, and it told her how much this land meant to him. He did care about something more than himself and his wild adventures, she realized. It was a side of the man Mara had never seen, and it intrigued her more than she liked to admit.

"So, you decided to use your cattle money to improve the house?'' she asked.

"Afraid this is oil money.'' He pushed open a heavy door. "The ranch keeps itself going, but we're not setting the world on fire. I'm still working on that. Here's where you'll stay.''

Mara stepped into the huge room and squeezed Abby so tightly the baby whimpered in surprise. Her whole apartment could have fit into this place! And the decor... Thick wool rugs covered the oak floor, a large old bed with enormous posts anchored one wall and two huge chairs flanked a conical beehive fireplace that filled one whole corner.

"A fireplace!'' She tried to bite back her gasp, but Brock heard it and his mouth lifted in a grin of pleasure.

"I built one in every room.''

"It's... nice,'' she said as she walked toward the line of windows that banked an entire wall. Nice was hardly the word. The windows faced the plains at the base of the San Andres Mountains, now robed in shades of purple and indigo. Two tall French doors opened onto a deep porch on which sat wicker chairs and tables. A swing hung from the beams, its seat drifting back and forth in the slight breeze.

"This other door opens onto the courtyard,'' Brock said.

Startled from the spell the scene had cast over her, Mara crossed the room and stood beside him to peer into the dimly lit garden. She could just make out the faint outline of the swimming pool and covered terrace.

"I put a little waterfall by the pool,'' he said. "I planted a Xeriscape garden with native wildflowers, cactus, other stuff that can take the heat and dryness. On my property over by the mountains, I found some great rocks. Big ol' things. The water runs over them, you know. It's terrific at night when you can't sleep."

Mara looked up, wondering what could ever disturb Brock Barnett's sleep. Highlighted by the setting sun, his stony profile belied the softness in his brown eyes. Odd. All she had ever noticed about him in the past were those severely carved angles of jaw, cheekbone and brow. She'd seen the swagger and the cocky grin, heard the curt sentences, tasted the bitterness the man could leave in his wake.

Who was this person with gardens, art, waterfalls in his soul? Why had he built a beehive fireplace in every room? And what kept him awake at night?

"The baby's room is next door," he said. "Come on."

Mara walked beside him into the adjoining room. Everything he had mentioned sat in perfect showroom newness—crib, high chair, swing, bathtub.

"A rocker!" she exclaimed, delighted at the sight of the large, smooth wood chair with its high arms and comfortably curved back. "This will be wonderful for nursing Abby."

She went straight to the rocker and eased her sore body into its cradling cushions. The chair glided evenly back and forth on the floor without a creak or a bump. Immediately, Abby turned her face toward Mara's breast and her face puckered into hungry desire. Mara lifted her eyes to Brock.

He stood in the gathering shadows, hands in his pockets and hat pulled low. "You like the chair?"

"This is perfect." She let out a breath. "I love it."

As Abby began to whimper, Brock turned away. "I'll go see what's for supper."

Mara watched the door shut behind him, then she unbuttoned her blouse. She could get used to this, she realized. She really could.

"Knock, knock?"

Mara looked up from the crib where Abby lay sleeping peacefully. Rosa Maria Hernandez beckoned from the door.

"Pierre sent me to tell you it's almost time for dinner," the housekeeper said as Mara crossed the room to her. "He wants to know, will you eat in the main dining room or in the lounge?"

"There's a lounge?"

"Sure. It's right down the hall there."

Mara gave Abby a last check, content that her daughter would be secure without her for a few minutes. As she stepped into her own room, she tried to envision this lounge Pierre was talking about. It made the house sound like a hotel.

"You haven't seen it?" Rosa Maria followed Mara into the room and began turning down the bed. "It's a big area with tables and chairs, bar, dancing floor, movie screen, pool tables, everything. Mr. Barnett has parties there, you know?"

"No, I didn't know."

"Sure! He has a big crowd of friends from Las Cruces. They come up to visit. Sometimes they stay all night."

I'll bet they do, Mara thought. Just when she was trying to accommodate the image of an art-loving Brock, the old party boy stepped back in. Maybe the other Brock was a persona he adopted to impress her. Or maybe he liked to play with his money, spending it on expensive stuff to impress his friends.

She flipped open the clasps on her suitcase and wondered how long she could endure living right down the hall from Brock Barnett's Bar and Grill. How long before the Las Cruces crowd decided it was time to party? Would there be strange men sleeping in the empty rooms up and down the corridor? Women lolling around the pool? Sleeping in Brock's bed?

She felt lonely enough without family to help her celebrate Abby's birth, without a mother to help her tend the newborn, and with her few friends miles down the highway. But to have Brock's pack of revelers around would be too much. Jerking a pair of jeans from the top of her suitcase, Mara frowned at the picture her mind had conjured.

"I don't think a lounge is the right place to bring up a baby," she said firmly.

"Oh, everyone will love Abby. Mr. B.'s friends are...well, they're..." Rosa Maria's voice faded off, and Mara glanced at her.

"They're what?"

"I was just thinking about some of the ones who come. I don't know if he has told anyone."

"About me?"

"About the wedding."

"Don't worry about that. This marriage is on paper only. Brock and I have been very frank about that, and everyone else should be aware of it, too."

"He told us—the ones who work here—that he doesn't know you very well." The housekeeper plumped Mara's pillows. "You're his best friend's wife?"

"Todd Rosemond was my husband."

"I'm very sorry about what happened."

Mara tried to think of a response as she placed her jeans, shirts, socks and undies in the drawers of the large Victorian bureau near her bed. "I'm sorry, too."

"Mr. Rosemond was a good man."

Mara turned quickly. "You knew my husband?"

"Not very well. He stopped by the house a few times when he and Mr. B. were going on trips. I remember he came by once when they were hot-air ballooning and another time when they had explored a cave near Carlsbad. But we all understood how fine a boy that Mr. Rosemond was. Mr. B. was happy when he had been out on trips with your husband. He seemed...lighter, you know?"

Mara shrugged. "I'm not sure."

Uncomfortable at the turn of the conversation, she only knew she didn't like to be reminded of Todd's friendship with Brock. If the two had never known each other, Todd would be alive today. He would hold his newborn daughter and kiss his wife. The world would be normal, instead of a mess. It was hard enough to lose a husband, without the reminder that his presence had been valued by someone else. Valued by the man who ultimately failed him.

"Mr. B. is very...lonely," Rosa Maria said. "He's so hard and tough on the outside, you know? He's closed off like a

torreón with thick walls built for protection. He doesn't
open up for people."

"What about all those Las Cruces party friends?" Mara
said under her breath.

"Them?" Rosa Maria chuckled as she set a crystal water
carafe and glass on the bedside table. "Oh, no. They don't
talk together, those people. They dance, drink, swim, have
fun. Nothing serious."

"Sounds like Brock is pretty lighthearted to me."

"Maybe for a few minutes. Then he goes back to the same
way. Quiet, working too hard, a little bit angry, you know?
But after spending time with Mr. Rosemond, he always relaxed. He whistled at his work. He made jokes and teased
Pierre . . . like today. I'll tell you, when Mr. B. came back
from a trip with your husband, we could always know. How
did we know, you ask?"

Mara hadn't asked, but she figured she was going to get
an answer anyway.

"He put his feet on the dining room table, that's how."

"What?" she said with a sudden laugh. "His feet?"

"Boots and all. You see, usually Mr. B. sits there in the
morning very stiff and brooding with his Powerbook and
tape recorder and cordless phone and all his pencils and
pens. While he eats breakfast, he plans out everything he
wants to do that day. He talks into his little machine, scrib-
bles on the paper, scowls at everybody. He makes us nervous."

"I can see why."

"But for a few days after he'd gotten back from his trips,
he would be happy. Relaxed. He would leave the notebook
and machine in his car or his study. And he would lean back
in his chair and put his feet on the table."

Mara couldn't hold in her smile. It wasn't only the image
of Brock with his boots on the table that warmed her. It was
Todd. Her husband had touched everyone he knew with his
special brand of affection.

"Mr. B., he hasn't been the same since your husband was
killed," Rosa Maria said. "For months now, he doesn't talk

to anyone. He's very difficult, very edgy. Everything has to be done the right way."

"I know about that. When I was in labor with the baby, he told me I hadn't done things logically."

Rosa Maria laughed out loud. "Yes, logic. That's Mr. B. Logic, order, organization, structure and perfection are all that matter to him. Do it right, Rosa Maria, he tells me. Everything must be excellent."

Mara shook her head. "I don't know how you put up with him."

"Oh, Mr. B. has a very big heart, very great tenderness. But his heart is buried deep inside. Locked away. I don't know anybody who ever got in there but his best friend."

"Ya'll, Pierre's having a fit!" Ermaline Criddle called from the door. "He's banging pots and flinging flour everywhere. He says he sent Rosa Maria down here half an hour ago to find out where the *madame* wants to eat her dinner. The lounge or the dining room?"

Rosa Maria set her hands on her hips. "Ermaline, you tell that damn cook—"

"Please, now!" Ermaline cut in. "He's got to know. Mrs. B., where do you want your supper?"

"It's Mara, and I'll..." She debated for a moment. The lounge would be closer to the baby, but she didn't like the idea of eating in a bar and pool hall. On the other hand, she didn't want to encounter Brock more often than necessary. At the same time, she couldn't deny she was curious about this man with the hidden heart.

"Oh, eat in the dining room," Rosa Maria said. "You can hear the baby on the intercom."

"Intercom?"

"Go on, Ermaline. Tell the old buzzard to set his precious dinner in the main dining room."

"But I'm not sure I—"

It was too late. Ermaline had fled, and Rosa Maria was right behind her.

"Just pray Pierre hasn't cooked those snails," she sang out as she vanished down the hall.

Mara stared at the empty doorway. All of a sudden she felt tired. Todd was gone, and she had bonded herself to a man who had built himself a house with a bar. A man who rarely smiled, who constantly drove himself toward perfection, and who made even his closest companions nervous. She could hardly wait for dinner.

Brock was checking his watch when Mara walked into the dining room, her doughnut cushion in hand.

"Dinner's usually at seven," he said as she set down the cushion and eased her sore body onto the chair.

"Newborn babies don't have schedules," she returned. "I was feeding Abby."

"You just nurse her whenever she cries? That doesn't sound very regulated to me."

"It's called feeding on demand." Mara was in such pain from her stitches and from nursing that her appetite had vanished. Even though she was exhausted, sleep seemed a long way off and she couldn't suppress her irritation. "You might recall I don't have Todd or a mother of my own around to help out, and babies aren't into efficiency, Brock. They follow their instincts."

Brock studied his bowl as Ermaline poured a ladleful of soup into it. He hadn't thought about Mara being lonely or needing help. Nor had he considered how often a baby might need to eat. In the hospital, the nurses had brought Abby into Mara's room and the baby had always suckled, but he had never noticed much about it. In fact, he'd usually been so uncomfortable with the process he'd left.

"Suppose she'll be hungry in the middle of the night?" he asked.

"I hear they usually are." Mara unfolded her napkin into her lap as Ermaline approached with the soup. "Let me do that, Ermaline. I don't want to be waited on."

"Oh, Mrs. B—"

"It's Mara."

"But we always serve—"

"No, let me—"

"It's okay, Ermaline," Brock cut in. "Set the tureen on the table."

With an anxious glance at Mara, the maid placed the soup dish beside the arrangement of fresh flowers. As Ermaline hurried back toward the kitchen, Mara let out a breath.

"I'm sorry," she said to Brock. "I shouldn't have snapped at her. I'm just not used to this."

"Is something wrong?"

"It's all so grand. So formal." She dipped out a ladle of vegetable soup and poured it into her bowl. "Rosa Maria turned down my sheets, for Pete's sake."

"What's wrong with that? She's turned down the sheets every night of my life."

"I can turn down my own sheets, Brock." Mara lifted her head and met his eyes. "I want my life to go the way I say."

"Fine."

"I don't want to be called Mrs. Barnett."

"It's your name."

"I'm Mara. I don't want people fawning over me, either, waiting on me hand and foot. And I don't want parties in my wing."

"Parties?" Brock tried to read the message in Mara's tired green eyes without success.

"That lounge," she said. "That bar down the hall from Abby's room. I won't have your wild parties in there."

"Wild parties? Mara, what in hell are you talking about?" He dunked his spoon in the soup.

"Are you going to eat?"

"Of course I'm going to eat. The soup's sitting here getting cold while you go on about wild parties in the den."

"Rosa Maria called it a lounge, not a den. She said you have parties with your friends from Las Cruces. And don't you say grace at the dinner table?"

Brock stared at her. Tears perched just on the edge of her lower eyelashes, threatening to spill over. If those tears slid down her cheeks, he'd be lost. He was already lost. What was she upset about? Was it this business about wild parties? Or eating before saying grace? Or what?

"I pray before I eat," she enunciated, as if speaking to someone a little slow on the uptake. "To thank God for the food, you know?"

"Sure." Brock set his spoon back in the bowl. "Go ahead."

Mara let out a breath. The dining room felt cavernous and almost cold in spite of the bright fire in the huge hearth. She and Brock sat facing each other at one end of a long, sleek table rimmed with twelve chairs. Between them burned a pair of white tapers in silver holders that matched the utensils and bowls. The china was stark white and chilly. Mara shivered. She had never felt so out of place, so confused and emotionally ravaged in her life. If only...

"Todd and I," she said softly, "we held hands."

Brock looked at the wedding bands still on her finger, then lifted his eyes to hers, finally understanding. "I guess you miss him a lot."

She nodded, unable to speak.

"Mara...you can hold my hands."

Startled, she glanced up to find him waiting, his arms stretched across the table and his palms spread open. Slowly she placed one of her hands in each of his. As his fingers closed around hers, she felt his sun-toughened skin and the hard ridges of calluses on his palms. How different from Todd this man was.

He bowed his head. "Go ahead."

"You," she countered in a whisper. "I don't think I can."

Brock swallowed and glanced up, only to find himself staring at the top of Mara's blond hair. He'd been to church in Las Cruces a few times as a boy, but he didn't have the first clue about praying out loud. Any other time, he'd have rejected the request. Then he thought about those tears on her eyelashes.

"Dear God," he began, "here we are at the table. Well...I guess you already knew that. Anyway, we're thinking about Todd, and we both miss him a hell of a lot."

Brock cleared his throat and peered at Mara. Had he blown the prayer? She sat in silence, head low and eyes closed.

"We wish Todd was here with us," he continued. "Wish he could see Abby. We thank you for the baby, for giving her to us...to Mara. And for the food, too. Thanks for that. Amen."

When he opened his eyes, he realized he had blown it. Mara was crying. He ducked his head and went for the soup. Damn! He didn't know what to do with her. Didn't know what to say or how to act. Mara was his wife, but he didn't have a clue how to be a husband to her. Besides, he knew whatever he tried he would never live up to Todd's example.

"Thank you," she whispered, dabbing her napkin in the corner of her eye. "For praying about Abby."

"You're welcome."

"I don't want anything to happen to her."

"It won't, Mara. She's safe here." He downed another spoonful of soup, but it was tasteless. Mara didn't trust him with her baby, and why should she? Look what had happened when he'd gone off with her husband.

"Could you have your parties in the east wing?" she asked.

"What is this about parties?"

"Rosa Maria told me you have a bunch of friends from Las Cruces who come out to the ranch for parties in your lounge. You have a bar and a pool table, and they spend the night. Brock, I can't have drunk strangers around Abby."

"Drunk strangers?" He set his spoon beside his bowl. "My friends come out here a couple of times a year, and they don't get drunk."

Her voice went hostile again. "Well, I don't want them near my daughter."

"Mara, they're good people. They're old college friends, business associates, ranchers."

"They play pool, watch movies, swim, dance and drink."

"They sure do. It's called having fun."

"I know about fun!" Her green eyes blazed. The tears had vanished, and so had the moment of tenderness between them. Mara was glad. She didn't want to hold Brock's hands or hear him pray. She didn't want him to care about Abby.

"You just keep your friends away from my baby," she said.

"What are you going to do—hide for the rest of your life?"

"Hide?"

"Lick your wounds?"

"Oh, what do you know about pain?" Mara stood and grabbed her doughnut pillow. "Abby's mine, and I'll raise her the way I want to. You have no say in it whatsoever. Abby's the one I'm protecting, and if that means hiding her from bad influences, that's what I'll do. The wounds that need to be tended are Abby's—and the man who wounded her is you."

Tucking the pillow against her tender breasts, Mara stalked across the dining room toward the hall.

"You're the one who's hurting," Brock said behind her. "You're the one who's wounded. But I don't know what it would take to fix you."

Mara slipped into the corridor and leaned against the wall as tears streamed down her cheeks.

Chapter 7

"Rosa Maria, where's my Powerbook?" Brock hollered the next morning as he strode into the dining room and tossed his Stetson onto the table. "I left it in the study next to the fax machine, and I'll be damned if it's there now."

He thunked his briefcase on the floor and dropped a shower of pencils beside his plate. Where could that Powerbook be? He stored all his files for the ranch in the small computer, and his backup disks were buried in the safe—those that he hadn't already locked in a deposit box at his bank in Las Cruces.

"Leave things in somebody else's hands for a week," he muttered as he dropped into his chair. "Chaos."

"Eggs Benedict," Ermaline announced. Breezing into the dining room, she balanced a silver tray on her upturned palm. "Hey, where's Mrs. B.?"

"Where's Rosa Maria?" Brock demanded in return. "I've called her three times."

"Isn't she in the living room? That's where she always starts dusting in the morning."

"She's not there now." Pushing back from the table, Brock grimaced. He'd let everything get out of control. For

most of the night he'd sat on his porch or wandered the
courtyard and tried to figure a way to put a stamp of order
back on his life. Now he was dead tired, he'd misplaced his
computer, his housekeeper had vanished and he was supposed to be in the north section in fifteen minutes checking
the cattle.

He walked to the intercom and flipped the master control switch. "Rosa Maria," he barked. "If you're anywhere in this damn house, get yourself to the dining room."

He waited a moment, then opened the intercom to every
room in the house. A baby's loud wail flooded through the
mesh screen and filled the dining room.

"Oh, no," Mara's voice groaned from her own bedroom
in the west wing. "Thanks a lot, Brock. It's okay, Abby.
Mommy's coming."

Standing half a house away, Brock winced. He hadn't realized he might wake the baby. Well, that was the crux of the
problem. With Mara and Abby in the house, things weren't
functioning the way they always had. Things didn't feel
normal.

"Here she is, Mrs. B.," Rosa Maria's voice said softly
through the intercom. "Here's your baby girl. You stay in
bed there. You've been up all night, haven't you?"

"Most of the night. Well, hello there, precious girl. Are
you hungry? Oh, Rosa Maria, I'm so tired and sore. It's really great to have your help. Thanks for bringing her to me."

"I'm glad to do it. I was here checking on Abby, anyway. Look at that, she doesn't want to nurse. She was just
scared by that darn Mr. Barnett yelling over the intercom.
Tsk. He doesn't even think sometimes, that man."

"I believe he wants you in the dining room, Rosa Maria."

"I heard him bellowing like one of his old cows. He's
forgotten he put his precious Powerbook in his car when he
went to the hospital to visit you. He can't get through
breakfast without his computer and all his pencils and pa-
pers."

Standing in the dining room, Brock scowled at the intercom. Half tempted to turn off the eavesdropping and half

tempted to throw both women out of his house for their disrespect and ingratitude, he shoved his hands into his pockets.

Come to think of it, he *had* left the Powerbook in his car.

"Do you think Abby's all right, Rosa Maria?" Mara asked in a low voice. "I'm worried she's sick or something. Is it normal for her to be awake so much of the night?"

"She doesn't know it's night. All she knows is she's hungry or wet or lonely in that big new crib. Remember this was only the first night. She'll start to sleep better after a while. In the meantime, you're the one who needs some sleep."

"I feel like I've been run over by a truck."

Rosa Maria chuckled. "I know, I know. I remember with all of mine how it was. But you're doing good. It's hard by yourself. If you had a nice man to look after you—" She caught herself, then tried again. "I'm sure Mr. Rosemond would have stayed by your side... Oh, I'm sorry. I shouldn't talk about your husband—"

Brock snapped off the intercom. *He* was Mara's husband, not Todd. As much as everybody missed him, Todd was gone. Never coming back. But Todd—who'd never actually been a father—was doing a better job of it than Brock.

He studied the lumps of eggs Benedict in their cold white hollandaise sauce. He might be Mara's husband, but he wasn't Abby's father. Mara had made that clear enough last night. Even if he wanted to go to Mara...comfort her...support her...she didn't want him. So, she could just cope with motherhood on her own.

Mara and Abby were nothing more than another of Brock's financial obligations. He had committed his resources to their care. He had offered a place to stay, food to eat, money to spend. But he didn't owe them anything else.

Besides, he thought as he grabbed his hat from the table, he wouldn't know the first thing about helping Mara with her baby. He had never learned how to be a husband or a father, and he wasn't inclined in that direction, anyway. Good enough.

He settled his hat on his brow and headed for the back door. So, there were two extra people in the house? He would put them into a file in his computer like a couple head of cattle he might have bought at the state fair. He'd factor them into the equation, calculate the cost of food, add their projected medical expenses and figure the outlay for wintering them. They wouldn't be economical, and he would never recoup his losses.

But those were the breaks.

Mara finished nursing Abby and clipped her bra cup into the strap. For a moment she gazed down at the tiny face nestled in the crook of her elbow. Her daughter's eyes had dropped shut, their long, curling lashes brushing the round apples of her cheeks. Her miniature nose bore a blush from being pressed against Mara's full breast. Like a pale pink rose, her mouth formed a delicate bud, barely open with lips so soft and sweet, Mara thought her heart might break.

Four days had passed since Abby's birth, and already Mara loved this child more than she had ever known she could love anyone or anything. Long nights awake didn't matter. Tender nipples and a sore tailbone didn't matter. Nothing mattered but this precious weight in her arms.

Mara blinked back tears, wondering if she was ever going to be in control of her emotions again. Had she actually yelled at Brock last night? Had she really admonished the man for failing to pray before dinner? And what did she know about his Las Cruces friends, anyway?

Shaking her head, Mara tucked the warm white blanket she had crocheted during the summer around Abby's neck. Brock had been nothing but kind and good to her since Todd's death, while she had chastised him and found fault with everything he did. She owed him an apology.

Easing herself up out of the rocking chair, Mara started toward the crib with its billowy white canopy. Halfway across the room, she stopped. Maybe she would just go and find Brock right now. It was almost noon, and he'd be home for lunch. With Abby sleeping in her arms, maybe they wouldn't be so tempted to argue with each other. Maybe she could tell him how she felt.

For a moment, she hesitated again. She hadn't had a shower this morning, and she was still in her ragged blue bathrobe. But she couldn't bear to put her maternity clothes back on, even though she had a sinking certainty they were all she could fit into.

Lifting her chin, she decided it hardly mattered how she looked to Brock Barnett. She walked out of the nursery and started down the hall. "Brock I wanted to thank you for taking Abby and me in," she would say. "You've been so kind."

Kind? Brock Barnett? Mara had to smile. The word hardly fit her image of the man. Tucking Abby more closely into her embrace, she passed the lounge. Remembering her discussion with Brock the night before, she felt a sudden temptation to clarify as much as she could about him. She paused briefly, and then she pushed open the door to his den of iniquity.

"Oh, you scared the living daylights out of me!" Ermaline gasped as she lifted her head from behind the long wooden bar. Feather duster in one hand and spray wax in the other, she leaned her elbows on the sleek aged wood. "Well, hey there, Mrs. B. What are you doing in here?"

"Just looking around. What about you?"

"I clean this place every morning before I go to the kitchen to help Pierre with the lunch. My job is the west wing and the meal serving. Rosa Maria takes care of Mr. B.'s rooms and the main living areas. Pierre's in charge of the kitchen, and Mr. Potter keeps up the gardens and courtyard. So, what do you think? Ever seen the likes of this little playroom?"

Mara surveyed the long room with its warm *saltillo* tile floor, comfortable seating area, entertainment center, pool table and neat kitchenette. "I thought... I thought it would be... different."

"This place hardly gets used anymore," Ermaline said. "Shame. Mr. B. used to have some dandy parties. Folks would come out from Las Cruces and make use of the pool, the barbecue pit, the whole shebang. There'd be lanterns strung across the courtyard and a band playing and everybody having a big ol' time. Christmas we'd have a bonfire and dancing. Frank and me got to come, too. He invited everybody, Mr. B. did. New Year's we'd have a big time, too. Things are sure quiet now.''

Mara studied the long linen drapes that covered the wall of windows, blocking out the late November light. ''What happened?''

''Mr. B. told us there's no time for parties now. Pierre was the one who finally faced him head-on about it. You know how Pierre likes to cook, and he gets tired of making meals for one. You should have seen the French stuff he used to turn out of that kitchen for Mr. B.'s parties. You'd have thought you were in gay Paree sure enough.''

''Brock is too busy doing what?''

''Running this ranch. I'm telling you, that's all he does day and night. He's either branding or roping or breeding or doing something to those crazy cows. He rounds them up and moves them here, moves them there. He goes to market, goes to shows, goes to the fair. He buys a prize bull, and we all have to take a gander at it. 'Come on, Ermaline,' he'll say. 'Don't you and Rosa Maria want to take a look at my new Simmental?' As if I'd know one kind of cow from another.''

''Why doesn't he take those friends of his to look at his cattle?''

''Well, he used to take your husband.''

''Oh.'' Mara lowered her head and focused on the wedding band Todd had given her. Again, she had been brought face-to-face with the realization that he had not belonged to her alone.

''They'd go look the ranch over, your husband and Mr. B.,'' Ermaline went on. ''There's some ruins over toward the mountains where the cliffs are, you know. Them two couldn't get enough of rooting around there and talking about the olden days. Oh, sometimes a bunch of Mr. B.'s friends from Las Cruces still come out here. The truth is, he's got nothing in common with them anymore, but he just doesn't like to admit it.''

''Has Brock changed so much over the years?''

''Sure he has.'' Ermaline shot a stream of foamy spray onto the top of the bar and began to rub it with a cloth she dug out of her apron pocket. ''Used to be, Mr. B. was out all night and slept most of the day. That was in high school and college when his daddy—we always called him Mr. Barnett, too—ran this place. The boy had lots of girlfriends, lots of fancy cars, big stereos, that kind of thing. Now, he just works all the time. His Las Cruces friends have become accountants and bankers and office types. They don't care about Simmental bulls, and Mr. B. knows it. I suspect they want him back the way he was with his freewheeling life, easy money, fast cars and all that. But he wants this ranch to do good, and that can't happen if you're up all night with the girls. You know how Mr. B. is. He doesn't do a thing unless he wants to.''

''I've learned that.''

Ermaline laughed. ''It's his way or no way.''

Mara strolled down to the end of the room, admiring the bold paintings on the walls and the thick wool rugs on the floors. A huge fireplace dominated the end of the lounge, its grate loaded with heavy, unburned logs.

Beside the hearth sat an intricately crafted chair built from the sinuous branches of an alligator juniper. Mara touched the strange piece, its arms constructed from whole limbs twisted together and then jointed into the massive legs. A soft green cushion formed the seat, and she couldn't resist settling into it with Abby.

''He made that chair, you know,'' Ermaline called from the other end of the room where she was dusting lamps. ''Mr. B. did. He builds stuff.''

Mara glanced at the piece in surprise. ''This?''

''You didn't know? He's got a big workshop over the other side of the house with all his tools. When he can't sleep, that's where he'll be if he's not in the courtyard. Half this stuff I dust every day is furniture he made. That table there, the bench over yonder, that cabinet by the window. He made you that rocker."

"The one in the baby's room?"

"Sure. Every day last week after he got back from the hospital, he'd come into the house, change clothes and go straight to the shop. Sawdust just flew, I'm telling you. He was a man possessed. Now, Rosa Maria and me remember what he told us about this marriage being only to take care of you because you're his best friend's wife, and all. But we think he's got a heart for you anyway, Mrs. B. You, or maybe the baby. Either way, he made that rocking chair just for you, no doubt about it."

"Oh, Ermaline, I don't—"

"When he brought it into the house, he said, 'Put this in the nursery, Ermaline. It's for the baby's mama.' That's what he said."

Mara stared at Abby, trying to absorb this news. Brock had made that beautiful rocker—for her? She could hardly believe it. She'd treated him so coldly. Because of what had happened to Todd, she'd thought nothing but the worst of Brock. And all the while he'd been building her a rocking chair.

"I'm going to talk to him this minute," she announced, standing suddenly. "We need to clear up some things."

"Good luck finding him," Ermaline said as Mara carried Abby to the door. "He's usually gone from sunup to way past dark."

Mara paused in the hall. "He doesn't come home for lunch?"

"Not even for supper sometimes. Likes to eat with the ranch hands, you know. Drives Pierre crazy when he doesn't show up for supper, which is more times than not. I reckon I've gone a whole week without laying eyes on that man."

"But this is his house."

Ermaline squirted the top of a table with the spray wax. "Sure it's his house, all fixed up and perfect. But what's a house if you don't have anything to come home to?"

She tossed her damp rag on the table and began to rub. "Let me know if you find him, Mrs. B. I've been needing a case of window cleaner in the worst way."

After lunch alone in her room and a deep afternoon nap, Mara showered and changed into a long, pink, knitted sweater-tunic. She told herself it didn't look as much like maternity wear as some of her other clothes. With a pair of pink leggings and the top hanging to her midthighs, she almost felt presentable.

After checking the sleeping Abby, Mara brushed out her hair, then braided it into a full French plait and tied the end with a pink ribbon. For the first time since Abby's birth, she smoothed makeup onto her face, dusted her cheeks with blush and puffed a little translucent powder over her skin. With a touch of liner, shadow and mascara on her eyes, she felt as though she were almost seeing the familiar face of Mara Rosemond in the mirror again.

But she wasn't that Mara anymore. Whether she liked it or not, she was Mrs. Barnett, rancher's wife. She was a mother, too. And she was jobless, penniless, almost homeless. The least she could do was offer her caretaker a polite thank you.

Mara again checked Abby, then headed down the long hall toward the dining room. She still felt awkward and uncomfortable in the huge, empty house, but some things were looking up. She had discovered she could walk without cringing in pain. In the shower, she had noticed her breasts were full but not quite as tender. Even her stomach seemed to be shrinking.

"There you are!" Ermaline swung into the dining room from the kitchen just as Mara entered from the hall. "Pierre's fixed the best chicken you ever tasted. He's baked his famous hot rolls, too."

"Is Brock coming?"

"Doubt it. We haven't seen hide nor hair of him all day. You?"

"No, I haven't seen him."

"Better get used to it." She grabbed a serving dish from the cupboard and hurried into the kitchen.

Mara pulled back the chair she had sat in the night before. This was her place at the table, she supposed. As she settled onto the chair, a memory suddenly surfaced. Growing up in a series of foster homes, she had never had her own place at a table. Then after she married Todd, she had begun setting their plates anywhere on the little dinette, sometimes at one end, sometimes at the other. Sometimes they ate on the couch, sometimes the kitchen counter, and once or twice even standing up.

"From now on you sit here, Mara," Todd had told her one night, holding out a chair at the table. "This is your place."

For the next five years she had sat right there. Her place. How normal it had seemed to face her husband across their laminated table with their plastic plates and their chipped glasses in between. How comfortable.

"Pierre sends you his regards," Ermaline announced as she sashayed back into the dining room, her arms laden with a heavy silver salver and covered dishes. "Chicken marsala," she continued as she swept aside a silver dome. "That means he cooked it in wine. And here's some veggies, some of those rolls, a little salad with tee-tiny onions in it, and I'll bring in the dessert when you're done. It's cheesecake. I peeked."

She started to spoon the chicken onto Mara's plate, then she caught herself. "Oops, I forgot."

Mara gave her a nod. "It's okay, Ermaline. Do it the way you always have."

With a sigh of relief, the maid loaded Mara's plate with food. "I've been working here a long time, first for old Mr. Barnett and now for young Mr. B. You learn to do things a certain way, you know?"

Mara nodded. "I was used to things a certain way, too."

"I reckon so. You live with someone a while and things kind of fall into a pattern. You get familiar with each other's habits, and you get real cozy with those ordinary little day-to-day things. Gee, I don't know what I'd do if I lost

Frank. Me and him go back a long ways. We've kind of got ourselves a routine after all these years being married. But, I guess you can't keep looking back at what you had. You've got Abby now, and Mr. B. You've got a lot right there.''

"I don't think I do have Mr. B."

"Well, nobody really has him. He doesn't think he wants to be had, but that could be remedied.'' She clanged the domed lids onto their dishes and swept the tray into her arms. "Want some music? I can turn on the stereo in the living room and pipe it in here.''

Mara stared down at her meal, then looked at the long empty table. "Is the intercom on? I want to hear Abby.''

"Oh, sure.'' Ermaline marched across the room and flipped a few switches. "You'll hear the slightest peep. This is the eeriest durn machine. Never know if someone's listening in. Okay, well, just ring that little bell if you need anything.''

"Thank you.'' Mara watched as Ermaline vanished into the kitchen.

She had eaten alone before. Ever since Todd's death, she had sat alone in her apartment, cooked alone, dined alone, slept alone. Why did this meal feel so strange and uncomfortable?

She inserted a fork and knife into the chicken and cut a few bites. The flavor was delicious, and at the same time the food tasted completely bland. Maybe she still had the baby blues. She should call Sherry and invite her best friend over for the weekend. Mara could show off the baby. Sherry could fill her in on things at church, people they both knew, events at the boutique where Sherry worked and the historical museum where Mara used to spend so much time.

She shouldn't need Sherry to keep her company. She shouldn't feel lonely at all. The three members of the household staff were in the kitchen. Abby was just down the hall. And Mara hardly even liked the man whose absence made the house seem empty.

Chewing on another bite of chicken, she tried to recall what she had hated so much about Brock. He had caused Todd's death, of course. Well, she had never learned the whole truth about that experience, and she didn't want to. But there was no doubt Brock was responsible for luring Todd off to another reckless adventure, and he had been responsible as Todd's anchor on the cliffs. She had lost her husband forever because of Brock's foolhardiness. Abby would never know a father. Mara would never truly be loved again.

So, why couldn't she summon up the proper anger toward Brock? Mara stabbed a bite of salad. Because Brock had come to the hospital? Because he'd helped her give birth? Because he'd built a rocking chair? Those things didn't erase his part in Todd's death.

But she couldn't hate him, either. Maybe she just hadn't seen enough of the man lately to remember how to despise him. It had always been so easy before.

"Dessert?" Ermaline's head popped around the door. "Chocolate cheesecake? Pierre put cherries on top and drizzled his rum-flavored chocolate syrup all around."

"Sounds good."

"It's delicious. We tasted it already, me and Rosa Maria."

"All right."

"She wants the cheesecake!" the older woman hollered over her shoulder into the kitchen. "You liked the chicken? Pierre wants to know."

"Very good."

"She liked it!" Ermaline called back again. "She said it was *très bon.*"

Mara watched the maid giggle, her oversize teeth suddenly seeming twice as large. She had to smile in return. *"Très bon?"*

"Pierre loves it when people talk French about his food." Ermaline cleared the dishes. "So what do you think, Mrs. B.? You think you'll like it here? You think you'll stay?"

Mara smoothed her napkin across her lap. "For a while."

"Me and the other staff hope you'll stay. We think Mr. B. will get used to you after a while."

"Pretty hard to get used to someone you never see."

"Oh, he just drove in. Didn't I tell you? He'll probably stop by for the cheesecake."

Ermaline sailed out of the room before Mara could call out. Suddenly her mouth felt like the bottom of an old shoe. Her heart skittered into a crazy dance, and she couldn't catch her breath. Grabbing the napkin, she debated bolting. She really didn't want to see Brock after all. She certainly couldn't bring herself to thank this man she'd always disliked.

No, she *did* want to see him. She wanted to understand why her palms had gone damp at the prospect of his appearance in the room. She wanted to know why he wouldn't be owned by anyone and why he'd locked his heart away. She wanted to feel that strange curl in the base of her spine when he looked at her. She wanted to hear his voice.

No, she didn't! She jumped up and pushed her chair back from the table.

"Hey, Mara." Brock walked into the room and took off his hat.

She stared. He was tall. He was tan. He was black-haired and brown-eyed and handsome. Too handsome. That pulsing curl slid down into the pit of her stomach and skittered down her thighs. This always happened when she saw him, she reminded herself. It always had, even from the beginning. But when he talked and swaggered and tried to control everything and everybody, she hated him. She really did.

"You already ate?" he asked.

"You told me supper's at seven."

He gave an apologetic smile. "When I'm here, it's at seven. I ate at the bunkhouse."

"You missed the chicken marsala."

"I hear it was *très bon.*"

"It was." Mara swallowed. He was holding her with those brown eyes of his. She couldn't move. Surely she could summon up her familiar dislike of him, couldn't she? He had let Todd fall. He had destroyed her life. Why on earth was she shaking? It had to be a hormone imbalance. Childbirth did that to a woman.

"I guess I'll have some cheesecake," he said, walking toward her. "Pierre's is the best."

"The *pièce de résistance* of this meal."

His mouth curved into a grin. "You learn fast. Speak French to Pierre, and he'll love you forever."

Mara grabbed the back of the chair to keep herself from asking the question that rolled to the tip of her tongue. *What would make you love a woman forever, Brock?*

Ridiculous! She didn't care how he felt or what went on inside his frigid heart. It was time to sit down. No, it was time to get out of this room and away from this man who was walking closer and closer.

"How was your day, Mara?"

"Fine."

"Get any rest?"

"A little."

"The baby okay?"

"Sleeping."

"That's good."

"Yeah." She tried to give a nonchalant smile. "Someone woke her up awfully early this morning."

"Sorry about that." He set his hat on the table. "You look different tonight."

She flushed and hated herself for it. "I took a shower."

"You have on regular clothes." He glanced down at her and regretted it instantly. Mara was beautiful. In the past four days, her body had become a vision of soft pink curves, delicious hills and welcoming valleys. Her breasts stood out more tempting than any dessert. Her long, slender legs wore nothing but a thin skin of tight fabric.

"At least I can see my feet again," she said.

It was meant to be a joke, a reminder of their adventure in the tiny apartment bathroom, but he didn't laugh. He lifted his head and looked into her eyes. Gray-green, they beckoned him. Her long, dark lashes fluttered down, then up. She moistened her lips, and it was all he could do to keep from devouring that soft, tender mouth.

"I have a long way to go before I feel normal." She was talking again, and he watched entranced as her lips formed the words. "I need to start exercising. Right now, I feel like I'm doing well just to walk down the hall without hurting too much."

"Hurting?" He reached out and touched her hand. "I'm sorry, Mara. I didn't realize... I know you went through a lot the other day. You want to use the spa? It's in my wing."

"Oh..." She should pull her hand away. The man was so close she could smell his scent, wild and somehow earthy after his day in the dust and wind and chilly, late-autumn sunshine. It cast a spell, like a fragile net, over her shoulders. She knew she could escape the spell, but she couldn't make herself want to.

"Feels good after a hard day," he said. "Warm water swirling around. Bubbles. Steam."

"Not tonight. Thank you." She instructed her knees to bend, and she managed to sit on her chair. "I'm tired. Very tired."

He studied the top of her head, the golden strands of hair that had fallen loose from her braid and the pale line down the center of her part. "Whatever feels right."

"Cheesecake!" Ermaline sang out as she swept into the dining room. "Have a seat, Mr. B. You want a dessert wine with this?"

Brock pulled away from Mara and forced himself to walk around the table. "No, thanks," he said. "I think I'm a little off center tonight already."

"You boys ought to lay off that beer down at the bunk-house, Mr. B. Especially on a work night."

Ermaline bustled out of the dining room, and Brock picked up his fork. "I haven't had a thing to drink," he said.

Chapter 8

For the first time in his life, Brock considered turning away a slice of Pierre's cheesecake. He stared down at the creamy confection dripping in chocolate and cherries, and all he could think about was Mara. She sat an arm's length away across the table, the scent of her perfume mingling with the fragrance of burning wax from the candles between them. He shouldn't have looked at her again. Only the day before, he'd made himself a promise to stay away from the woman. But the minute he'd heard she was in the dining room, he'd galloped right in like a stud stallion on the scent of a mare.

He twiddled his fork back and forth, then stuck it into the cheesecake and broke off a bite. As he chewed, he realized the stuff felt like quick-drying carpenter's glue in his mouth. His attempt to swallow only lodged the bite right at Adam's apple level where it stuck firm and made any chance at conversation impossible. Just as well.

He had no business daydreaming up a bunch of romantic nonsense about a woman who had nearly ruined his peaceful life. In spite of his best intentions, he'd thought about Mara all day long. While loading a steer or checking his barns or driving down a dusty dirt road, he would catch himself in the realization that her face had appeared right in front of him. He might picture her straining to give birth to little Abby or smiling with that half shy, secret smile or lashing out at him like lightning in a summer storm.

From any angle and in any circumstance Mara looked beautiful to him. Her blond hair sifted around her shoulders like a silk sheet. Her eyes glowed with an inner light of determination and intelligence that had always fascinated him. Her mouth... oh, Mara's mouth...

"I dropped by the lounge this morning," she said. "The one in my wing."

He worked at swallowing the gluey lump of cheesecake. "Oh, yeah?"

"It was very nice."

"Mmm-hmm." He couldn't lift his head or he'd have to see her face again. But he couldn't take another bite or he'd be so gummed up he'd choke. Instead, he intently mashed the cheesecake into a pattern of geometric fork marks.

"I feel like I misjudged you, Brock," she said in a low voice. "It's just that I'm a quiet person, and I don't enjoy parties all that much. Especially with a baby around."

"Mmm."

"I was worried there might be too much going on in my wing."

He glanced up, but focused on the window behind her. "No, it's uh... quiet around here."

"It is very quiet." Mara toyed with the crust of her dessert. "You're gone a lot, aren't you?"

He nodded. "Lots to be done, you know."

"Cows."

"Yeah."

"Well, I wanted to talk to you tonight," she began. "There are some things I thought I should tell you."

Again he lifted his eyes, but this time he couldn't resist looking at her. Mara was studying her own cheesecake as intently as he'd studied his. A soft flush had spread across her cheeks to light her skin with a pink glow. He couldn't remember when he'd ever seen a woman look so gentle, so tender. In her pink sweater and golden hair, she was almost a vision. He had to get out of the dining room. And fast.

"Don't worry about parties," he said quickly as he pushed back from the table and stood up. "I keep things pretty dull around here. Well, I reckon I'll just—"

"Thank you," she cut in, lifting her eyes to his. "For everything."

He stopped. "What?"

"For all this. The house, the food. I'm grateful to you for paying my hospital and doctor bills. And the nursery…thank you for all the furniture. For the rocking chair."

Rubbing his palm around the back of his neck beneath his collar, Brock let out a breath. "Somebody say something to you about that rocker?"

"Ermaline told me you built it."

"Figures." He debated how to handle this inevitable situation. While Mara had been in the hospital, he could think of nothing but finding a way to please her. He had felt almost obsessed with crafting the rocker for her. More than with any other piece of furniture, he had poured the sum of his carpentry expertise into that chair. Telling himself it was for the baby's comfort, he had known all along he was building it for Mara. When the piece sat finished, he had felt certain it was perfect. Only then had he begun to wonder what had possessed him to work so hard for a woman who despised him, and to worry how she might interpret his gesture.

"I do a lot of carpentry," he said, his voice carefully nonchalant. "Keeps my mind off things."

"Well, I appreciate it." Mara stood and rounded the table toward him. "Brock, you've done more than—"

"I'd do just about anything for Todd," he said quickly. She was suddenly too close. He could smell the scent of her freshly washed hair, like flowers after a rainstorm. Terrified he might touch her, he threw out the only barrier he could think of to push her away.

"Todd was my best friend, remember?" he said, his voice harsher than he intended. "I can't do anything to bring him back, but I know how to manage the business end of things.

You and the baby are already figured into my budget. Consider yourselves part of the general household operation, like Pierre, the maids, the gardener. You know what I mean? You've just been absorbed right into the equation. Don't start thinking about the money I'm out for furniture, food and all that. I know what my obligations are, and I never let anything slip by me.''

Mara studied his brown eyes as he spoke. He was staring at something above and behind her, as though she didn't really exist. This wasn't the Brock she knew—the head-on, take the bull by the horns, confrontational man whose glance could wither a person.

Either he was evading her for some reason she couldn't fathom, or he really didn't see her as a human being worthy of congenial conversation. He'd told her she was an obligation, a factor in his budget and nothing more. How could she think a hand-built rocker made it otherwise?

"I'm not accustomed to thinking of myself as a line item in somebody's budget," she said.

Brock looked at her, and the realization that she was easily within his grasp sent a solid weight to the pit of his stomach. He swallowed hard and shifted from one foot to the other. Her gray-green eyes were fastened to him as she waited for some response, but all he could think about was squelching the urge to take her in his arms and kiss her lips.

"I realize you're trying to do right by Todd," she continued. "But I prefer to be treated as a human being."

"Is anyone here treating you badly, Mara?"

Her shoulders sagged. How could she explain that this day had been almost unbearably lonely? A woman with a new baby and a house full of servants, stereos, CD players, televisions and phones had no right to feel alone. But Mara had, and she wasn't even sure why.

"I'm being treated very well," she acknowledged.

"Has the staff said anything unkind about our arrangement or the baby or anything?"

"Oh, no. They've all been polite."

"Do you need anything? More clothes? Shoes? A different room?"

"No, I have all I need. More than enough."

"Then what's the problem?"

She ran a finger along the back of the chair. "I'm a human, Brock," she said, lifting her eyes to his. "I have feelings. I have needs that have nothing to do with clothes and shoes. It's hard to live with the realization that you're resented."

"No one resents you."

"I'm trying to tell you that I want to be treated like a woman, not a budget cost. Can't you see that?"

"I see that." He took her shoulders firmly. "Mara, don't ask anything more of me. I'm doing all I can to...to manage this situation."

"You don't have to manage me, Brock. And I'm not a situation, I'm a human being. I'd like someone to talk to once in a while. I could use a little company at the dinner table."

Struggling for control, he stared into her eyes. "I told you I can't bring Todd back. I can't fix that."

"I know you can't bring him back."

"I can't take his place, either. I'm not Todd. I never will be."

"Am I asking you to be Todd?"

He shook his head slowly. Beneath his fingers, her sweater was warm and soft. Her shoulders felt so small and fragile. With one tilt of his thumbs he could pull her against him and know the sweet pressure of her body. "You're asking too much, Mara."

"Why?" The word was a breath against his skin.

He searched her face, hoping to find the hatred and disgust he had seen so often in her eyes. Instead he saw only vulnerability. Loneliness. Sorrow. But he couldn't melt the wall of resolve he'd built to keep her and everyone else out of his life. This woman, more than any other, was forbidden. She wore another man's wedding band, and she belonged to him.

"You're Todd's wife," he said, determined to restore the barrier she had begun to topple. "If I'm going to take care of his business—and I am—then I have to work hard. You may have feelings and needs, but you're going to have to handle them without me around. I don't have time to eat here at the house every meal and then sit around visiting with you. I have to pay my bills, which are bigger now than they were before you came along, and that means I need to be out on the range whenever I can."

He dropped his hands from her shoulders and leaned over the table to grab his hat. Mara clenched her teeth as he turned his back on her and headed for the door.

"Todd never walked away from me in the middle of a conversation," she snapped.

He halted. "I told you—I'm not Todd."

"My husband never thought of me as a bill to pay."

"I'm not your husband."

"Yes, you are, Brock." Mara glared at the square set to his broad shoulders. "You know, after walking through your home and meeting your friends and seeing the rocker you built, I thought I had caught a glimpse of a man I might be able to forgive. I thought there might be room for a measure of cordiality between us. In fact, I almost forgot why I originally refused to marry you that day in my apartment. Thank you for reminding me."

"You're welcome," he said.

As his shoulders vanished into the shadows of the long hall, Mara realized he had never even turned to look back at her.

"So, how's Brock these days?" Sherry asked over the telephone. "Is he doing anything to help out with the baby?"

Mara frowned at the pile of white cotton infant T-shirts she had been folding as she sat on the bed with the receiver in the crook of her neck. "I haven't seen the man for more than a week, Sher. I doubt he's been home long enough to read his mail, let alone help out with Abby."

"How could you not see Brock for a week? Aren't you living in the same house?"

"You should take a look at this place sometime. We could live here forever and not run into each other."

"What about meals and evenings?"

"He's never here. Works all the time." Mara dropped a T-shirt onto the stack. "Brock informed me he has a lot more bills to pay these days, thanks to Abby and me."

"Ooh, what a rat. You don't suppose he's trying to turn the tables, do you? Maybe he wants to make you feel like you owe him, instead of the other way around."

"Who knows? I never think about the man."

As soon as she'd said the words, Mara realized they were a lie. She thought about Brock Barnett all the time during her long, empty days. As she had studied each painting up and down every hall in his house, she had wondered what about the artistry had touched him. As she had examined every stick of furniture, she had imagined his hands smoothing over the hard wood, planing it and polishing it to a high, silken sheen. She'd looked through his living room library, reading the notations he'd penned in the margins and noting the titles of the books he'd obviously read more than once.

Every morning, she dressed for breakfast and wondered if she would run into him on his way to the day's labors. Every evening, she listened for the sound of his pickup pulling up to the house. At night, after nursing Abby, she wandered onto her porch and sat in the long wooden swing to try to figure out why this man had possessed her thoughts.

It had to be that hormone imbalance.

"Well, I wouldn't think about Brock, either," Sherry said. "Abby must keep you awfully busy."

"Actually, she sleeps a lot."

"Just being around to nurse her all the time is such a responsibility, though. Don't you feel tied down?"

"That's not really the way I would describe it." Mara looked around at the huge, empty room. "I love Abby so much, and I'm thankful I can have this time with her. I feel like I've been given a chance to rest and recover from the birth."

"But? Come on, Mara, I know you too well. What's the problem?"

"It's awfully quiet here. When Abby's sleeping, there are long spaces of time when it's just me."

"You're missing Todd, aren't you?"

Mara shut her eyes. Yes, she missed Todd, but she couldn't deny that much of that pain had eased. She didn't think about him all the time anymore. She didn't experience his loss as sharply as she once had. Should she feel guilty about that? Sometimes she did.

"I miss Todd," she acknowledged. "I miss people."

"Why don't you come into town for church this Sunday? Everyone's been asking about you, Mara."

"I couldn't leave Abby in the nursery yet. She's still hungry too often. Besides, I don't have anything to wear that doesn't make me look like I'm still pregnant."

"Oh, Mara, I bet you look like you always have—Ms. Toothpick Perfection. How about if I drive out to visit you? I'd love to take a gander at that mansion of Brock's."

"It's not a mansion, Sherry. It's just a big house. A very big house." Mara let out a breath, realizing she couldn't even work up much enthusiasm to see her best friend.

"I've got some Christmas presents for Abby," Sherry said. "I could drop them off."

"Christmas? Gosh, I haven't even given that a thought. I don't suppose much will change around here. I'm married to the original Grinch, you know."

Sherry chuckled. "Maybe you should give Brock a chance. Didn't the Grinch's heart grow two sizes after he felt all that love and affection? You never can tell what might happen to Brock with you around. Be nice to him, and he might turn into Prince Charming one of these days."

"Dream on." Mara shook her head. "Why don't you come out for a visit in a week or two? Maybe by that time I'll even be able to put on a pair of jeans."

"How about next Sunday afternoon? I'll give you a rundown on the sermon."

Mara laughed. It was a standing joke with Sherry that their pastor—though good-hearted—was the most boring preacher in the world.

"It's a deal. See you then. Bye, Sher."

"Bye, Mar."

Mara hung up the receiver and stretched out on the bed among the piles of miniature dresses and nightgowns. She wasn't the least bit tired, and she knew Abby wouldn't wake up for at least an hour. Maybe two. Of course, she couldn't leave the house, just in case Abby surprised her, but what could she do with all the empty time until dinner?

She had already walked up and down every inch of this place. The art might be beautiful and the architecture grand, but the house was a prison nonetheless. Mara felt trapped, and she could see no way out. In the midst of winter there could be no gardening, no wading in the pool and few warm days for picnics or walks with the stroller.

Indoors, things were only worse. With effort, Mara had convinced Rosa Maria to let her take on some of the laundry duties. But Pierre wouldn't dream of allowing her in the kitchen, and Ermaline refused to give up her dust rags. They had brought in a stack of jigsaw puzzles.

Mara rolled onto her bottom and hauled herself to her feet. Brock certainly had enough to do. Once or twice she had caught sight of him from a distance. Mostly she had seen his pickup pulling in or out of the drive. If he came home for dinner, he ordered the meal sent to his study. If the weather was too bad to work outside, he spent the day in his workshop. Several nights while Mara was up feeding the baby, she had realized his light was on. His room lay directly across the courtyard from hers, but it might have been a thousand miles.

She had to find something to do or she'd go stark raving mad. Mara thought about the old days when she had rushed here and there—teaching school all day at the academy, racing to the grocery store, throwing a meal in the oven, wolfing down dinner with her husband, poring over her students' homework or helping Todd with his research for the fort project and finally falling into bed too tired to move. What she wouldn't give for one hectic day.

Wandering down the hall, she trailed her fingers along the smooth adobe wall. She had loved working with Todd on the fort restoration. Though he had been in charge of the project, she had done much of the research. In fact, her files lay abandoned in a box in the bedroom closet, awaiting the decision of the fort supervisors.

If Mara was forced to sell her husband's company, the buyers would be able to claim her research. But Brock had assured her he was going to manage Todd's business. She realized she hadn't even asked him what had become of the company. Was it possible the project might continue?

The first tingle of enthusiasm she had felt in days ran through Mara's veins. If Brock could find a way to keep the restoration company going, find someone to take Todd's place renovating the old buildings, then Mara's work was still in demand. Instantly, she recalled a section in Brock's library devoted to the Civil War and the ensuing settlement of New Mexico. Might there be some mention of the old military forts? Of Fort Selden?

She almost ran down the hall and into the living room. The library formed one whole wall of bookshelves devoted primarily to history, archaeology and anthropology texts. Mara strode directly to the section of titles that she had perused the day before.

In moments, she had loaded a stack of books in her arms, mounded a pile of sofa pillows against one wall and created a nook that would provide hours of quiet reading before dinner. Fort Selden had been built in 1865 to protect settlers moving into the Mesilla Valley and those embarking on the Journey of the Dead to northern New Mexico. Indians had never been much of a threat, so no wall surrounded the fort, but the structures themselves were distinctive.

Mara flipped open a book and ran her finger down the index. After she dug her files and note cards out of the closet, she would use Brock's library to add to her research. Todd had acknowledged more than once that Mara knew more about the history of the fort than he did. His job was tied to engineering and construction, while she had provided the background details he needed.

"If you're going to go to the trouble to track me down in the middle of a cow pasture," Brock's deep voice boomed suddenly from the entry hall, "you might as well come on in and have a drink."

"It's Saturday afternoon, Brock," a woman responded lightly. "You're not supposed to be working. This is play-time, remember?"

Hidden in the shadows of her reading nook, Mara peered around the corner of the library shelving into the living area. A group of young adults—two men and three women—were following Brock into the room. Cheeks bright pink from the cold, they began shrugging out of heavy wool coats and leather gloves, rubbing their hands together, stamping their feet.

"It's bitter out there. Stoke up that fire, Brock." The woman who spoke was a tall, willowy redhead with copper lipstick and long matching nails. She gave Brock a wink and patted his rear end. "Do it for Sandy, won't you?"

"Anything for Sandy," he said.

Mara gripped the book as he leaned over and gave the redhead a peck on the cheek. Who were these people? Some woman had just touched Brock's bottom! And he'd kissed the woman in return! Mara felt a flash of outrage before she remembered she had no claim on the man. He could do whatever he wanted in his own house with his own friends.

Mara cringed, aware that she should emerge from her cubby and introduce herself. Suddenly feeling foolish tucked away with her pillows and books, she debated staying put. That morning she had dressed in a pair of black leotards and a turquoise T-shirt that hung almost to her knees. She had bought the oversize men's shirt at the start of her preg-nancy to cover the growing bulge in her stomach. The last thing she wanted was for these suave men and their svelte girlfriends to see that the bulge was still there—even though the baby wasn't.

"So are you coming with us to the party or not, Brock?" Sandy asked. "Stephanie and I have a bet riding on this. She says you won't come, and I say you will. You're not going to disappoint me, are you?"

"What are the stakes?" Brock asked. He had thrown a couple of logs on the stack of kindling in the fireplace, and he was holding a box of long matches in his hands.

Mara felt her stomach sink to her knees. Brock looked so good in the late-afternoon light, his denim shirt a little dusty and his jeans scuffed at the knees. He had taken off his hat, and Mara could see the glint of sun that softened his thick black hair. No wonder these women wanted him.

"A double margarita," Sandy said. She balanced her weight on one leg, which threw her slender hip in Brock's direction. Clad in a short black leather skirt, opaque black stockings, boots and a skintight purple turtleneck, she might have stepped out of an ad in *Elle*. She certainly hadn't had a baby two weeks ago.

"Double booze, huh?" Brock said, turning his attention from the redhead to her statuesque blond companion. "Stephanie, what possessed you?"

"I knew you wouldn't do it. We haven't seen your hide in six months, honey. Even when Joe and Travis cooked up the idea of driving out here to nab you bodily, I told them you wouldn't leave. You've become a regular hermit."

Brock shrugged. "I've been busy."

"Busy." One of the two men took the matches from Brock and knelt by the fire. "Bunch of cows."

"Bovines," the other one hooted. "Brock, what the hell is going on? You haven't been without female company this long since you were five years old."

"Yeah, Brock," Sandy cooed, "you used to call me once in a while. What's up? You found yourself another woman or something?"

Mara held her breath. She *had* to emerge. Shoving the books off her lap, she cleared her throat.

"Well, I have been on the run," Brock began. "There are a few things I haven't told you all, but—"

"Excuse me, Brock," Mara said. Everyone in the room turned to stare at her. She attempted to smooth the T-shirt over her stomach and thighs as she stepped into the light. "I was reading in the corner. Would you introduce me to your friends?''

Five pairs of eyes swiveled to Brock. He jammed his hands in his pockets. "Uh ... this is Stephanie, Sandy, and Justine's over there. This is Joe, and that's Travis." He glanced at his friends. "This is Mara. My wife."

A stunned silence ensued as the five pairs of eyes darted back to Mara.

"Brock!" Sandy said with a gasp. "You didn't! You got married?"

"The other day. Well, it's a different sort of a deal than you might think."

"Brock married me to help take care of my baby," Mara said.

"Baby!" Sandy's voice lifted into a near shriek. "You have a baby?"

"Not Brock's baby," Mara said quickly. "My husband died. He was killed. Brock was his best friend, and he wanted to help out. I was having some difficulties, and he offered to take care of us financially for the time being."

"You married this woman?" Sandy's blue eyes raked Mara up and down. "Brock, you married your best friend's wife?"

"It's a long story. Just take it at face value, Sandy. I'm a married man, and I figured I'd hang out here at the ranch. Seemed the appropriate thing to do under the circumstances."

"You don't need to stay here on my account," Mara said, crossing her arms. "I'm fine. Go ahead with your friends, Brock."

"Jeez, I don't believe this!" Sandy plopped onto one of Brock's long leather couches. She threw her arm over her eyes and let out a deep breath.

"Guess you owe me a double margarita," Stephanie said. "You're on your own tonight, lady."

Sandy laughed without humor. "The man is married. I can't believe it. Tell me I'm in some kind of a time warp."

"It's an arrangement." Mara glanced expectantly at Brock. He turned his back on the group and began prodding the fire with a poker. No help there, she thought. "Brock felt responsible for me because of my difficult pregnancy and the problems I was having with some business debts my husband had incurred. Our marriage is nothing more than a way to provide insurance coverage and establish long-term assistance for Abby."

"Abby?" Sandy peered out from under her arm.

"My daughter."

"He's got a daughter."

"Abby is my daughter. Brock is her...her financial caretaker. Sort of a guardian or a godfather. Right, Brock?"

"That's what you keep telling me," he said to the fire.

She glared at his back. These people were his friends, not hers. Why did she feel compelled to explain his behavior?

"He likes to remind me I'm a line item on his budget," Mara said. "That ought to give you some idea of where this marriage thing stands. It's certainly fine with me if he goes out for a night on the town."

"Ooh, hostility," Sandy said, sitting up. "This is sounding better. Your husband must have been that archaeology friend of Brock's. The guy who fell off the cliff when they were playing Indiana Jones. So, did you blackmail Brock or something?"

"No, she didn't." Brock swung around, red-hot poker in his hand. He narrowed his eyes at Sandy, then fixed Mara with a cutting stare. "I offered to take care of you and the baby."

"I thanked you for that."

"Yes, you did."

"Brock , you don't owe me anything. Especially not some misguided sense of spousal loyalty. If you want to go out with your girlfriend, go ahead."

Mara watched his face harden as his hand knotted into a fist around the iron poker. He was angry, she knew. She had provoked him and backed him into a corner. He hated that. But what else could she have done? If he didn't go out with his friends because of his marriage, he would resent her even more.

Though her heart begged him not to go, her mouth formed words of separation. "Go on," she said softly. "They're waiting."

Chapter 9

Jaw clenched, Brock fought the emotion that had welled up inside him the moment Mara stepped out of the shadows. There she stood, tall and golden-haired, her arms locked protectively around her waist and her chin lifted in a gesture of defiance. She wore blue—turquoise blue that made her gray-green eyes shine. Her long legs were sheathed in black. No wonder Sandy was acting so catty, he thought. Mara looked terrific.

There she stood, the sum of everything he had come to desire most, pushing him away. She didn't want him.

She would take his money, sure. She'd live in his house and raise her baby there. But Abby was *her* daughter, she reminded him again and again. Those long legs belonged to another man, even though he had been gone for many months. Brock wondered if those sparkling eyes would ever look at him with anything but rejection and distaste.

Between Mara and himself stood Brock's past, this group of men and women who did want him. They wanted his jokes to laugh at. They wanted his good looks to enhance their own at parties and gatherings. They welcomed his adventures, his daredevil stunts, his freewheeling joyride through life.

And the women. They wanted him very much. If he chose, he could have Sandy in his bed before the sun was up. She seemed willing enough. So did Stephanie, for that matter. And quiet Justine over in the corner had been biding her time, giving him little hints that she, too, would appreciate his attention.

Joe and Travis didn't mind. They were used to Brock Barnett and his women. Theirs was a sort of trade-around group—young business executives searching for the right person to marry eventually, and trying out everyone else in the meantime.

It had been fun.

Sort of.

Brock tossed the poker onto the hearth. Metal clanged against stone, an echoing sound that reverberated in the awkward silence. He looked at Mara, needing her and knowing she would never be his. Then he looked at his friends. For some odd reason, the choice was simple.

"I believe I'll stick around here," he said in a low voice. "Keep the home fires burning."

Joe chuckled as the others headed for the foyer. "Well, Mrs. Barnett—sorry, I forgot your first name—you take care of old Brock."

Joe slapped his friend on the back as he passed through the doorway. "I've got to admit, Brock, you've pulled off some strange stunts in your time. But marrying your best friend's pregnant widow? This has got to take the cake."

"Later, Joe." Brock leaned against the doorframe as his friends strolled to their cars.

"I thought the stark-naked bungee jumping was pretty wild," Travis said, the last one out. He leaned toward Brock. "Your new bride's a looker, though. You might as well get some mileage out of the old marriage license, pal."

"Get your butt out of here, Travis," Brock said, giving his friend a shove.

Travis laughed and waved. "See ya later, Daddy Barnett."

Brock shut the door and stared at the beveled wood for a moment. Had he really enjoyed those people? He knew he had. Once, there had been nothing better than a room full of good-looking women, fast-talking men, and lots of booze and loud metallic music. Beer bashes, cocktail parties. Nightclubs, dance halls, strip joints, bars. Sandy, Stephanie, Suzy, Sheri, Sheila. He'd been enmeshed in that life. Now, he could care less.

As he turned back to the living room, he had the sensation that he'd once been a hollow man. He had grown up without a mother, with a father who was always distant, and with nothing to fill in the emptiness. So he had spent his time and money on thrill sports, taunting fate as he tested the limits of his strength. And he had used those people who were driving away from his house. He had plugged up the hole in his heart with their noise, fast cars, beer, sex, drugs, music, money, anything that life-style could offer.

He might have run them off tonight, but the truth was he still felt hollow. Only these days he was filling his emptiness with work. Branding, roping, breeding, castrating, marking, rounding up. Cows. Bovines.

He shook his head, wondering if his life would ever change. As he entered the living room, he spotted Mara standing next to the blazing fire, her arms still crossed and her mouth set in an angry line.

"Why didn't you go with them?" she demanded.

"I didn't want to."

"Why not?"

"Work."

She let out a growl of exasperation and set her hands on her hips. "You could take one evening off to go to their party."

"Look, I'm not going to drive in to some shindig in Las Cruces, so you might as well get used to the idea. Number one, I have a sick cow to take care of. She's down in the barn, and I have to check on her every hour or so tonight. Number two, I'm your husband, and people are beginning to find that out. If I go to a party with Sandy Hamilton draped around my neck, that's not going to look too great, is it?''

Mara swallowed at the image of the slinky redhead lavishing her attention on Brock. Even now, the thought of those long, copper-nailed fingers patting Brock's bottom filled her with outrage. On the other hand, why should she care if some woman blatantly lusted after the man? She might be Brock's wife, but she held absolutely no claim to his affection—or even his attention.

"I don't want your misguided chivalry, Brock," she said, deliberately hardening her voice. "You may be my husband, but I know better than to expect loyalty and celibacy out of you."

"You don't know a damn thing about me."

"I heard the way your friends talked. You're not exactly known for long-term relationships."

"Yeah, but I've never been married before."

"Oh, come on, Brock!" Dismayed, Mara absently twisted the wedding band Todd had given her. She didn't want him to talk this way. "We're not really married, and you know it."

"Are you trying to tell me you want out of this thing?"

"I'm telling you I don't want you to feel trapped."

"If I'm trapped, you're trapped, too. We're in this thing together, Mara, and it's the biggest damned tangle I've ever stepped into."

"Whose fault is that? Are you implying I tricked you into this marriage, like your friend Sandy said? Are you trying to insinuate you were blackmailed?"

"I said we're both caught. You, too."

Mara stared into his brown eyes. "You offered me a way out of one trap. Sometimes I feel like I walked right into another one."

"What kind of a trap are you in, Mara?"

"This crazy marriage." She swung her arms out. "We obviously don't love each other."

"Don't we?"

"Well, no." Staring at him, she heard her breath go shallow. "Of course not."

"So, I'm trapped in this crazy, loveless marriage, which keeps me from going out to parties with Sandy and her pals. Big loss. What's it keeping you from?"

Mara willed her heart to slow down. Brock was walking toward her, his hands at his sides and his eyes fastened on hers. He had looked this way before. Consuming. He would devour her, and against all reason she suddenly wanted him to.

No! The man couldn't be trusted. He was every woman's dream and every woman's worst nightmare. He was a devil with black hair and bedroom eyes. If she allowed him to find one chink in her armor, he could destroy her.

"This marriage is keeping me a prisoner," she said.

"How?"

"This house."

"You can walk out of here any time. Take your baby and go. You've told me I'm useless to you. That I'll never be Abby's father."

"Todd is her father."

He stopped a foot away. "Todd is your prison, not this marriage," he said. "Look at the rings on your hand. You're still married to him, aren't you?"

"Yes," Mara whispered.

"You made a lifetime commitment to a man who died a long time ago."

"It's only been six months."

"Seven."

"So what? It doesn't matter how many months have gone by. He's still my husband."

"Todd isn't coming back, Mara."

"I know!" She fought the tears those words always evoked. Yet even as she struggled with her grief, she realized she was capable of dealing her husband's memory an ultimate treachery. She wanted desperately to know the touch of his betrayer.

"Mara," he said, holding out a hand toward her.

"You're as committed to Todd as I am," she flung at him. "You're just as bound and imprisoned by his memory. You married me out of that sense of obligation."

"And I'll never break that vow."

"What do you mean?"

What had he meant? Brock turned aside and walked past her to the fire. He knelt on the hearth, one knee on the rough stone and the other supporting his arm. As he stared into the licking flames, he wondered what was happening to him. Had he turned down a chance to enjoy his friends so he could spend a lifetime with a woman he could never touch? Had he given up a life of freedom and pleasure . . . for this?

"Todd," he said to the fire, and he realized the word had somehow changed in meaning for him. "I'm loyal to Todd. I'll never break my vow to you because of him."

"Todd is gone," Mara whispered behind him. "You keep telling me that."

"I know."

"How long can you honor a promise to a dead man?"

Brock slammed his hands on his thighs as he swung around and stood to face her. "How long, Mara? You tell me."

"I don't know!"

"I don't know, either."

They stared at each other, neither daring to move. Mara could hear the blood hammering in her temples. How could this have happened? How could she be standing a breath away from him, willing him to be the first to break the barrier between them?

If he said one word. If he reached out to her. If he touched her hand. Everything would collapse, and she would walk straight into his arms. She despised her own weakness.

"Abby's probably hungry," she said to fill in the silence between them. "I'm going. I don't want to talk to you anymore."

He caught her arm and gripped it so hard the blood stopped. "Mara, admit it. You know I didn't let Todd fall off that cliff."

"Don't!" She tried to break away, but his iron fingers closed tighter around her wrist.

"If you won't hear me out, you'll never let it go, Mara. You'll never forgive me."

"I'm not sure I want to forgive you."

"Because you'd have to admit I'm not all bad? You'd have to see some of what Todd saw in me. If you forgave me, you'd know me."

"Do your friends know you? They're not holding anything against you. I don't think anyone really knows you, Brock. I'm not sure you know yourself."

He dropped her arm. "Todd knew me."

"Maybe." Mara faced him, trying to put conviction in her words. "But I don't want to know you."

He nodded, his mouth a bitter line. "You want to nurture your hatred like that little baby you keep hidden away in the back room. You know I loved Todd. You know I'd never hurt him. He fell off that cliff, and I did every *damn* thing I could to save him, but he—"

"Stop talking about it!"

"You're going to hold on to your bitterness and nurse it every day of your life until it grows big enough to eat you alive."

"Why do you care what I do?" she exploded. "What difference does it make? What do you want from me?"

He grabbed her and jerked her against him. "I want... I want..." With every ounce of strength he could summon, he fought the need to stroke and caress her.

"Oh, Brock," she said softly.

"Go feed your baby." He set her aside and turned his back on her. "I've got a sick cow."

Mara watched him stride across the living room and through the foyer. He threw the front door open and flung it so hard it bounced against the wall before slamming behind him. In a moment, his pickup roared to life and gravel crunched beneath its wheels as it blasted down the driveway.

Mara sank onto the couch and buried her face in her hands. She had married Brock Barnett to escape the mess in her life. But things were worse now. Much worse. As she searched her mind for a way out, she realized there was no escape. Abby's waking cry through the intercom reminded her she had more than herself to think about.

Brock glanced at the old grandfather clock on his way down the hall to his bedroom. A little past one in the morning. He felt dead on his feet but he was hungry enough to eat his own horse. Tending the ailing cow all evening, he'd missed supper, drunk nothing but black coffee and shot his nerves to hell.

At least the animal had pulled through. She must have eaten some kind of nasty weed out on the range. With the onset of winter, the good grass had died back, and the cattle sometimes poked their noses where they shouldn't. This cow had been a good breeder, often giving birth to twins, and Brock hated to lose her. He had hauled her down from the pasture and tended her until she'd passed the poison.

Though he was no veterinarian, he had learned how to handle most ailments, and he kept a good stock of medicines on hand. Now the animal was in the head man's care, and she should be back on her feet by morning. Pedro Chavez cared almost as much about the ranch as Brock did, and Pedro never balked at being roused from his sleep after midnight.

After tossing his hat on his bed, Brock raked his fingers through his hair and gave a long stretch. His back ached from bending over for hours without a break. His muscles felt like they'd been tied in knots. At least he hadn't had time to think about Mara all night.

Unwilling to permit even her name to slip into his mind, he stripped off his shirt, tugged the tail of his thermal underwear out of his jeans' waist and rubbed a hand across his flat belly. Empty. But he'd better take a shower before he ate. He pulled his undershirt over his head and unbuckled his belt. His stomach gave a loud rumble.

On second thought, he decided the shower could wait another fifteen minutes, while his appetite couldn't. Still in his boots and jeans, Brock walked silently down the darkened hall to the kitchen. He flipped on a low light over the stove and opened the refrigerator as he wondered if he'd find anything besides Pierre's sauces, marinades and fresh vegetables. He could use a thick roast beef sandwich and a couple of dill pickles.

Opening a few plastic-lidded boxes, he located some cheese, chicken breasts and carrots. He set them on the work table and pondered the usual absence of mayonnaise in the house. Pierre disliked mayonnaise even though Brock had complained that it was damned hard to make a decent sandwich without the stuff.

As usual, butter would have to do. There was never any sliced white bread, either, but Pierre's famous rolls usually could be found in the pantry. Brock was crossing the kitchen toward the smaller room when he spotted a shadow moving slowly across the courtyard outside. He stopped in his tracks and studied the ephemeral shape.

Blinking, he wondered if he'd imagined the movement. Two strides took him to the window. He leaned across the sink and peered into the darkness. In the moonless night, a shrouded, bulky figure vanished behind a thicket of shrubbery.

Brock frowned. In all his years on the ranch, he'd never had a thief. But everyone who worked for him knew payday was getting close, and Christmas bonuses already were stashed in the house's safe. Any familiarity with Brock's habits told a potential burglar that the master of the house was often away and inner doors were never locked. The courtyard wall was an easy climb. Too easy.

Brock slipped down the length of the counter and opened a cabinet door. Sliding across the top shelf, his fingers found the cool, slick steel of a pistol. He brought the weapon to chest level and checked the chamber. Loaded.

His heart thudding in his chest, he snagged a sheepskin coat from the hook by the door and slipped it over his bare skin. Gun in one hand, he turned the doorknob with the other. The hinges barely creaked as he eased the door open. Hugging the wall, Brock edged out into the darkness.

"Hush little baby, don't say a word," Mara's voice sang softly, "Mama's gonna buy you a..."

I'll be damned, Brock thought. His thief was a tired mother with a fussy baby. He let out his breath as Mara emerged along the starlit path, her hair hanging loose around her shoulders and a whimpering Abby nestled in her arms.

"Mockingbird," she went on, her voice a little quavery. "And if that mockingbird won't sing…Mama's gonna buy you a diamond ring."

She strolled past Brock, unaware that he stood two steps away in the shadows, his gun hanging loose in his hand and his eyes following her. He could see the round, pale curve of Abby's head tucked in the crook of her mother's elbow. How long had it been since he'd laid eyes on the baby? Mara had kept her daughter away from him ever since her birth. Brock tried to swallow the ache that tightened in his throat as he recalled the moment the doctor had placed that tiny bundle in his arms.

Two weeks ago, he'd have done anything for Abby. Now he could hardly remember how she looked. In the hospital, he had watched the baby being carried in and out through Mara's door. Half the time, he had wheeled her bassinet down the hall himself. As she lay in the small plastic cart, he had studied Abby's petal pink skin and wispy eyelashes. He had brushed his fingertip over her rosebud mouth. But once inside his own home, Abby had been kept from him. She was Mara's daughter. Todd's baby.

As Mara hummed her way around the courtyard, Brock gritted his teeth. In spite of his good intentions, had he made a terrible mistake bringing this woman into his house? Had he given up what little pleasure he had in life for a woman who was bitter and unforgiving? If it weren't for Todd, he never would have married a woman like Mara. He never would have married at all. Period.

Did he resent Todd? Maybe. But how could he be angry at a man for dying?

Once again, the memory of that afternoon on the cliffs at Hueco Tanks clicked on in Brock's mind. Though he knew he had done all he could to save his friend's life, he blamed himself as much as Mara did. Todd had never been the natural athlete Brock was, and he had neither studied as much about rock climbing nor practiced as often as his friend. Todd had trusted Brock to keep him safe on the cliffs—and Brock had trusted himself. But Brock had failed. Todd was dead . . . and the angry Mara would make him pay any way she could.

"And if that billy goat won't . . ." she sang tiredly, pausing to search for the words to the lullaby. "And if that billy goat won't . . . eat, Mama's gonna buy you a . . . piece of meat."

She was making up the song. The edges of her nubby pink robe drifted around her slippered feet as she padded back and forth, back and forth, swaying Abby to the rhythm of her footsteps. Her breath made little puffs of steam in the crisp night air.

"And if that piece of meat won't . . . cook," she went on in a low, almost tuneless voice, "Mama's gonna buy you a crochet hook. And if that crochet hook . . . gets bent, Mama's gonna buy you a canvas tent."

At the inane words to her song, Brock fought the grin that tickled the corners of his mouth. He definitely resented Mara and her self-righteous intolerance, but at the same time he was drawn to her. He needed her forgiveness. Hell, he needed more than that from this woman who somehow had become his wife.

"And if that canvas tent falls down, Mama's gonna buy you a wedding gown." She was over by the swimming pool now, walking past the empty, covered hole. Rocking Abby, she gazed into her baby's face as she sang.

What did Brock truly want from Mara? Acceptance? Peace? At this point he would gladly accept the barest smile.

"And if that wedding gown . . ." Mara stopped singing, stopped walking, stopped rocking. Her voice trembled as she went on. "If that wedding gown falls apart, Mama's gonna mend your broken heart. And if your broken heart won't . . . stop hurting . . ."

Brock watched her from a distance. She stood like a statue at the edge of the pool, unmoving, silent. The baby had stopped whimpering, and Mara let out a deep, lingering breath.

"Oh, Abby," she said softly.

Brock recognized the tone in her voice. She had said the same thing to him. *Oh, Brock.* But what did Mara want? What could he give her? Never in his life had he felt such a tangle of emotions.

"Let's go back inside," she said softly.

She started toward her room, and Brock stepped out from the wall. In less than a minute, Mara would be gone. He wouldn't see Abby again for days, maybe weeks. Hard telling when he would even catch a glimpse of Mara. But he had to let her go. He had no right to her.

Just as Mara pushed open her door, Abby let out a loud wail. *"Weh, weh, wehhh!"*

"Oh, no." Mara stopped and leaned her head against the doorframe. "Not again, Abby. Please, I'm so...so tired."

She clutched the sobbing baby to her breast and lifted her eyes to the sky. Clearly frustrated and teetering at the edge of exhaustion, she swallowed back tears. Brock studied her, his own impulse to help manacled and impotent. With Abby howling at the top of her tiny lungs, Mara turned into the darkness of her bedroom and shut the door behind her.

Brock leaned back against the chilly wall and listened to the sounds of a baby crying and a mother attempting to sing once again. In the darkness, his stomach grumbled loudly, and he recalled the makings of his chicken dinner spread out on the kitchen table. He had been on his way to fetch a roll. Definitely, he was hungry. Too hungry to be walking across the courtyard toward Mara's door. He should head for the kitchen, eat his sandwich, take his shower. He shouldn't knock on her door. Absolutely not.

"Brock?" Still holding Abby, Mara peered through the slit between the open door and the frame. "Is that you?"

Chapter 10

"I heard the baby," Brock said. He couldn't believe what he had just done. Two minutes ago, he had been hungry and tired. Two minutes ago, he had been determined to stay as far from Mara as possible. Now he was struggling to keep from lifting her into his arms, carrying her into bed and kissing her to sleep.

"Is Abby okay?" he asked.

"I don't know," Mara said over Abby's wails. Brock could barely hear her. "I can't get her to sleep."

"Maybe she's hungry."

"I've nursed her until I have nothing left. I've changed her diaper, burped her, checked her temperature, everything I can think of. I can't understand why she won't sleep."

They both looked down at the subject herself. The baby's tiny fists pumped the air, now and then batting her mother's breast. Her little feet churned inside the white crocheted blanket. Cheeks bright red, her head was thrown back against Mara's arm as though she desperately wanted to escape but couldn't.

"She's raising quite a ruckus," Brock said.

"What?" Mara asked above the cries.

"She's loud."

The gray-green eyes lifted to his face, and Brock could see they were swimming. "Well, I'm sorry she bothered you. I'd better try rocking her again."

Mara turned to go, but Brock caught her arm. "Let me."

Before he had thought through a plan of action and its consequences, he found himself ushering Mara back into her room, flipping on a low light and guiding her to her bed. Then he took the squirming bundle from her arms and gave her a valiant grin.

"You get some rest."

"Are you sure?"

"No problem."

Spotting the rocker beside Mara's bed, Brock headed for it. Mara must have moved the chair from the nursery into her own quarters so she could rock Abby during the night. How many hours the two of them spent together, while he saw little or nothing of either one.

He could hardly believe he was actually holding this baby whose birth had played such a significant part in his own life. In his arms, Abby was almost weightless, her small, rounded body nestling easily against the soft contours of his sheepskin coat. Weightless, maybe, but definitely loud. The kid could raise the roof.

Brock glanced at Mara, who had fallen across her bed in a heap, then he shrugged out of his jacket and kicked off his dusty boots. Gathering the baby closer to him, he eased his large frame down into the chair. Abby was a mess of rumpled blankets and twisted nightgown, so he peeled her out of everything that would come off. Then he laid her against his bare chest, pressed her little round head to his warm skin, and began to rock back and forth.

"Now then, quit your squallin'," he murmured. Abby pushed her mouth into his chest to nose around for milk. Brock shook his head. "You ain't gonna have any luck there, little gal. Might as well get used to it. About all this ol' boy's got for you is a pair of strong hands and a big hairy hide.... Ouch. Yeah, that's it. You got yourself a handful now.''

As he rocked, Brock leaned his head back on the chair and shut his eyes. Abby's wails gradually mellowed into whimpers. Her fingers worked the hair on his chest and her nose nestled into his skin. She sure was little. He figured he could easily hold her in one hand.

Lowering his head, he drank in the scent of her downy hair. Baby shampoo and talcum powder. Something tugged at his heart, and he swallowed against the tide of emotion. He brushed the baby's forehead with his lips and let out a deep breath.

"You planning to sleep sometime tonight, girl?" he whispered. "Don't you know you've about worn your mama plumb out? I was on my way for a roast beef sandwich and a warm shower, myself. But you decide to set up a holler and everybody comes running, don't they?"

He studied the diminutive face pressed against his skin. Abby was perfect. From her soft eyes to her small nose to her bowed lips, she was the image of her beautiful mother. Even her ears fit against her head like tiny seashells. Again, he kissed her, and this time her fussy cries wound down into a sigh. "This is what we call nighttime, Abby," he murmured against her shoulder. "It's dark outside the window, see? The stars are hanging in the sky. The moon's tucked away. Even the coyotes have gone to bed. Sleep now, baby. That's my girl."

As Abby fell silent, Brock lifted his feet up onto Mara's bed and stretched out his long, tired legs. The creak of the rocker was replaced by the whisper of winter wind against the window pane. In the quiet, Brock let his eyes drift shut and his cheek settle against the top of the baby's head.

"And if your broken heart's too deep," Mara's soft voice filtered through the cobwebs of sleep gathering in his brain, "Papa's gonna come and rock you to sleep."

Brock opened his eyes. From the pillow where her head lay, Mara was gazing at him. She lifted her bare foot and touched the tip of her toe to the end of his sock. Running her toe along his sole to the hem of his jeans, she continued humming the lullaby. Then she slipped her toes inside his jeans and touched his leg.

"And if my baby girl goes to sleep," she murmured, "I think we might have found a man to keep."

She broke into a smile that lit the room like sunrise on a summer morning. Brock stared at her, his heart suddenly galloping inside his chest.

"Mara," he whispered. "What do you—"

"Shh." She held one finger to her lips and glanced at Abby. "Good night, Brock."

When Mara opened her eyes the next morning, she realized it was the first time since Abby's birth that she had not awakened to the sound of a baby. In fact, there was no sound at all in the room, nothing but the chitter of birds and the rustle of bare branches in the courtyard outside. Sunshine lay like a pool of melted butter on the tile floor. A slice of cloudless blue sky peeped through the open curtains. An old, beat-up sheepskin jacket hung over the arm of the empty rocker.

Empty! Mara sat up in bed. Where was Abby? Where was Brock? She swung her legs to the floor and sat for a minute, breathing hard. Her breasts were swollen and damp inside her robe. Abby hadn't nursed since midnight!

Mara retied the belt of her chenille robe as she padded across the floor. She jerked open the door to the nursery and hurried to the crib. Empty. Brushing a hand over her forehead, she tried to think. It had been a difficult night—Abby restless and whiny, Mara tired and sore—until Brock showed up at the courtyard door.

The last thing Mara had seen before falling into an exhausted sleep was her daughter snuggled against Brock's bare chest. Brock had her. Mara walked down the hall, her throat tightening with worry. Brock had witnessed Abby's birth, but he knew nothing about babies. He'd only held Abby once. What if he dropped her? What if he spilled something on her? What if he laid her down on a couch or a kitchen counter and she rolled off? If she landed on the hard tile floor—

"Once you get your teeth," Brock's distinctively deep voice said from the kitchen, "you'll be eating eggs and bacon for breakfast."

Mara came to a sudden stop in the doorway. With Abby neatly tucked like a football in one arm, Brock was stirring a batch of scrambled eggs with his free hand.

"Now, don't frown at me, girl," he said to the baby. Oblivious to the observing woman, he poured the egg mixture into a hot skillet on the stove and returned his attention to the baby. "You can have some milk, too, when you get bigger. But you'll drink it out of a cup, and it'll be cow's milk. Cows are what we do here on the ranch, so you'll have to learn to drink big glasses of bubbly milk and chow down on prime rib. That is, if we can get Pierre to leave us alone in the kitchen for a few hours so we can cook together."

Mara stared at the expanse of Brock's bare chest and Abby's pink cheek snuggled comfortably against the mat of black hair. As he tended to his breakfast, the man looked as though he'd spent his whole life with a baby wedged in the crook of his arm. One-handed, he salted and peppered his steaming eggs. He sauntered to the refrigerator and hauled out two jars of jelly. Next he opened the oven door and set a couple of croissants onto the rack.

"You'll have to get used to French grub," he said to the baby. "But when you get really hungry, we'll sneak out to the bunkhouse and chow down with the men."

"Wuh," Abby said.

"I know just what you mean," Brock concurred. "Let me tell you about my head man, Pedro Chavez. Now, he can cook enchiladas like you never tasted. Brings homemade tortillas his wife makes on the weekends when he's home. And Nick Jefferson is our steak man. Loads us down with T-bones, baked beans and biscuits."

From the open doorway, Mara watched as Brock set a plate, silverware and napkin on the kitchen work table. Whistling, he took a mug down from the shelf.

"You know, for such a pretty little girl, you're smelling mighty whiffy," he told Abby as he walked toward the coffeemaker. "I reckon you're due for a diaper change."

"Uh-behhh," Abby burbled.

"I'll tell you what. If you'll hang on till after breakfast, I'll do what I can to clean you up. Maybe between the two of us we can figure out what it is your mama does to keep you feeling bright-eyed and bushy tailed."

He reached for the coffeepot and held it over the mug, which sat on the counter only an inch from Abby's tiny bare leg. As the steaming black liquid splashed into the cup, Mara opened her mouth and made a gasping sound. Brock swung around.

"Whoa. You scared the hell out of me and Abby." He gave her a broad grin. "Coffee?"

"I was afraid you might spill it." Mara shoved her hands deep into the pockets of her robe as she walked toward Brock. "I'd love some. But let me pour."

"Don't trust me?"

"Not much." She took down another mug and filled them both with hot black coffee. "But more today than I did yesterday."

"Keep that up and you might start to like me." His voice held a light, teasing note.

"I doubt it." She set the mugs on the table and leaned toward him. "Brock, thank you for helping me last night. I haven't slept that many hours in a row since Abby was born."

"You were wrung out. I'll tell you what," he said, studying the baby in his arms, "I never knew someone who weighed less than ten pounds could wiggle like a rattler on a hot skillet, raise the rafters with her hollering and odor up an entire kitchen."

Mara had to laugh. "I'd better change her."

"I thought I'd give it a shot, but I wasn't sure what kind of a surprise I'd find when I opened the package."

"Not a pretty one, I can promise you that."

He held Abby at arms' length and peered into her tiny face. "You leak, you drool, you squall, you mess your britches and you keep us awake half the night. What do you have to say for yourself, young lady?"

"Bah," Abby gurgled.

Brock laughed out loud. Hugging her close, he planted a kiss on top of her head. "Yeah, you'd steal my heart, wouldn't you? Go on, now, your mama's waiting."

He placed the damp little bundle in Mara's arms. "When you're done, come back and have some breakfast," he said. "No point in waiting for Pierre. It's Sunday, and we're on our own."

Mara snuggled her daughter, aware of the tiny lips rooting against her neck. "Abby's hungry, too. You go ahead with your breakfast. I'll nurse her, and then I'll fix something later."

"No point in that." He snagged a chair and pulled it back from the table. "Feed her in here. Might as well all eat together."

Mara stared at him as he sat down, leaned back in his chair and propped his feet on the table right next to his plate. He cocked his hands behind his head, giving her a full view of bare, dark-haired chest and ropy muscle. His black hair gleamed and his smile was as broad as all New Mexico.

"I've watched you nurse her before," he said. "Go on, now. I'll keep the eggs warm."

Carrying her fragrant little bundle, Mara strolled down the hall. Abby whimpered, as if dismayed at the feel of chenille robe against her cheek instead of a coarse mat of male hair. Mara frowned.

"You like him, don't you?" she whispered. "Scamp. I heard you cooing and gurgling over that man. You just wrapped him right around your little finger, didn't you?"

Mara carried Abby into the nursery and quickly changed her diaper. A strange sense of satisfaction came over her as she realized how easy the task had become. She could bathe, diaper, nurse, rock, burp and sing lullabies like a pro. In fact, in the last couple of weeks she had become a pretty darned good mother.

"So, the old feller wants to watch you have your breakfast, does he?" she said, hefting Abby up in her arms. "All right then. Here we go."

As Mara walked toward the dining room, she thought of the man who waited there, his feet resting on the table and his broad, bare chest comfortably exposed to view. She recalled Rosa Maria's statement about Brock.

After spending time with your husband, Mr. Barnett always relaxed. He would be happy. He would lean back in his chair and put his feet on the table.

Feet on the table. Relaxed. This was a man she could tolerate a lot better than the driven perfectionist she had always known. What had calmed Brock? Was it Sunday, a quiet house and a sunny December morning that had soothed him? Was it Abby and her snuggling acceptance? Or could Mara herself have had something to do with mellowing the man? For some odd reason, she hoped she had played a part.

As she stepped into the kitchen, she again knew a sense of guilty betrayal. The picture was all wrong. It should be Todd, his wife and their baby gathering in the little apartment kitchen. They should sit around their dinette, talking and laughing in the comfortable way they had together. A family.

She walked toward Brock, suddenly overwhelmed with the guile in her heart. How could she actually look forward to spending time with this man? How could it be fair that he held Abby and rocked her to sleep? Worst of all...how could Mara herself be feeling the wayward desires and emotions she felt every time she was in Brock's presence?

"Hey there," he said, looking up at her. In worn and slightly wrinkled jeans, his long legs stretched across the expanse from chair to table. His feet were comfortably crossed at the ankles. "You'll never guess what just skedaddled past the window there."

Uncomfortable at being drawn into an easy banter with him, Mara settled on the edge of her chair. She tucked Abby close and fought the swirl of tingles that curled through her spine as she looked into Brock's brown eyes.

"A roadrunner," he said. "A chaparral bird. Ran right through the courtyard. Never seen one this close to the house."

Tearing her focus from his eyes, Mara searched the walled enclosure for the fabled bird, but it had vanished. "Maybe it was hungry."

"I don't know about the roadrunner, but I know about me." Brock set his feet on the floor, stood and headed for the stove. In moments, he had served up two plates of scrambled eggs, bacon, hot croissants, farm butter and jelly. He refilled Mara's coffee mug.

As he sat down and reached for the pepper grinder, Mara draped a cloth diaper over her shoulder to cover Abby's head. Beneath it, she pushed back her robe and gown to free her breast, and at the familiar ritual the baby began to whimper. Abby quickly found her mother's swollen nipple, took it into her mouth and began to suckle with loud, satisfied gulps.

At the sound, Mara flushed a bright pink as she lifted her eyes to Brock. He was grinning. "Reckon we can pray over that little barracuda?" he asked, holding out a hand toward Mara.

"Oh, Brock, really—"

"I decided you had a point about praying before meals, Mara. I wasn't brought up in the church, and I'm not too sure about my doctrines and theologies, but that doesn't mean I've locked the door."

Mara shut her eyes for a moment, hating herself for the happiness she felt at the sound of his voice and the prospect of touching his hand. It wouldn't be right to feel this euphoric about any man so soon after her husband's death. It was doubly wrong to be melting inside over Brock Barnett. He had been Todd's best friend. That made her attraction to him seem somehow incestuous. He had led Todd up those cliffs.

She planted her hand firmly in her lap and twisted her wedding band around and around. "Brock, I think—"

"There's been an empty place inside me, Mara," he said, still reaching out to her. "I got to thinking about it yesterday after the crowd from Las Cruces dropped by."

"Empty?"

"The hollowness that's built into everybody. It's uncomfortable, so you try to fill it up. I used to think I could ease it by partying. You know, keep a buzz on? Didn't do the trick. In the past few years, I've been trying to work it out of my system by putting in eighteen-hour days on the ranch. It's not going too well, either. Then you mentioned how you and Todd used to pray together, and I remembered that about him. Todd had a peace I couldn't touch."

Mara looked down at Abby and let out a breath. Maybe it wasn't as wrong as she thought to enjoy the same man her husband had loved so deeply. "Todd's faith filled in the hollowness in his life," she acknowledged. "He had a deep, personal relationship with God."

Brock nodded. "And with you, Mara."

She searched his eyes, trying to read the message in their brown depths. Did he understand what she felt? Did he want the same things she was beginning to want? Slowly she unknotted her fist and stretched out her hand. Brock's warm fingers closed around hers, covering the gold bands she wore. He cleared his throat, and she gave his hand a slight squeeze.

"Dear God," Mara said softly, "thank you for a good night's sleep. Please bless this food to the nourishment of our bodies... Thank you for Abby and...and for Brock...and teach me how to forgive. In Jesus' name I pray, amen."

"Amen." Brock glanced at her. Continuing to hold her hand, he picked up his fork. "Forgiveness. That's tough business."

Realizing she was immobilized—one arm wrapped around Abby and her free hand clasped firmly in Brock's—Mara watched him chew a bite of breakfast. She could feel Abby's mouth massaging her nipple, and though the sensation was anything but sexual it heightened her awareness of her own body and stimulated her nerves to a tingling tautness. Suddenly she didn't want to talk about forgiveness or faith. She wanted to stare at Brock Barnett's bare chest and his own flat brown nipples nestled in crisp black hair.

"I don't know how to forgive," he said bluntly. "Never have figured it out in all these years."

Mara studied their clasped hands, aware that his fingers were tanned and hard against her soft pale skin. She remembered how their fingers had been entwined during her labor, and she recalled how she had stared at them, loving them. She wanted his hand to touch more than her fingers. More than her arm. All he had done in the past two weeks was grab her, shake her, propel her here or there. But she craved those brown hands on her neck, sliding up and down, rubbing her shoulders, massaging her bare back.

"My mom, for one." He pointed his fork out the window, as though his mother were standing in the courtyard. "She left my dad when I was a kid. Took my sister and headed east. It was like I'd never been born. I watch you and Abby, and I wonder how she could do that to me. How do you forgive that?"

Mara focused on the man who was speaking and realized just how poorly she had been concentrating on his words. He had been baring his soul in a completely uncharacteristic flow of confession.

"I don't know," she said honestly. "I haven't had much to forgive in my life."

"Until recently."

She looked down at her plate. "It is hard to let go."

"If forgiving is the same thing as forgetting, I can't do it. My dad wasn't much better than my mom. I might as well have been invisible around the house. For most of my life, I've treated people the way he treated me. I see folks as pesky flies buzzing around my head. Tolerate them as long as you can, then swat them back if they get too close."

"You never treated Todd that way."

"Todd." Brock took a sip of coffee. "He was different."

Mara studied her cold eggs, unwilling to remove her hand from Brock's grasp. "I think Todd would have wanted me to forgive you," she whispered.

"Maybe."

"I don't know how."

"You could start by letting me tell you what happened on the cliffs."

"It doesn't matter what happened up there. What I can't forgive is the fact that you asked him to go."

"And I was responsible for him."

Mara bit her lower lip. "Please, I don't want to talk about it."

"All right."

"Does it really matter if I never completely get past this?"

"Sure it matters." He set his mug on the table and leaned toward her. "If Todd would want you to forgive me, then it matters. You owe him that. And it matters to me."

"Why?"

"Because I don't want to see you turn bitter. Bitterness will eat you up, Mara. It'll make you hard and tough and cold. It'll turn people away. It'll hurt Abby and everybody else you touch. Look at me. Hey, am I the kind of warm, loving guy a woman would want to spend the rest of her life with? Am I your basic family man—two kids, a wife and a dog? The truth is, you don't hold on to bitterness. It holds on to you."

Mara studied the cynical tilt to his mouth and realized how deeply his parents' rejection had cut him. Had he become too hard to give and receive love? She ran her eyes down his bare shoulders and gazed at his chest for a minute. Did it matter what kind of man he really was, when he could have any woman he wanted? When he could have Mara herself . . . if she wasn't careful.

Yes, it did matter.

"I watched you with Abby this morning," she said. She rubbed her thumb up and down the side of his finger. "You may be hurt and you may be bitter, Brock, but you're not cold. You loved Todd. You've won the hearts of your household staff. And you cooked breakfast with my daughter in your arms. Maybe you are just a basic family man."

His fingers tightened on hers as he struggled to control an emotion she had never seen in his eyes. He swallowed hard. "You reckon?"

"Maybe."

He studied her plate for a minute. "You're not eating."

"I can't," she replied, nodding toward their clenched hands.

"I'll be damned." He pulled his hand away, swept up her plate and strode to the microwave oven. "I'll zap these eggs for a few seconds, and you can chow down. Then I need to check on that cow. What would you say to a drive around the ranch?"

Mara glanced at him. He was studiously watching the plate revolve in the oven. She wasn't sure why he had opened up to her. But she was intrigued.

"Can I bring Abby?" she asked.

He turned, and the smile on his face warmed the edges of her soul. "You bet," he said.

Chapter 11

The ranch on the western plains beneath the San Andres Mountains welcomed Mara like the mother she had never known. As Brock's pickup sped down long, dusty roads, she felt warm, sunny arms enfold her. Dry grass, old mesquite and gnarled juniper decorated an arid landscape that welcomed her more than any house she had lived in. The nip of crisp mountain breeze against her cheeks nurtured her as profoundly as did the up-and-down warble of meadowlarks and the coo of doves. Yuccas pointed toward the turquoise sky and the pale yellow winter sun.

Mara gazed down at her own child, tucked safely beside her in the car seat, eyes closed in peaceful slumber. No bigger than a pearl, Abby's nose drank in the clean New Mexico air as her tiny chest rose and fell. Layered beneath a pile of flannel blankets, quilts and crocheted afghans, her infant tummy was warmly filled with nourishing mother's milk. Little hands, curled like miniature sweet rolls, were nestled against her chin. A few wisps of hair as pale and soft as corn silk escaped her white knitted cap.

How could this child be so new, so small, and yet so essential? Mara could no longer remember life without Abby, nor could she imagine it. Her thoughts were consumed with images, plans and dreams for her baby. Her arms were rarely empty. Even her body was so connected with the child that their rhythms of sleeping and eating had meshed. Without Abby, what would Mara do?

Swallowing back tears of love mingled with fear, she stroked her daughter's round cheek. What would Abby do without her mother? If Mara were to die, as Todd had died—as Mara's own parents had died—what would become of this baby?

Would she be dumped into the welfare system as Mara had been at her own parents' death? Would she be passed from foster home to foster home, never allowed to form personal bonds? Would she struggle the rest of her life with a fear of abandonment and a reluctance to entrust her heart to anyone?

Nearly overwhelmed with her own imaginings, Mara lifted her eyes to the man who sat on the other side of Abby's little car seat. Black hair ruffling away from his forehead in the breeze from the open window, Brock stared evenly ahead at the dirt road. With one strong, sunbaked hand he worked the gears, with the other he steadied the jerky steering wheel. His deep-set brown eyes surveyed the landscape, back and forth, up and down. His domain.

"Glad we checked on that cow this morning," he said, unaware of Mara's turmoil. "She's looking as good as new again. The trick will be to keep her out of the weeds." He drove on, speaking almost as if to himself. "I've got a new Simmental bull over here in this pasture. He ought to make a fine breeder come spring. The Simmental is a Swiss breed, you know. Big, sturdy animals. Good beef and milk. Usually they're either a buff color or a dull red and white. Whoa, there he is."

Brock swung the pickup off the road, crossed the borrow ditch and pulled up against a fenced pasture. In the distance, a lone animal lifted its head to stare. For a moment, the bull studied the intruding vehicle, then it returned to the monotonous task of grazing the stubbly winter range. Brock cut the pickup's engine and stretched his arm along the back of the seat.

"You wouldn't think a bull would be much to look at," he commented, "but sometimes I drive out here and just stare at that young fellow. He's got the future of this place locked up inside him. Of course, he doesn't know that. Doesn't have a clue. It's up to me to see that he does his job."

He looked at Mara and when their focus met, his eyes softened to brown molasses. As they stared at each other, she felt herself melt inside like a crock of thick, creamy butter in the summer heat. Half afraid she might slide right into his gaze, she struggled to pull away. It was useless. Her heartbeat slowed to a dull, lopsided thudding, her breath hung in her throat.

"I guess you're not too interested in cows, are you?" he asked in a low voice.

She watched his mouth form the words, moving over every syllable in a mesmerizing dance. "I don't know much about cows," she whispered.

"I guess not." With one finger, Brock touched the ribbed neckline of her blue sweater. He could feel Mara scrutinizing him with her gray-green eyes, her dark lashes shadowing their hidden depths. Between them lay her baby and all the built-up anger, resentment and sorrow that could possibly separate two people.

So why did he read a sense of longing in those magical, mysterious eyes of hers? Were they merely reflecting his own desires? Or did she want him as badly as he wanted her?

"I suppose I could be interested in cows," she said, dropping her gaze, "if I knew more about them."

"They're not as complicated as some animals. They're pretty basic. If you live out here long enough, you'll catch on."

He allowed his focus to trail down her cheek to her long neck. Her hair, soft and slightly fluffy after her morning shower, lay scattered across her shoulders. One strand had trickled over to rest on her arm. Unable to stop himself from touching, he picked it up and fingered the wispy ends of the hairs.

"Is it working out for you two to live here, Mara?" he asked. "Well enough to stay a while?"

"Maybe," she said, incapable of lifting her eyes to meet his. "It depends."

"On what?"

"Lots of things." She tried to keep breathing steadily as he wound her hair around his finger. The lock shortened and grew tighter. His finger touched the tip of her earlobe. She gave a silent gasp, then slowly let out her breath. "I have to do what's right for Abby."

"What about you, Mara? Seems to me if you're happy, she'll be happy, too."

"I'm not sure I can be happy here."

"Too boring?"

"I found your library. I'm not bored."

"Neither am I."

She glanced up, and he captured her eyes. In them he read fear, uncertainty, dismay. But she wasn't pushing him away.

"It's difficult to think about Abby's future," she said. "Or mine. I know I can't allow us to live on your goodwill forever."

"Why not?"

"I need something of my own. Something to do."

She sucked in a breath as his finger traced the outer edge of her ear. If she didn't cut him off soon, he would thaw what was left of the frozen core of her heart. And then what? Did she want to know what could happen between them? Again, she tossed out the barrier she knew would stop him.

"Todd has been on my mind," she said quickly. His hand paused. "I was thinking about his restoration business. You said you were going to keep Rosemond Restoration solvent. You had written a letter to the Bureau of Land Management. Have you heard from the project director?"

"Dr. Long." He let his finger slide out of her hair. "I got a letter Thursday. The BLM concedes the contract is still in effect, but Long wants to know who's going to run the restoration. If we can't come up with something pretty fast, he's going to terminate the contract. He claims they have grounds."

"What grounds?"

"Time. A limitation was written into the contract as to when the restoration had to be complete. Since Todd's death, nothing's been done at the fort. Even if skilled adobe workers could be found, it would be next to impossible to finish the project on time."

Mara studied the bull wandering toward the pickup. "What are you going to do?"

"It's legally your company. What do you want to do?"

"I think I could pull it back together myself. I think I can run the whole show."

"You do?"

"I did a great deal of the research for Todd, so I know the historical period well and Fort Selden in particular. I studied all the plans Todd had drawn up. I have everything collected in a box in my closet, and it's basically ready to go. If I could find a competent builder who knows adobe and would be willing to take on the project, I could supervise it."

Deciding his bull should be left in peace on a Sunday morning, Brock turned the keys in the ignition and gunned the pickup. Beside him, Abby stirred as the vehicle bounced back onto the road, then she slipped back into slumber.

"You think the BLM would let you run the project?" Brock asked as he drove toward the mountains.

"I don't see why not. I have a degree in history."

"You're a teacher, Mara. An educator. You don't have any experience in reconstruction and restoration. You're not qualified."

"That's bunk. I went to Fort Selden umpteen times with Todd. I've studied it inside and out. I've read and memorized every last inch of those plans. I have a concrete understanding of the historical period. Most important, I have an intuitive feel for that era and how to re-create it. In the long run, that's what counts."

"Intuition as a credential?" He shrugged. "That won't cut any ice with BLM."

"Brock, I can manage a restoration project as efficiently and effectively as anyone else, including Todd. Maybe I can't run heavy equipment myself, and maybe I don't have the experience in engineering and construction he had. But I could hire out the heavy labor. I think what really matters is the end result. The detail work is what lends authenticity to any restoration. And yes, intuition plays a part in that. If I employed a builder to follow Todd's plans and then I supplied the historical accuracy, I believe the project would be a success. Why can't you understand that?"

He gave her a sly grin. "Just playing devil's advocate there. Thought I'd see if you could summon the gumption to fight for a dream."

Mara frowned. "Well, of all the—"

"Whoa, there are my horses." He slowed the pickup again. "Beautiful, aren't they? I ride every day if I can find the time. Evenings around sunset are the best. Once you get to feeling better, I'll take you out for a ride."

Still a little off-kilter at the mental game Brock had played with her, Mara looked over his shoulder at six fine-looking horses grazing in the open pasture. Sleek and healthy, they pawed at the grass and shook their manes in the chill air. Behind them, the mountain range loomed in shades of purple, brown and sage.

"I've got cattle spread out all over this range," he said as he pushed the gas pedal. "This is the dream I'm fighting for."

The pickup wheeled past miles of neat barbed-wire fencing, herds of grazing cattle, windmills creaking in the breeze, lonely yuccas and prickly pears, half-filled sinkholes and clumps of foxtails and catclaws. The vehicle's riders fell silent, Brock mapping the future of his ranch, Mara focusing on the possibilities in her own life.

"Do you think I could do it, Brock?" she asked finally. "You think I could run the restoration company?"

"Give it a shot. Nothing to lose."

Mara stared unseeing at the passing landscape. "I'd need to contact builders in Las Cruces. I'd have to take bids and line up my team before I could write to the BLM myself."

"Use the phone all you want. My house is your house."

She felt a smile tug at her lips. "You know, even though I enjoyed my students and I felt good about teaching, I always liked researching for the fort project better. I felt I was touching history—my real passion—more directly."

"Why didn't you quit teaching sooner?"

"Todd always discouraged that."

"How come?"

"In the beginning, we needed my income. Later...I don't know. I guess the restoration company was his private dream. Todd was never a selfish person, but I don't think he wanted to share that."

"Maybe not. Shame, though. A person ought to be able to do what she wants to do."

Mara leaned her head back and thought over this turn of conversation. It felt somehow oddly releasing to be angry with Todd—to use that resentment to help her let go of him. Why *had* he held her back? More important, why couldn't she now pursue her own dreams?

"If you want to touch history," Brock said, "you ought to see this place coming up. Todd and I came out here once in a while to explore. It's an old adobe house, just about melted. Walls look like velvet, don't they?"

Mara focused on the rippled mahogany-hued structure in the distance. Behind the old walls rose a line of steep cliffs dotted with sharp stones and overhanging mesquite shrubs. At the familiar anticipation of solving the mystery contained within any historical site, Mara's heart sped up and she leaned forward for a better look.

"What was the building's function?" she asked. "Was it somebody's homestead?"

"An old trading post, I think. I've found bullets, broken glassware, tools, rusty nails, even a shoe sole."

"Can you put a date on the place?"

"Never have. You'd think a document somewhere would mention it. Believe me, I've looked. Searched every book in my library and the one downtown. *Nada*. Not a word."

He pulled the pickup into the scant shade of a huge old cottonwood tree. In silent but mutual agreement, he and

Mara leaned toward the baby between them and began to unbuckle her from the seat. For the first time since Todd's death, Mara knew a heady sense of self-confidence. Within her grasp she had both a dream and a plan. More than that, she felt a hope for building her own future—without anyone's charity.

At the recognition of that freedom, she looked up at Brock, the man who had somehow pointed her toward it. He was gathering Abby into his arms and settling her wobbly head against his chest. Holding her securely with one hand, he used the other to tuck blankets and quilts tightly around her little body. As he backed out of the truck, he brushed a kiss across the baby's forehead.

At the simple gesture, Mara felt a weight of unexpected heat flood through her. Brock's lips had touched Abby. His large hands held and comforted the baby. His chest supported her head; his muscled arms cradled her weight.

Mara stared, stunned at the realization rocketing through her. The moment Brock's mouth had left Abby's skin, Mara had wanted to take her baby and press her own lips to that spot. A sudden urge came over her to bury her nose in Abby's blankets just to smell Brock's scent. Just to know she was touching places he had touched.

Dear Lord, she prayed silently. What was happening? Holding onto the pickup door handle for support, she watched as Brock strolled toward the adobe ruin, his boots kicking up little spirals of dust. His legs moved in an easy stride, his narrow hips tightening inside his jeans at each step. The tip of Abby's white-capped head appeared just over one broad shoulder, her cheek resting comfortably on his suede sheepskin jacket.

"I figure this was the entrance," Brock called, turning back toward Mara. "It's a wide opening, and there are a few old planks lying around that might have been the boardwalk."

She gazed at him, riveted.

"You coming?" he asked. "There's nothing to be scared of. I've checked for rattlers."

Realizing how foolish she looked, Mara started toward him, willing common sense back into her head. Her blood had pooled in her knees, and her thighs felt like butter. She felt sure it was almost time for Abby to nurse, because her breasts had swollen and gone damp inside her bra. That must have been the reason her nipples felt so tight and tender.

As she approached, Brock's eyes surveyed her up and down. She could almost feel the heat burning through her sweater and into her skin as his focus fastened first on her face, then skimmed to her breasts, then slid slowly to her hips and legs.

"You know, Mara, you look damn good for so soon after having a baby," he commented, lifting his eyes again. "I figured it would take you a long time to get over what you went through."

Mara tried to squelch the flush that had spread across her cheeks. He was standing just inside the ruin, one hand holding Abby and the other stretched out to her. How could it be fair for one man to look so earthy and carnal? And how could she be feeling hungrily lascivious in broad daylight, in a baggy old sweater, in a body that had given birth only a few weeks before?

It just wasn't possible. But when she placed her hand in his and his fingers wove through hers, she knew it was more than possible. Her breath trembled as she lifted her focus to his eyes.

"This must have been the front of the store," he said, speaking to her eyes. "When I was a kid, I found an old coffee grinder in this room. Rusted clean through."

Mara nodded, fighting the urge to move closer to him. "Did you find anything else? Signs? Glass? Scraps of fabric?"

As if sensing her unspoken desire, he pulled her toward him until the lengths of their arms touched. It hardly mattered that they wore coats and sweaters against the December chill. At his touch, Mara went as hot as if it were midsummer.

"I carried everything back to the ranch house," he said, looking at her mouth. "It's in my workshop. Labeled."

She swallowed. "I guess you made diagrams."

"Yeah."

"Done any digging?"

"No."

Neither spoke again. Neither looked at the ruin. Or the baby. Brock ran his eyes over Mara's face, across her lips, down her neck. Her fingers gripped his so tightly they throbbed. He studied her mouth, the parted lips, the pale pink hue. He imagined her breasts, full and blue-veined and ripe. He thought about Abby's mouth closing around Mara's nipple, and how often he had wished it was his own mouth, his own lips.

With other women, he had never prefaced a kiss with explanations, rationales or apologies—but for some reason, he felt the need to talk everything over with Mara. She wasn't just any woman. She was different, a very special treasure who had stepped into his life and might walk back out at any moment. The night before and during the past few hours, he had grown into the realization that he couldn't startle or frighten her. He couldn't take the risk that she might bolt.

At the same time, how could he deny his own urgent need for her? They were two adults. Married adults, for heaven's sake. Could one chaste kiss hurt?

"Mara..." he tried. "Listen, I..."

"Brock," she said softly, "I'm...so..." Mara swallowed again. Her mouth felt dry and her skin prickly with damp heat. What was she? Excited, afraid, uncertain, eager, delirious? "I'm...very..."

"Mara, you and I...we..."

"I think it's...just..."

"Things are... What I'm trying to say is...if you..."

"No, it's really..."

"I...uh...would never want to..."

"Do you...do you...do you think there might be a record of the trading post in the county courthouse?" She pulled her hand out of his, swung away from him and headed across the lumpy ground. "The deeds office, or something? Have you looked there?"

"No." He clutched the baby and walked the other way. It would have been a mistake. A terrible mistake. If he had kissed her, they could never have gotten past it. What little goodwill they'd built would have come tumbling down.

"I guess there might be an old title in the record books," he said, studying a fallen wall.

"Or a survey." She hugged herself tightly, fighting the dizzy sensation that had swept over her. He would have kissed her. She would have let him. Dear God!

"Next time I'm in Las Cruces, I'll check it out."

"Good idea." Trembling, she walked along the length of crumbled wall. How could this irrational, illogical thing be happening to her? She felt like a child—lost, uncertain, even afraid. And she felt like a woman for the first time in months. Her body tingled with delicious electricity. She was moist and eager and hungry. Had she ever felt this wanton with her husband... her comfortable, teddy-bear Todd?

Where *was* Todd at a time like this? She needed him! How dare he die and leave her in turmoil. How dare he abandon his wife and daughter when his calming presence was required. She clenched her jaw and marched around the perimeter of the ruin without seeing anything.

Her parents had deserted her when she was six. How could they die in a car wreck just like that? She had needed them. Then Todd did the same thing. Vanished from her life. Would everyone?

She could hear Brock talking somewhere in the distance, explaining his theories about the old trading post. She ventured a glance at him, and instantly a ripple ran through her, tightening her nipples and shimmering into the pit of her stomach.

Oh, no. This was not good.

If Todd were around, he would laugh and tell a joke and everything would feel normal. But he had to go off and die, didn't he? He had to leave his wife with a belly full of baby and a mountain of debt. Now look. She was living with Brock! Brock Barnett—the man she'd always resented and hated. And she was gazing like a lost sheep into his brown eyes and aching for him to take her in his arms and kiss her.

Damn Todd! Damn, damn, damn!

"Back here it looks like there might have been a wood-burning stove at one time," Brock was saying. He had stepped through the doorway of the main room and into the quarters behind. "There's a hole in the wall where the pipe would have gone. Maybe somebody lived here. Do you reckon the trader's family made a home at the back of his store?"

Mara scowled at the ground. She didn't want to chat. She didn't want any of this. "I suppose. They usually did."

"Then there ought to be a trash pile buried somewhere. I heard those are the richest digging places. You can usually tell a lot from someone's garbage, can't you?"

"Depends."

"Reckon we might be able to date the place if we found some old bottles or china plates or something?"

"Maybe." She stepped over the raised threshold between the front room and the back.

Brock was standing by the back wall, looking through a hole that had once been a window. A fragment of wood frame remained, nothing else. "I think this was the bedroom," he said.

Mara swallowed. She wanted him to hand over her daughter and then turn over his car keys. She wanted to drive to Sherry's house, lay Abby in a crib and bury herself in bed where she wouldn't have to see Brock Barnett or hear him or smell him ever again.

"If this was your bedroom," he was saying, "you could lie in bed and look right out the window at those cliffs."

"Why on earth would I want to look at a blank wall?" She realized her voice sounded harsher than she had intended.

"The cliffs aren't blank. They're a canvas of shadow and light." He glanced at her. "Come here."

When she didn't move, he stepped backward and took her hand. At his touch, a shower of sparks scattered down her spine and flickered between her thighs. Not again. Moving as stiffly as a wooden puppet, she followed him to the window. There she removed her fingers from his and tucked her hand safely under her arm.

"See, Mara, the cliffs protected the trading post from the mountain winds." His voice was low, almost hypnotic. "At sunrise, these cliffs turn a deep purple. Velvety purple-black like an overripe plum. At dusk when the setting sun shines on them, they change from bright pink to beet red. And at noon, they're blazing white-hot. You touch a bare rock and your fingertips just about blister. You have to watch for scorpions and sunning rattlers, too, when you're up there."

"You go up?" Mara craned her neck, trying to see the top of the enormous bluff. "To the top?"

"It's where I train. I climb—"

"You climb these cliffs?" Todd's face flashed before her eyes. She could hear the animation in his voice. *Brock trains all the time. He's got his own cliffs where he practices. He's good, Mara. Brock knows what he's doing.*

"Yeah, I climb here," Brock admitted in a low voice. "This is a good place to practice technique. It's a fifth-class rock face, which means to climb it you need rope and special equipment. Every year or two I take a training course at a rock-climbing school. In between, I continue upgrading my skills and adding to my equipment."

He studied her, reading her mind clearly. She was remembering her husband and all the unanswered questions. How had Todd fallen? Why had he fallen? And why hadn't his best friend saved him? Brock knew he could answer those questions if Mara would let him . . . if only she would ask. But, of course, she would never ask.

She turned her head and scrutinized the cliff again. He could see the little muscle working in her jaw as she pondered the rock face. Her mouth went hard, uncompromising.

"Do you still plan to climb, Brock?" she demanded suddenly, facing him with cold, gray eyes. "Now?"

He could feel his heart thudding against the sleeping body of her daughter. "Does it matter to you, Mara?"

"I asked you a question. Do you still plan to climb?"

"Climbing helps me relax and let go of tension. When I'm up on those cliffs, I feel a peace I can't touch anyplace else." He clutched the baby tighter. "Yeah, I guess I still plan to climb."

Mara stared at him, a whirlwind of emotion tearing through her. Was it the death of her parents...or the loss of her husband...or the fear of abandonment...or the insecurity of her future? Or was it this man himself? Was the thought of losing Brock too much to bear?

Mara cut off the answer to her question before it had time to form. It was only Abby's future that mattered, after all, she told herself.

"Well," she said evenly, "if you're planning to continue climbing cliffs, I hope you've updated your will to include my daughter."

Chapter 12

Brock lifted his head and studied the hues of gray, gold and pink mingled in the rock face he had scaled countless times. He knew the easiest routes up the slab, where balance and friction were more essential than brute strength. And he knew more challenging paths that followed the natural line of cracks and required such techniques as smearing, edging, clinging and fist jamming. He had been up the cliff alone countless times; he had led skilled companions; he had guided groups of novice climbers. More than once, he had successfully free-soloed the cliff using neither rope nor equipment. He was never careless or casual, but he understood the soaring wall of stone so well it seemed like a comfortable old friend.

Yet to Mara, the precipice represented death. He understood that, too. And for the first time in his life, another person's feelings mattered more than his own.

"I have updated my will," he said gently. "Two weeks ago in Las Cruces I met with my lawyer to discuss the situation. A few days later I approved the revisions. When I die, my estate will belong to Abby... and to you, Mara."

At the simplicity of Brock's statement, Mara realized how harsh and unfeeling her mercenary demand had sounded. She didn't want him to think she was hoping he would keel over any minute. But could she confess what the thought of losing him had done to her heart?

"It's not that I don't care what happens to you," she tried. "Of course, I wouldn't want you to... I mean, I'm certainly not hoping that anything..."

"You just want to make sure your daughter has a future."

"That's right."

"If I'm going to keep spelunking and parasailing and white-water rafting and rock climbing, you want to be certain that you and Abby have something you can depend on."

"I'm not hoping something happens to you. But, Brock, I just know I don't trust—"

"You know you don't trust a man who would let Abby's father fall off a cliff. But there are too many things you don't know, Mara. You don't know that Todd and I practiced out here on this slab until he could just about run up the thing. And you don't know that I bought double of every piece of equipment so Todd would be outfitted safely. You don't know that he made up for any lack of dexterity with his uncanny sense of technique. Todd could climb just about anything."

"Obviously not the cliffs at Hueco Tanks."

"He did climb there. All the way up. We were on our way down when he fell." The image of that inescapable moment flashed itself before Brock once again. "It was late in the afternoon, and since it was getting dark, we decided not to rappel. Rappelling can take a lot of time because you have to secure the ropes, anchor and slings. Todd was afraid we'd have to leave some of the equipment behind, and he never liked to do that. We checked to see that the route was free of loose or rotten rock, and we began down-climbing the crag without ropes. I led, since I'd been there before a few times. So we started down, face out with our backs to the wall—"

"All right," Mara cut in. "I know what happened."

She squeezed her eyes shut as her heart hammered against her ribcage. How many times would she have to command Brock's silence before he understood? She didn't want to hear it. She couldn't hear it. When she looked up, he was staring at the cliffs above him.

"I know what happened," she repeated, her voice tense. "Todd fell."

"Not there, at the top. It was later." Oblivious to her consternation, he kept talking. "The angle got steeper, so we knew we needed to turn around and face the cliff wall. I decided we should use a rope at that point, just to be safe. I tossed mine up to Todd." Brock could almost see the moment when his friend had caught the end of the rope. "We had it tightly stretched between us, and he was working to anchor it—"

"Stop it!" Mara burst out.

"You need to know what happened."

"No, I don't. I don't want to hear the details."

"Why not?"

"Why should I? To hear how Todd suffered? To be able to picture his pain more clearly? Why do you insist on telling me?"

"So you'll know, so you won't just imagine what happened for the rest of your life."

Hot tears stung the corners of her eyes. "You want to tell me for your own sake! You think you can get rid of the memory and pain and guilt by dumping it on me."

"You think you're not wallowing in it right now? You'll never get over Todd's death. You're going to let it haunt you forever."

"Who's it haunting?" she burst out. "Me, or you?"

"Us!" He grabbed her arm and pulled her tightly against him. Pressed between them, Abby let out a muffled cry. "It's haunting us."

"There is no us."

"You're lying to yourself, and you know it. Until we talk about what happened, Todd is as alive between us as this baby."

"It's Abby, Brock," she choked out, her anger suddenly evaporating. "I'm so afraid for her. Todd's gone. What if something happens to me?"

"Mara, I'm here for her. For you."

She swallowed a sob as his mouth brushed over her lips. The kiss was light, unexpected and over before she could respond, but it burned on her lips like a wildfire out of control. Near her ear, Abby squealed as her tiny arms pummeled against the sheath of quilts, but the only sensation Mara absorbed was the scent of Brock's skin as his hand slid up the side of her damp cheek.

"Mara," he ground out, "I know you still love Abby's father. I know you're not over Todd."

"You don't know anything, Brock." She couldn't breathe. "You don't know anything about me." His fingers wove through her hair, lighting sparks across her scalp. His breath was warm and clean, his mouth so very close to her own. And she wanted his kiss again.

"I know you'll always love Todd," he murmured. "I know that. I understand it. I'm trying to honor that."

Beneath the blurred veil of tears clinging to her eyelashes she watched his lips form each word. She saw the tiny, dark point of each whisker on his jaw. She tasted his kiss on her salty lips.

Somewhere in the background, like a crazy symphony, the sound of little Abby's wails pierced the air. Mara tried to think maternal thoughts. She attempted to focus on her need to nurse, but instead of Abby's mouth clinging to her breast, she saw Brock's sunbaked fingers caressing and stroking the sensitive skin. She imagined his lips moving down her neck. She fantasized his tongue flicking over the tip of her nipple.

"Brock!" she gasped as she caught his arm with her hand. She couldn't think this way. She couldn't let him near. "I do love Todd. I'm sure I do. It wouldn't be right to feel any other way, would it?"

Brock felt every muscle in his arms go rigid with tension. Was she asking? Did she really want to know what he thought? Her scent drifted around his head like an intoxicating liqueur. The warmth of her silken hair spilled through his fingers, and her mouth beckoned. He gazed at her lips, aching to kiss her again in spite of a wailing baby and the threat of tears for a lost husband.

"It might be all right," he said slowly. "It might, Mara."

She trembled with anticipation as his eyes traveled to her mouth. Ragged breath escaped his chest. His hand slipped to cup the back of her neck. He drew her so close her breasts crushed against his chest and her thighs pushed against his. He wanted her so badly his body throbbed. Every male instinct he possessed told him she was eager for his kiss. But he was scared...so damned scared that he would frighten her.

"Mara," he began, demanding order of words that tumbled through his brain like falling building blocks. "I don't understand everything that's happening between us—"

"Nothing's happening." She blinked back the mist of confusion as her head demanded separation from this man and her heart demanded his kiss. "Between us there's just...we both loved Todd, and now...now there's Abby to take care of..."

"There's more than that, Mara." His mouth covered hers. Gently searching, he explored, testing the soft curves and pillowed rises of her lips. Against all reason, she responded, reveling in the feel of rough male skin against her chin and the pressure of his urgent demand. She could hear her baby crying with hunger, and all she cared about was her own hunger, the explosion of throbbing drums inside her body as his mouth moved over her own.

His hand behind her head drew her closer, increasing the pressure of his kiss. Her lips grew damp as his mouth heated her skin. Allowing her hand to slide up his arm, she groped the rigid mounds of muscle and sinew. Her knees went as warm and soft as melted butter, but she boldly wove her fingers through the coarse dark hair above his collar. The short, crisp ends feathered against her palm. The longer strands sifted back and forth between her fingertips.

An ache settled in the pit of her stomach as his mouth covered hers again and again, now tender and ministering, now hard and demanding. She danced with him through the kiss, absorbing every nuance, waiting like a butterfly poised on the tip of a petal.

And then his tongue slipped over her lower lip in a hot, damp line that sent a shower of liquid down her spine. Parting her mouth, she took him inside and caressed with her own tongue the hard, male reminder of his desire.

For minutes she could never have counted, they drank each other, lost to the winter sun, the scent of dried grasses, the mournful wail of a baby. Mara explored his mouth, memorized his taste, his heat, his texture. She bared herself for his caresses as he probed and stroked the silken lining of her mouth. Against her thigh, she felt him stiffen with desire, and she realized how deeply she coveted his male hunger for her body. She wanted his hands on her. She wanted his mouth. She wanted his penetration.

The image of the husband she had once loved evaporated like mist on a hot day, leaving in its place this bold, determined man whose touch lit a fire on her skin. His mouth consumed her as his hand drew flame down the line of her back. Their tongues reveled, and she inwardly begged him to stroke her breasts. Her nipples ripened, swelled, contracted . . . and they began to seep.

As mother's milk wept slowly into her clothing, she heard her baby's hungry squalls. She remembered her body's limitations so soon after childbirth. She remembered stitches and torn muscle and stretch marks and engorged breasts.

"Oh, no," she broke away from him, gasping for breath. What had she done? What had she done?

"Mara—"

"No, Brock, we have to stop this right now." She stepped backward, breaking out of his arms. "I have to feed Abby. I have to take care of my daughter."

She reached for her child, and his hand locked around her arm. "Mara, don't go."

"Let me have my baby!" Lifting Abby away from him, she turned and half ran across the broken ground, stumbling over fallen debris and skirting the raised walls of doorways.

At the entrance to the trading post, she spotted the huge cottonwood tree near the pickup. Its denuded gray branches whispered in the chill air. Desperate for refuge, Mara carried her howling bundle toward it. A fallen limb provided a sturdy seat, and she crouched on it, tucking her baby into the nest of her lap. With expertise born of practice, she tossed a blanket over her shoulder and lifted her sweater.

In a swift motion, she freed her breast and settled her sobbing daughter against it. Abby's loud screams faded instantly to urgent sucking, her lips pulling at the nipple and her stomach filling with warm comfort. But Mara felt nothing close to comfort and warmth. She stared down at the wedding band on her free hand and focused on the shimmering gold.

What had she done? She had kissed Brock Barnett, that's what. She had more than kissed him. She had devoured him, plundered him, lusted for him. Every ribbon of moral constraint and decency had unraveled and shredded and been blown to the wind. Had there been no baby, she would have tumbled into the dry grass and rolled in his arms until ecstasy exploded through her body.

How wonderful! How terrible. She had never acted this way with Todd. They had been compassionate and gentle and never, never impulsive. Todd had been Mara's first and only lover. Never for all the world would she have broken their bond of trust and faithfulness.

But less than a year after his death she had fallen into Brock Barnett's arms like a wanton teenager crazed with hormones firing out of control. Even now, she could feel her thighs throbbing and hear her breath coming in tiny, hot gasps. Her lips were swollen and still damp, and her mouth tingled from the pressure of his kiss. She ran her tongue over her lower lip, tasting him.

Oh, God! She lifted her eyes to the bare limbs in a prayer for heavenly aid. She needed help. She needed escape. She needed a miracle. How could they ever pretend it hadn't happened? How could they go on in their distant, uninvolved circles of life? But they had to.

Brock was wrong. There was no "us." There was nothing happening between them. It was far too soon, and she didn't even like him.

But she did like him. He was kind to her baby, he loved his ranch and he cared about Mara's thoughts and feelings. He was everything a woman would want.

That was the whole problem! Women went wildly crazy for him, and he knew it. He took advantage of his sensuality with every available female—including Mara. She had fallen for his wiles like a silly schoolgirl. What a fool she was.

Abby continued nursing as Mara lifted back the blanket and studied her tiny daughter. Her face was still a bright mottled pink from her distress, and her miniature fingers gripped her mother's breast in desperation as she suckled. The knitted white cap had fallen away somewhere, leaving the baby's wispy tufts of pale hair to blow and drift in the chilly winter wind.

A flood of guilt washed through Mara as she tucked blankets around the precious little face. In Brock's arms, she had forgotten all about her own child. What evidence of his treacherous hypnotism could be more damning than that? She gently released Abby's mouth from her nipple, turned the baby on her lap and settled her against the other breast.

When she lifted her head, Brock stood ten paces away.

"Mara, don't run away from me again," he said, his voice deep and tinged with anger.

She slipped her arms around Abby and drew her closer. "What happened back there was a mistake."

"I don't make mistakes."

"Everyone makes mistakes."

"Not that kind. Not with you."

"You have to leave me alone, Brock."

"Don't try to stop this. It's right, and you know it."

"It's not right." She shook her head. "No, I will not be seduced into this game with you."

"This is no game. You're my wife."

"Stop it! You know why we got married. It was for Abby, for Todd. Not for us. Not for thoughtless... stupid... mistakes."

"I won't stop. I won't quit on you, Mara."

"What do you want?"

"The same thing you want."

She studied him as he observed her. Tall, confident, he waited for her admission of desire. Shaded beneath the brim of his Stetson, his brown eyes regarded her. He had settled his hands in his pockets, waiting.

"What I want," she said evenly, forcing her wayward heart and her impetuous body into silence, "is to be left alone."

"Why?"

"Because I need room to breathe, to grieve. I need to heal and grow past everything that has happened to me. I need to be Abby's mother. I need to be Todd's widow."

He took a deep breath, then released it slowly. "Maybe that is what you need. What you want is another thing. I think you know what you want, and it doesn't have a damn thing to do with being a mother or a widow." Giving her a last glance, he turned his back on her. "I'll take you and Abby back to the ranch house when you're done."

Mara watched him walk away, his broad shoulders outlined in morning sunlight.

Brock did give Mara room. He decided if she needed time to think things over, she could have it. He hadn't learned to bury himself in work for nothing.

He spent two weeks putting up new barbed-wire fencing on the far side of the ranch. Nights, he slept in the bunkhouse with the men he had rounded up to crew the project. They ate beans and steaks, drank beer, played their guitars and sang ballads, and he told himself he wasn't thinking about Mara at all. Hardly at all, anyway.

The week before Christmas, he flew his plane to Santa Fe to buy a few things for his staff. It was a tradition he had. He stayed at the La Fonda Hotel near the plaza and looked through the galleries for Indian paintings, pottery and jewelry. He bought Rosa Maria a turquoise-and-silver squash blossom necklace with rows of blue stones. He found a coral-encrusted silver hair clip for Ermaline and some videos for her kids. At a gourmet boutique he located the new grill attachment Pierre had been wanting for his stove. The chef would be in seventh heaven over that.

For his men, Brock bought heavy, waterproof canvas duster coats. Good protection against the howling winds and driving rains of New Mexico's vast plains. He picked up a few new lariats, a good saddle and a bundle of wool blankets woven by a Hispanic family who lived near Chimayo. He ate blue corn enchiladas at The Shed one afternoon and a big bowl of *posole* at The Pink Adobe another night.

Trying to push Mara out of his mind, he drove to a bar and introduced himself to a nice-looking woman, an attorney for the state. They talked a while, and he bought her a drink. She was smart, confident, aware of her sensuality. When she asked him to dance, he considered it...for about two seconds. He begged off and spent the rest of the evening walking the cold, empty streets of Santa Fe.

He didn't want another woman. Couldn't imagine ever wanting anyone but Mara. He wasn't sure how such a thing had happened to him. Maybe it came about the day he watched her give birth, or maybe in those long hours at the hospital while she learned to be a mother. Maybe he had lost himself to her only that morning in the old adobe ruin when she had looked into his eyes and welcomed his kiss.

But he thought it had probably happened a long, long time before. Images of Mara had floated through his life for years, beginning with the evening Todd had first introduced them at an art gallery. She'd talked about the Anasazi tribe and some research paper she was working on. They had been in college then—he was edgy, wild and cocky as hell; she was serious and high-minded and acted supremely certain of herself. They had nothing in common. But the moment he met her he saw something in her gray-green eyes...something that touched the hidden essence of himself...and he hadn't been able to let it go. Not even during all the years when she was his best friend's wife.

Now she was his own wife. In spite of another man's rings on her finger, she wanted Brock as deeply as he had always wanted her. Their kiss had proved that. But she was scared and confused. She had built herself a wall of protection—nearly as insurmountable as his own. Out of respect for her, and for Todd, he knew he ought to let that barrier stand.

He flew back to Las Cruces and drove out to his ranch the morning of Christmas Eve. Every year his friends threw a party in Las Cruces, and he'd never missed it. This would be his first time to go alone. He dreaded the thought of unwinding Sandy's tentacles all evening. As he pulled his Jaguar into the garage in midafternoon, he again turned over the option of asking Mara to go with him.

But to take her into that den of lions? She'd never go. Besides, he hadn't seen her since the incident at the cliffs three weeks before. He wasn't even sure she still lived at his house. Maybe she had moved away and taken the whirlwind of emotion with her.

As he walked across the drive toward the kitchen door at the rear of the home, a light flurry of snowflakes sifted out of the gray sky. Loaded with packages, he elbowed the door open and backed into the room. When he turned around, he heard someone give a loud gasp.

"Brock," Mara said, her voice almost a whisper. "You came back."

"Mara." Looking at her, he felt like a starving man unexpectedly set before a feast. "You're still here."

She was standing by the open refrigerator door, a carton of eggnog in one hand and a string of Christmas tree lights in the other. She had pulled her hair up into a high ponytail fastened with a garland of silver tinsel. A tight red sweater skimmed over her high, round breasts and ended at the waist of a pair of black slacks. Her shoeless feet wore bright crimson socks decorated with little white snowmen.

He set his packages on the counter and kicked the door shut behind him with his boot. She was beautiful. Too beautiful. He had to make conversation or he would do something he'd regret.

"How's Abby?" he asked.

"Big."

"She's a month old now?"

"More." She watched him take off his hat and brush the snowflakes from the brim. He had been away so long, and she had prayed so hard to forget how he looked. She hadn't. Her heart thudded against her ribs as his gaze settled on her.

"You okay, Mara?" he asked.

"I'm fine. I've been busy. Calling builders, completing the fort research, contacting the BLM." She tucked the carton of eggnog against her chest and closed the refrigerator door. "How are you?"

"Good." He held her eyes, unable to pull away. "You look great."

A pink flush blossomed on her cheeks. "Pierre and I have been working on meals to help me trim down. He's even cut down on the butter and cream sauces."

"Whoa. You must have won his heart."

She smiled. "We like to work together. I asked him how he made éclairs, so he invited me into the kitchen. Now I take lessons almost every day."

Brock drank in the sight of her mouth, her white teeth, her almond eyes. Every wall he had worked to erect came tumbling down the moment she smiled. He shoved his hands into his pockets to keep from taking her in his arms.

"Sounds like you're getting used to things around here," he said.

"Everyone's been wonderful. Rosa Maria's daughter helps me look after Abby."

"Ramona?"

"Yes, she's fabulous. I've even been able to leave the baby with her and go into Las Cruces a couple of times for meetings. I found out about your trading post, too, by the way. It was built in 1887. I have copies of the deed in my room. And Ermaline's teaching me how to quilt. We found a pieced quilt top up in a cupboard in the lounge, so we're finishing it. I really like her."

"You haven't been lonely."

"Oh, no." She said the words so easily she almost believed them herself. How many times had she wondered at the utter stillness in the house? People had come and gone, but without Brock every room had seemed quiet and empty.

"Sherry drove out for a visit," she told him quickly. "She brought Abby some Christmas presents. Which reminds me...I invited the staff and their families over tonight. Sort of a thank-you get-together and tree decorating party. I didn't expect you ... and I thought it might be fun to share Christmas with someone."

He nodded. "Sounds good."

"I was just pouring the eggnog."

"I won't be in your way. I have a party in Las Cruces tonight."

"Oh." She swallowed, images of his friends welling up inside her. He would be with Sandy, Stephanie, Justine, and how many other women? Sherry had reminded Mara just what kind of a man Brock was. Together the two friends had restored the old picture of the bullheaded, insensitive womanizer who had always angered Mara. Sherry had been right, of course. Brock was no different now than he'd ever been.

"I have another load of things out in the car," he said. "Go ahead with your party fixings."

"Sure." She swung around and hurried out of the kitchen into the living room. Abby lay on a thick, pink blanket spread across the floor. Beside her rose a towering pine tree that Ermaline's husband, Frank, had cut and brought in.

Bowls of popcorn and cranberries sat beside the fire. Boxes of old ornaments that had been in the Barnett family for generations were stacked against a wall. Rosa Maria had dug the decorations out of a storage closet, lamenting how rarely they had been used through the years. Christmas at the ranch had always been more of an off-again on-again whim than a cherished tradition, the housekeeper had told Mara.

Mara had been determined to change that. Now bayberry and cinnamon scented candles burned on the mantel. Christmas carols drifted through the room. An evergreen wreath hung on the front door. Everything was ready, just perfect ...

Swallowing the unexpected lump in her throat, she opened the carton of eggnog and poured the creamy liquid into a huge punch bowl. The aroma of rum and nutmeg swirled upward to mingle with the fragrance of newly cut pine and fresh popcorn. The scents said Christmas... hope, peace, joy. They spoke of past years with a loving husband. They whispered of precious memories, laughter around a spindly tree, a first turkey cooked in a too small oven, gifts wrapped in newsprint and tied with twine, two voices lifted in carols at a small church. They spoke of Todd.

Why had Brock come back?

Mara blinked at the sting of pain. She didn't want Brock. It was his fault this Christmas had hurt and aching loss at its core. She might paint a bright veneer of tradition and happiness, but beneath it all she was faced with the truth. Her husband was dead.

Now Brock had returned—the focus, the cause of her sorrow. And all she could think of was how giddily happy she felt to see him...how much she had missed him...how desperately she had longed for his touch, his voice, his kiss.

"Oh, Abby." She knelt beside her baby and lifted the gurgling infant into her arms. "What am I going to do?"

But there was no time for reflection as the front door burst open. Rosa Maria and her husband, Fernando, brought in a swirl of snowflakes and laughter.

"¡Feliz Navidad!" Fernando said. He worked on the ranch, and he was one of Brock's longest employed cowhands. "Merry Christmas, Mrs. B. How's the little one?"

"Wonderful, Fernando." Mara greeted them as their youngest daughter, Ramona, followed her parents into the house.

Ramona reflected the contentment of a happy upbringing in her love for little Abby. At nineteen, she had graduated from high school the past spring, and she was hoping to become a kindergarten teacher. She had confessed a desire for a family of her own one day, but first she wanted to earn enough money for a college education. After laying a collection of presents under the tree, she hurried to Mara's side and lifted Abby out of her mother's arms.

Ermaline's happy clan was only moments behind the others. Frank carried a load of firewood, and the four children had each brought an empty stocking. Mara had promised to fill them to the brim. They swirled around the room, cooing over the baby, sampling the popcorn, chattering with excitement over the prospect of Christmas morning.

Into their midst entered Pierre and his plump wife, Yvonne, who was every bit as jolly and effusive as her husband was stiff. She hugged everyone in the room, her French accent bouncing off the vigas as she wished the gathering a *"Joyeux Noël!"* Pierre had brought boxes of pastries and a bottle of champagne.

"And where is Mr. Barnett?" he demanded loudly. "I have seen his car on the road not ten minutes ago."

"Mr. B. is back?" Rosa Maria turned to Mara. "Oh, how happy! I thought he would miss this Christmas with the baby."

"He won't be here tonight," Mara said. "He's going to a—"

"A party in Las Cruces," Brock finished as he walked into the room. He had changed into a black shirt and jeans, black leather coat and boots. A silver bolo tie echoed the heavy silver of his belt buckle. In his somber colors and jet black hat, he looked anything but merry. "You know the one I always go to. At Joe's house."

"Oh, that one." Again, Rosa Maria looked at Mara. Her eyes softened. "Well, then you must go, too, Mrs. B. We'll have our party here while you two go into town together."

"Yes! That's a great idea. We'll watch Abby for you." Ramona hugged the baby against her cheek. "Go on with him, Mrs. B. You've stored enough milk in the freezer to feed the baby for one evening. I'll take care of her."

"I think it is best," Pierre intoned, nodding sagely. "The friends will expect it."

"A husband and wife together—*oui!*" Yvonne clapped her hands. "And when the cats are away, the mice can play. We will have a lovely time here. Go on with you both!"

Mara shook her head. "Oh, no, really. I don't want—"

"I'd like you to come." Brock held out his hand to her. "We'll be back before midnight."

"But Abby—"

"She'll be fine," Ramona said. "You've been away before, Mrs. B. We'll take care of her."

"But I've spent all day getting things ready—"

"Come with me, Mara." Brock took a step toward her. "Please."

"Go on, go on!"

Mara stared at Brock's outstretched hand. It would be a terrible mistake. She knew it even as she placed her palm on his. She was going away with him, leaving her home, her friends, her baby, her security. And she felt as happy as a child on Christmas morning.

Chapter 13

Mara stared in horror at her ankles as Brock's Jaguar sped down the highway toward Las Cruces. In the rush, she hadn't thought to change her socks. She was stuck with the bright red pair decorated with white snowmen. Perfect for a party with loving friends; absolutely appalling for a gathering of the young, snobbish elite. Sandy would probably laugh her right out of the room.

Groaning inwardly, Mara lifted her eyes to the man at the wheel. Dark, silent, Brock was absorbed in thoughts he obviously didn't care to share. Maybe he was regretting the impulse that had led him to invite Mara. He had no reason to be happy about going to a party with a woman in snowman socks.

As foreboding as he looked in his black clothes and hat, he had been a different man back at the house. Before they left, he had walked over to Ramona and had taken Abby from the young woman's arms. While Mara tugged on her coat and gave instructions about the party food, she had observed Brock stroking the baby's cheek. His brown eyes had gone as soft as molasses, and the hard set to his jaw had relaxed. Abby had cooed and batted him on the nose, and his mouth had curved into a gentle smile. Before he was bustled out of the house by Rosa Maria and Ermaline, Mara had caught sight of Brock returning the baby to Ramona. Bending over the cuddly bundle, he had brushed a kiss on Abby's forehead. And as she gave her daughter a kiss of her own, Mara had melted inside.

Did he truly care about Abby? Had the little girl really captured his heart? Mara couldn't help but want his affection to be genuine. Even as she felt her thoughts betray Abby's birth father, she admitted how deeply she longed for her daughter to know Brock's love.

"Did Abby look any bigger to you?" she asked into the silence.

Brock glanced at her as if surprised there was someone else in the car with him. But as their eyes met, his deepened. He shifted gears with a leather-gloved hand and returned his focus to the road.

"She's grown a lot," he said. After a moment he spoke again. "I missed three weeks."

"I guess you were busy. Rosa Maria told me you're usually gone from the house a lot."

"Yeah." He turned on the wiper to deflect the snow-flakes that brushed onto the windshield. "This time I shouldn't have."

"You had to build a fence, didn't you?"

He nodded, silent again. When Mara decided he wasn't going to continue the conversation, she leaned her head against the backrest and shut her eyes. Then he spoke.

"My dad was always away building fences," he said, his voice deep. "Or checking on oil wells."

Mara opened her eyes and observed him. The solemn line of his mouth and the tension in his jaw wrote a message of pain. For the first time in her life, she knew exactly what the man was thinking.

"Your father missed out on your whole life," she said. "Your mother did, too."

"So did yours."

"Not by choice."

"No. You're not missing Abby's life, are you, Mara?" He ran his eyes over her face. "You're right there all the time. Todd would be, too, if he hadn't died. He'd be at her side. He wouldn't go off for three weeks to build a fence."

Mara took a deep breath. Brock was speaking honestly. Could she?

"I'm glad you came back, Brock," she said finally. "You're good with Abby."

"I missed her, even though she doesn't belong to me. And I missed you, Mara."

"Even though I don't belong to you, either," she reminded him.

"You belong with me."

"Brock, please don't start."

"You've had three weeks to think over what happened between us out there at the trading post. You've had three weeks to get used to motherhood and three weeks to continue coming to terms with Todd's death. I want to know where you stand."

The perfectionist was back, Mara thought as she stared at the snowflakes blowing against the windshield. Brock couldn't let things happen. He always had to control people, to put things in order.

"Don't push me, Brock," she said. "I have to think about practical things like the Fort Selden project and Abby's future. I want to forget about the trading post, okay?"

"No, it's not okay. In the past three weeks, I've done my best to put what happened between us out of my mind. I tried to convince myself it didn't mean anything. But this evening when I walked into the kitchen and saw you standing there, I knew I'd been lying."

Mara's heart slowed to a deadly rhythm as her blood puddled in her knees. The car had rolled into the outskirts of Las Cruces where Christmas lights cast a blue, green, yellow and red glow on the gathering snow. Brock said nothing, waiting for her response as he steered through a subdivision, past a park and up a gentle hill. Mara concentrated on her red snowman socks. It was impossible to believe he had said what she thought she had heard.

"Brock, what happened out at the trading post was just an impulsive reaction to the situation," she said carefully, trying to make sense of it even as she spoke. "It was something that occurred on the spur of the moment. It didn't mean anything."

He pulled the car up to the curb in front of a stucco executive home with a sloping front lawn and perfectly trimmed evergreens. Cutting the engine, he leaned back against his seat and let out a breath. Mara could see the muscles in his thighs tighten as he tapped his fingers on them. Suddenly his big shoulders turned and he pinned his focus on her.

"That kiss didn't mean anything to you?" he demanded. "Don't evade the question, and don't lie to me when you answer."

"You make me sound like a felon." Mara tried not to shiver at the intensity in his brown eyes. If she was timid, he would devour her. She had no choice but to stand up to him. "Listen, Brock, I'm doing my best to work through this issue. The bottom line is, I'm a mother and a widow. I can't let a kiss mean anything. I shouldn't even have let it happen."

"But you did. You wanted it."

She turned away. "Is this Joe's house?"

"You wanted to kiss me, Mara. I'm no fool. This has been brewing between us for years, from the first time we met. You know it has. We just couldn't do anything about it."

"No," she whispered, and her breath formed a circle of mist on the window. "I'm cold. Let's go inside."

"But you loved Todd, and so did I. Neither of us would have betrayed him for the world. All the same, we knew. Look at me, Mara."

"I'm going in."

"Damn it, Mara."

"Stop pushing me."

"Stop running away."

"I don't want to feel it."

"But you do. Mara, look at me and tell me you wanted that kiss."

"Leave me alone, Brock." She grabbed the handle and shoved the door with her shoulder. As she bolted into the snowy night, she heard him swearing behind her. She slammed the door shut on his words and ran up the hill, her heart hammering with every step.

This was not acceptable! She couldn't allow it. She couldn't let him say the things he was saying...and she couldn't feel what she knew she was feeling.

"Mara!" Stephanie hailed her across the huge foyer as Mara flung open the front door. "This is a surprise. Where's Brock? We had just about given up on him."

Mara found herself suddenly surrounded by strangers, men who removed her coat and placed a warm drink in her hands, women who stared appraisingly as they stepped aside to let her pass. She walked toward Stephanie on wooden legs.

"Brock's coming," she said. "He's locking the car."

"Well, come on in. Did you bring the baby?"

Mara shook her head. She glanced behind her to see Brock entering the foyer, a sprinkle of snowflakes scattered across his shoulders and the brim of his hat. Turning her back on him, she followed Stephanie into the cavernous living room. It was a modern home with chrome-and-glass tables, sleek leather sofas, plush gray carpet, recessed lighting. It smelled of cigarettes and expensive liquor and even more expensive perfume. An electric fire glowed in a fireplace that boasted a pair of potted green neon cacti on the hearth.

Fit-looking men and thin women clad in cashmere, silk and leather stood in laughing, talking clusters. The women sparkled with diamonds and gold. The men shone in silver and turquoise. Mara thought about her red snowman socks.

"Oh, God! It's her!" Sandy in a tight red skirt glided across the floor, trailed by three other women. "I didn't know you were still lurking around Brock. Ladies, this is Brock's kept woman. I'm sorry, I forgot your name, honey."

"Shut up, Sandy. You're drunk as a skunk." Stephanie rolled her eyes. "This is Mara Barnett. She's Brock's new wife."

"Wife? Wait a minute, I thought Brock told us it was a monetary arrangement," Sandy complained loudly. "You know, she gets the dough, he gets the sex."

"Excuse me," Mara said in a low voice. "I think I'll take a look around the house."

"Hey, love the socks!" Sandy said in a stage whisper as Mara brushed past the offensive woman. "Snowmen! God, those are great!"

Sandy turned to her group of giggling companions to give a loud reenactment of the evening visit to the Barnett ranch. Mara wished she could shrink into her snowman socks and disappear completely.

Why had she come? Back at the ranch house everyone would be enjoying the eggnog, sugar cookies and homemade *posole* she had worked so hard to prepare. They'd be stringing popcorn and cranberries, hanging ornaments and singing the Christmas carols she had been looking forward to all day. Abby would be the focus of love as everyone reveled in the contentment and peace of the season. Instead, Mara was here at a party with a female Attila the Hun.

Stephanie followed her to the ceiling-high tree decorated in silver and blue. Chromed icicles interspersed with tinsel gave the tree a chilly aura. The artificially flocked branches looked as though they were choking in their muffler of goopy fuzz.

"So, how are things going out at the ranch, Mara?" Stephanie asked. "Are you getting used to motherhood?"

Mara studied the woman for a moment and concluded she wouldn't bite. She let out a deep breath and tried to relax her shoulders.

"Motherhood is a slow process," she said. "I don't get much sleep at night. My nerves are a little frazzled."

"Are you, like, breast feeding your baby and all that?"

Mara smiled. "It's not hard once you get used to it. Do you plan to have children, Stephanie?"

"Who knows? At this rate, I'll hit menopause before I get married. That's part of Sandy's hang-up, you know. She's so damned bitter. A lot of us haven't found the right man, but we'd really like to start families. We date around— maybe live with somebody for a while. It's been a bust for Sandy and me. It seems like men are into experimentation more than commitment. I think Sandy was hoping Brock would be it for her. Anybody could have told her differently. A lot of us tried to warn her, but she wouldn't listen."

Taking a sip of the warm rum punch, Mara studied the tree. "Brock's not the kind to settle down, is he?"

"You ought to know that by now. He's a smooth talker, and when he runs those big brown eyes up and down a woman, there's no holding back, you know? But the man doesn't have a heart. Or if he does, he's not about to give it away."

"Sounds like you've been burned."

"Who hasn't? Every woman in this room has probably lusted after him. Just look at the guy."

Mara glanced behind her at the group gathered in the foyer. Brock stood head and shoulders above the others, his hard, suntanned face in sharp contrast to the pasty complexions of his citified companions. Holding a drink in one hand and his black Stetson in the other, he chuckled at a joke someone had told. Two women giggled, and one of them leaned her head against his shoulder for just a moment. He seemed oblivious to the flirtatious ploy.

Mara turned away. "Has his moves down pat, does he?"

"Oh, yeah. You don't hang around this scene for years without learning what makes a woman bend. And Brock's got charisma in spades. If he fixes his sights on someone, she'd better look out. It's like he has this uncanny sense for knowing what will make a woman melt. Once he has her in the palm of his hand, he uses her up. He's broken a lot of hearts in this room, I can tell you that."

"Yours included?"

"Sure. We dated a few years ago. I thought Brock was so intelligent, so handsome, the whole bit. But he was always holding back, you know? It was like his mind was somewhere else. His heart was locked up tight, and I sure wasn't the woman with the key. I don't believe there is such a person."

Mara recalled Rosa Maria's use of the same image to describe Brock. These were women who had known him longer and more intimately than she had. If they believed he was impossible to reach, they must be right. Certainly Mara didn't hold the key to Brock's heart. And she wasn't about to become another used-up piece of litter in the debris of his conquests.

"Anyway," Stephanie went on, "you're not as stupid as the rest of us have been. You're enjoying his money and his company without making a fool of yourself over the man. You've got your baby and your memories of a happy marriage. I wish I'd had your smarts where Brock was concerned."

"I'm just doing what has to be done to survive." Mara spotted Brock across the room again. Though surrounded by people, he was staring straight at her. When he left the group and started toward her, she turned away quickly. "Could you show me a phone, Stephanie? I'd like to check on Abby."

The rest of the evening became a cat-and-mouse game as Mara did her best to avoid Brock. Every time he appeared at her side, she invented an excuse to get away. She asked Joe for a tour of his house. She made three phone calls to the ranch. She went to the bathroom umpteen times. In fact, Joe's downstairs toilet became her ultimate refuge.

She sat on the closed lid of the stool and stared at her snowman socks. The truth was dismaying. She was no better off than Stephanie and Sandy and all the rest of the women at this party. Brock had spoken just the right words to weaken her heart. Every time he came near, her heart rate sped up to double time. When he spoke against her ear, she melted inside. If their hands brushed, she went weak in the knees. She was an absolute fool.

As she sat in the chrome-and-gold bathroom, Mara tried to pray through the situation. But she could only mouth a desperate plea for almighty help. Her prayers seemed to go as high as the marble-tiled ceiling and stop cold. She attempted to turn her thoughts to Todd; instead she tasted her own betrayal of her husband in Brock's arms. When she made the effort to focus on Abby, she pictured her daughter gurgling happily as Brock cooked breakfast.

The only way out, Mara finally decided, was literal escape. She would insist on a job with the fort project. If she could earn even a small income, she could rent an apartment in Las Cruces. She could take Abby on-site at Fort Selden, or she could leave her at the church day-care center. She would give herself a month to work out the details.

During that time, she would do her best to ignore Brock. She could have her meals brought to her room. She could spend her days in Las Cruces negotiating with builders. Brock would be out on the ranch somewhere, anyway. It could be done. She had no choice.

Stepping out of the bathroom, she took a deep breath. Brock stepped from the shadows and slipped his arm around her shoulders.

"You feeling okay, Mara?" he asked. "You've been in there an awful lot tonight."

Startled by his unexpected presence, she shrugged out of his arm and stepped to one side. Had he been waiting for her all this time? She felt like a wary rabbit around a lurking wolf.

"It's getting late," she said. "I'd like to go home."

Brock looked her up and down, worried. Mara seemed too thin and too pale tonight. Had she been sick? Was she worried about her baby? Had Sandy said something cruel to her? Maybe she was still upset about their discussion in the car. It hadn't been pleasant. Still, he'd had no choice but to confront her. He wasn't going to play this game of tag with her much longer.

"I'll get your coat," he said, taking her elbow. Again, she pulled away. Trying to read her mood, he walked beside her toward the foyer. "How's Abby?"

"She's fine. Ramona put her to sleep a couple of hours ago."

"Everyone still at the house?"

"They've all gone home but Ramona. She said she'd be happy to stay until we got back."

In the foyer, Brock tried to help Mara into her coat. With fingers as cold as ice, she took it from him and put it on herself. She avoided his eyes and kept her mouth pinched tight. As she thanked Joe for the party, she buttoned her coat clear up to her chin. If the front door hadn't been ajar, Brock would have sworn she was generating her own chilly breeze.

"You seemed to hit it off with Stephanie," he said as they walked to the car. Before she could get to it, he grabbed the door handle and pulled open the door. "She's a nice woman."

"She's a real-estate agent, you know." Mara glanced at him as she slid into her seat. "She thinks she can find me an apartment."

Pulling the door shut on him, she turned her focus to the swirling snow. It had been very important to reestablish the barrier, she reminded herself as she watched him stalk around to his side. If he had any thoughts of resuming their previous conversation in the car, she intended to squelch them right away. In fact, she thought she probably would tell him exactly what she intended to do about her situation. If that made him want to sever his financial commitment to Abby, so be it.

Brock climbed into the car and started the engine. As he pulled out onto the street, he looked briefly at Mara. She was as tight and rigid as he'd ever seen her. What the hell had happened? At the ranch house, she'd seemed eager to go with him to the party. Now she might have been a million miles away.

"You're moving out of the ranch house?" he asked.

"I'm going to start looking for a place of my own."

"Did Sandy say something to you? I know she's ticked at me, and she's got a mean streak."

Mara shook her head. "It was no big deal. She called me your kept woman. Implied we've got a sex for money arrangement going."

Brock bit off an expletive.

"Stephanie set her straight," Mara cut in. "Sandy was plastered, and everyone knew it. I'm not worried."

"I'd have set her straight if you hadn't kept dancing away from me all night."

"I wasn't dancing. You were stalking."

"I was under the impression we had come to this thing as a duo. It seemed appropriate to at least get within your range of vision once in a while. You are my wife."

"Oh, Brock—"

"And how soon do you expect to move out?"

"It's time now. I'm back on my feet physically. I can get a job either with the fort project or somewhere else."

"What's the point? You've got a place to stay now. You've got food, money. Why move?"

"You know why."

Brock knew. He had scared Mara with his determination to be open about what had happened at the trading post. But damn it, he didn't pussyfoot around things. If he wanted something, he pushed until he got it. And the minute he'd walked into the house after three weeks away from her, he knew what he wanted.

"You planning to run from the truth the rest of your life, Mara?" he asked.

"I'm not running from anything."

"You ran from me all night. You hid in the bathroom so you wouldn't have to face me."

"I needed to think. And after thinking things through, I decided it's time to move out of your house. I'm not running from you, I'm stepping into my own future."

"Bull. You're running from everything in your past. You lost your parents. You lost Todd. You're not about to let anyone else into your life, just in case you might lose him, too. Right?"

Mara clenched her fists inside the pockets of her coat. She felt trapped by this man. Trapped by his words. Trapped by her own desire for him. Again, she tried to turn her thoughts to something else, something less upsetting. Abby was probably awake and needing to nurse. Ramona would need to go home and rest for her family's Christmas celebrations. Ermaline... Rosa Maria... Todd...

No, she couldn't make anything stay in her mind. Not even Todd. For the first time, she wanted her husband's memory to release her. She wanted freedom from the turmoil. She wanted to stop hurting, to enjoy her own sensuality, to feel her own passion. And Brock was right. He was the man she wanted...even though she felt certain his words were hollow and his desire for her had no depth.

"Right?" Brock demanded. "You're running from the past. You're running from the future. You're even running from the present. You don't have the guts to find out what's going on between us."

Mara glared at him. "I'm no coward, Brock Barnett. If I'm running from you, it's because I have every reason to keep my distance. You want to know how I felt about you in the beginning? Right from the night I met you at the gallery, I didn't trust you. I still don't."

"Damn it, Mara." The muscle in his jaw worked as he steered the car through the driving snow that had begun to make the dark highway slick. She had pulled out her ammunition, and he knew it was going to hurt.

"Damn you, Brock," she snapped. "If I had to hide in the bathroom tonight, it's because you're a predator. You always have been. I don't want to be tracked down. I don't want to be devoured like Stephanie and Sandy and every other woman you've set your sights on."

"What makes you so sure I'd devour you? Have I taken advantage of you? Have I gone back on my word?"

"No, but you have a lousy track record. Stephanie told me you've gone out with just about every woman at that party, and you've left a trail of broken hearts. When Todd was alive, you had a different woman each time I saw you. You're not a long-term—"

"No, I'm not Todd. I didn't grow up in a solid home and on the first day of college meet the woman I knew I wanted to marry. My world was a broken family and a father who couldn't commit to anyone. Except for Todd, my circle of friends played the dating game endlessly. And don't believe

Stephanie and Sandy aren't using their wiles to play along just like Joe and Travis and every other person at that party tonight. It's a game, and I won't deny I played it, Mara.''

"Well, I don't want to play."

"Maybe I don't want to play anymore, either."

"Maybe, or maybe not. Like I said—I don't trust you."

"What the hell do I have to do?" He pulled the car over to the shoulder of the highway and jerked the emergency brake into place. Turning to her, he took her shoulders. "Mara, your mouth is saying one thing and your eyes are telling me something else. Damn the past and the future. I want the truth right now."

She stared at him, terrified she would blurt out everything that had built up inside her. If he came any closer...if he leaned toward her... "I'm going for a walk," she whispered.

She threw open the car door, letting in a rush of frigid air and snowflakes. Gasping with the cold, she slammed the door shut and strode out into the darkness. She shivered and buried her hands in her pockets. Her breasts felt swollen, her nipples tender with the need for her baby's suckling. If only she were home.

Home? Did she even have a home? Mara shook her head. Brock had given her his home. Why had she been so harsh with him? Maybe it was because she couldn't deny the truth in his words. She was running from the past. More important, she was running from him.

Even as she felt chagrined for hurling words of doubt at him, she heard Stephanie's voice. *If he fixes his sights on someone, she'd better look out. It's like he has this uncanny sense for knowing what will make a woman melt. Once he has her in the palm of his hand, he uses her up.* Had Brock fixed his sights on her? Would he use her up?

Why not? He had admitted he wasn't like Todd. He had played with women's hearts his whole adulthood. Why would it be different with Mara?

Huge flakes of snow drifted out of the black sky as though a feather pillow had burst. The highway was completely dark. No trucks blasted past. No cars traveled this late on Christmas Eve. Everyone was tucked away in warm houses, wrapping presents and waiting with bated breath for the following morning.

Behind her on the sloping shoulder of the road, Mara made out the black form of the silent Jaguar. Inside it she could see Brock's dark silhouette. He seemed to be staring off into the night, his gaze fixed on the falling snow. Her feet damp in the ankle-deep snow, Mara shifted uncomfortably. She shouldn't have shouted. She shouldn't have cut him. She shouldn't have lied.

Yes, her words were lies just as much as they were truth. She *had* felt that attraction between them from the day they'd met. She had known it was different, strong, unquenchable. And she had wanted his kiss that morning at the trading post. She wanted it now, which was why she couldn't go back to the car.

Again, she glanced at the shiny contours of the Jaguar. Brock was sitting in the utter hush of the night. Wind whispered against the icy windows. Snow gathered on the hood. If only the man would evaporate. But Brock wouldn't go away any more than her desire for him would. He would always be there waiting for her, tall, angry... and very warm beneath his black leather coat.

Her heart hammering in her ears, Mara squeezed her eyes shut for a moment. Yes, she would go back to the car. She would because, in spite of everything, she wanted to be with him.

She moved her feet through the deep snow. Dampness seeped over her shoes and into the soft cotton of her red socks as she walked toward the car. Her coat hem drifted at her knees. Her teeth chattered.

"Mara."

At his voice, she lifted her head. Startled to find him so close, she realized he had left the car and come to meet her.

"Mara, I'm sorry," he said, his voice ragged. "I'm pushing, I know that."

"No, it's me," she muttered. "I'm evading everything."

"Whether you can believe this or not, I have tried to hold back."

"I know."

"Just don't run from me, Mara."

She trembled inside her wet shoes as he lifted his hand to a strand of hair that had escaped her ponytail. At his slight touch her body went out of control, her heart slamming into her chest and her breath coming in tiny gasps. In the darkness, she could just make out the outline of his mouth, and she could feel his eyes on her face.

"Brock, I have to move out of your house," she said. "I have to."

His fingers closed on her shoulder. "Don't run, Mara."

"Please, don't try to keep me."

"Don't run from me, Mara."

She shook her head as his hands slipped around her and pulled her into the hard warmth of his body. "Brock, I can't trust—"

"Don't run."

"But you might hurt—"

"I won't." His mouth covered hers.

Chapter 14

Cursing her weakness, Mara drank his mouth. Brock's hands worked down her back as his lips took hers again and again. She was crazy to let him near, foolish to trust him, reprehensible to betray her husband's memory. But she didn't care. All she knew was the delicious ecstasy of his lips on hers. His tongue drew lines of sensual fire inside her mouth. His hands roved across her body, molding to the curve of her waist and the swell of her hips.

He pulled her closer, settling his hips against hers, and she sucked in a breath of delight at the jut of his pelvis against her stomach. As their lips sought satisfaction, she allowed her hands to move up his arms, over his neck, into his hair. She feathered the coarse blacks strands and touched the sides of his jaw with her thumbs.

Yes, he was aroused with his need for her. And yes, she was unbelievably pleased at the realization. How long since her body had been craved? How long since she had felt this throbbing melt of desire for a man? Giddy, she swam in his kiss, oblivious to the brush of snowflakes on her cheeks and eyelashes. All she knew was the taste of his tongue and the scent of his leather coat.

"Mara," he groaned, "I don't want to hold back from you any longer."

She shook her head. "Just kiss me."

At her admission of need, he caught her roughly and crushed her mouth to his. His hands found their way inside her coat, and his fingers kneaded the flesh of her back. He pressed her closer, cupping her buttocks as he eased his arousal against her pelvis.

Never had he wanted a woman this much. Never this urgently. But he knew he had to be careful. Mara wasn't ready to give herself completely, even though his body demanded satisfaction. He felt sure she wanted him, too, as she clung to him, her mouth exploring his lips, his cheeks, his eyelids. Her breasts, swollen and ripe, pushing against his chest, seemed to call to his eager hands. As her lips moved down the side of his neck, he let out a moan of disbelief.

"Touch me," she whispered against his skin.

"Mara," he breathed. If he could have resisted, he might have tried. But her neck wore the fragrance of incense and spice, and her mouth moved in damp blossoms over his skin.

His body hammering with need, he moved his hands from her back to her breasts. Heavy and large, they more than filled his palms as he cupped and weighed them. Against his chest, she let out a deep, sensual moan. He ran his fingertips in circles around and around each tip. Beneath her sweater, her nipples beaded up into tight, hard points.

"You're beautiful," he whispered. Her mouth trailed wet lines up and down his neck and behind his ear as he stroked her. "Mara, I've wanted to touch you so badly I could taste it."

"Taste me, Brock." The plea was hardly out of her mouth before she realized how brazen she had sounded. But he had slid her sweater up and over her breasts, and his lips began to trace the upper outline of her bra. She tried to think of seeping milk and the absorbent pad tucked into each cup. She told herself to be embarrassed. She wasn't.

His tongue slid down the line of her cleavage, and she sank hungrily against him. As they stood in the darkness, snow swirling around them, she reveled in the pressure of his hands as they lifted and massaged her breasts. His lips danced like butterflies over the soft, rounded skin that rose out of her bra. Absorbed in her, he moved his fingers around her bare waist, then back up to her bosom. She drank in the scent of his hair and ran her hands beneath his coat.

"I missed you those three weeks," she confessed. "But this scares me so much."

"I won't hurt you, Mara. God knows I don't want to drive you away."

"I can't think clearly."

"Don't think. Feel me, Mara. Feel how much I want you."

Her hands molded over the firm muscles of his chest. Touching him awakened her to sensations she had believed were gone forever. To smell the scent of an aroused man, to feel the taut smoothness of his skin, to taste his tongue in her mouth reminded her she was human. She was not just a mother, not just a widow; she was a woman. Todd had died, but at this moment Mara knew she was very much alive.

Like the snowflakes drifting around her head, images filtered through her mind. She pictured herself lying naked before the fire in the great room of the ranch house. Brock lay by her side, his fingers trickling over her body. She saw his hands tracing random patterns up and down the insides of her thighs, felt his fingertips exploring the moist folds of her hunger. And she was damp...even now...so ready for him she could hardly believe how fast it had happened....

Wrapped in the warmth of his arms and bathed in the soft glow of starlight, she watched in mesmerized fascination as Brock cupped her breast and raised it until the halo around her nipple peeked from the lacy fabric of her bra. He murmured things she couldn't understand as he ran his thumb back and forth over the rosy skin. Weak with wanting, she slid her hands inside his shirt and wove her fingers up through the coarse hair that covered his chest. Searching for his nipples, she kneaded and massaged him. His skin felt hot, burning against her fingertips.

"Mara..." Brock sucked in a breath as her magic touch wound through and over him. Throbbing with the pent-up pressure in his loins, he dipped his nose against the sensitive skin of her breast. He could hardly believe they were standing on a roadside in the middle of a snowstorm and all he could think about was undressing her.

Her breath came in tiny sighs as he rolled down the lace trim on her bra and let her nipple blossom into his hand. With one hand, he cradled her hips tightly against his arousal as he slowly ran his tongue around the tight crest of her breast. The taste of her dampness held him spellbound. Her nipple rolled like a tiny cherry on his tongue. As he took it between his lips and gave a gentle pull, he felt the sweet, primal taste of her milk seep into his mouth.

Lifting his head, he kissed her cheek and then found her lips again. "Mara," he murmured against her mouth, "Mara, this is right. This is the way it's supposed to feel."

"I feel out of control. My brain isn't working."

"Your body's in control. There's nothing wrong with that."

"Oh, Brock, kiss me again."

His mouth obeyed, smothering her lips as his pelvis ground into her hips. She slipped her hands behind him and covered his buttocks. Hard and tight, they held promises she had begun to covet. She wanted to touch all of him, to know the taut skin of his thighs and the taste of his firm belly. She wanted to run her tongue over his flat nipples and bury her nose in the hair on his chest. She was lost in him... lost to him... swirling through the snow in the utter darkness... aware only of his mouth and his hands... and a flashing red light....

"Excuse me," the voice came out of nowhere. "You folks all right here?"

Mara let out a muffled squeak. Brock stiffened and pulled her into the protection of his chest. "Who's there?" he barked.

A bright white light shone into his eyes, nearly blocking the blink of the red beam behind it. "Doña Ana County

Sheriff's Department," the voice said. "I spotted your car on the shoulder."

Blinded by the glare of the flashlight, Brock barely made out the face and uniform of a patrolman. "We're fine. Just...uh...enjoying the snow."

"You all right, ma'am?"

Flushing, Mara peered around Brock's shoulder. She had barely managed to tug her sweater over her breasts. "I'm fine. Thank you, officer."

"And the car's okay?"

"Car's fine," Brock said. "Running great."

The man nodded. "Well, I guess you know, we really prefer that people don't stop on the roadway. I reckon you didn't see the sign posted back there."

"Afraid not," Brock confessed.

"Could be mighty dangerous to park on the shoulder, especially on a snowy night like this. Since I'm here, sir, would you mind if I took a look at your license?"

Brock groaned. Tucking Mara against him, he pulled his wallet from his back pocket and handed his license to the patrolman. "I guess you'll want to see the car's registration?"

"Please. Proof of insurance, too."

"Come on," he said gently to Mara. "Let's get you out of the weather. It's freezing out here."

After what seemed like forever, Brock managed to satisfy the officer that he was a law-abiding citizen with a functioning car and no evil intent. The man spoke with Mara, apparently to make sure she hadn't been kidnapped, and then he let them off with a warning.

"Merry Christmas, now," the deputy called as Brock pulled out onto the highway. "You folks go on home. Santy Claus will be here before you know it."

Brock nodded and glanced at the clock on his dashboard. "It's Christmas morning," he said in a low voice.

Mara snuggled into the depths of her coat as the Jaguar's heater blew warm air on her wet feet. She felt dewy and aroused and unbearably happy in spite of the interruption. When Brock reached over to take her hand, she wove her fingers through his. Smiling, she leaned her head against the backrest.

He drove along in silence, his eyes focused on the swish of the wipers and the blur of snowflakes. Mara studied him through half-open lids, realizing that at this moment she didn't care what their future held. All she knew was the pleasurable memory of his kiss and the sensual pressure of his fingers stroking her breasts.

When a grin tilted the corner of his mouth, she savored it, tucking it away in her mind to think about when he was away.

"You know, you're grinning like the cat who ate the canary," she whispered. "What are you thinking about, Brock?"

He chuckled. "'Twas the night before Christmas, Mara. I'm having visions of sugarplums."

Ramona insisted she didn't mind the late hour. She seemed especially satisfied when Brock handed her a fifty-dollar bill and gave her a wink. After giving Mara a run-down of Abby's eating schedule for the evening, Ramona slipped on her coat and headed out to her car. With calls of "Merry Christmas," she drove away, leaving Mara and Brock in the silence of the big house.

"Looks like everyone had a good time," Brock said as he surveyed the great room. The tall tree glowed in the firelight, its myriad ornaments hanging between long garlands of red cranberries and white popcorn. The scented candles flickered on the mantel, logs popped and crackled on the grate.

"They left everything so tidy," Mara observed. She had taken off her coat, but she stood in the foyer, suddenly uncomfortable at being alone with Brock. "I guess that's what you get when you invite your housekeeping staff to a party."

He smiled. "I've never known Rosa Maria to leave a room anything but spotless. I wonder if she and Pierre got through the evening without one of their squabbles."

"They haven't been bad these past few weeks. Maybe they just like to argue over you."

Brock slung his leather jacket over his shoulder and gave the fire a stir with the poker. Orange sparks shot up the black wall of the chimney. Out of the corner of his eye, he could see Mara moving hesitantly into the great room. Her tightly clasped hands and pale face told him exactly how she felt. Mara was nervous.

As much as he hated to risk breaking the truce between them, Brock knew he couldn't keep up this elusive dance with her. The attraction between them was real, powerful and demanding. He had never been the kind of man to pussyfoot around an issue. If he didn't like something, he walked away. If he wanted it, he went after it until he got it.

He set the poker in its stand and straightened from the fire. What he wanted was Mara. But unlike some women he had known, she was no easy, willing partner. Mara was complicated—intelligent, passionate and, most significant, moral. As much as she might desire a night of lovemaking, she wouldn't just climb into Brock's bed. Mara would think about the future. She would dwell on consequences and ponder implications. Her deliberateness frustrated him, but he sensed it was one reason he had come to desire her as he had desired no one else in his life.

"I'd better check on Abby," she said as she skirted the leather sofa a safe distance from him. "It's been hours since I nursed. She's bound to be hungry."

He reached up to a panel on the wall and flipped a switch. "She's quiet," he said in a low voice. "Intercoms never lie."

"Then I guess I'll head for my room." She eyed him from her position across the open space. "I enjoyed the party, Brock. Stephanie's not so bad. Maybe she and some of the others could come out to the house one of these days. I realize I was being pretty silly about the lounge. I doubt it would be a prob—"

"Mara, come here." He held out a hand.

She glanced down the darkened hall as if making certain of her escape route. When she looked at him again, her eyes were luminous. She let out a deep breath. "I'm not ready to make love with you, Brock. It's too soon."

"I want to hold you."

"I'm sorry... but I can't trust you."

"You don't trust yourself."

"Maybe not. Back there on the road, I...I got carried away and didn't think. It was... wonderful...and I still feel so... Oh, Brock, I did want what happened between us. I won't deny that anymore. But I need time to think about this. You ought to think it over, too."

"I know how I feel. I know what I want. And God knows I'm willing to wait for it. I'll wait until you get it all figured out, if you want to try. But in the meantime, I'd like to sit by the fire and hold you."

She wrapped her arms around her stomach and shook her head. "Stephanie was right. You have all the words."

"This is no memorized speech, Mara." He walked toward her, frustration bubbling inside him again. "You make me out to be some kind of Casanova. I'm just a man. I speak my mind."

"Brock, stop right there."

He kept walking. "Don't run from me, Mara."

"This is Christmas. I should be thinking about Todd. I *am* thinking about him."

"I'm thinking about him, too." Pausing a pace away, he ran his hand up her arm. "I'm remembering the time I bought him a collection of baseball cards for Christmas. We were eleven years old, and we'd met for the first time that summer at camp. When Todd opened the box of cards, he was so happy he cried. He said it was the best present he'd ever gotten."

"Oh, Brock..."

"And I'm remembering when he gave me a decorated chest he'd made out of Popsicle sticks and glued-on shells. I kept my rock collection in it. I still have that chest in my bedroom. Todd was my best friend for seventeen years, Mara. I'll never live through a Christmas without thinking about him."

Her lower lip trembled as he pulled her closer. She unknotted her hands and allowed him to draw her into the warmth of his chest. "I miss Todd," she whispered.

"I miss him, too." He fought the lump that formed in his throat. "But it isn't helping anyone if he keeps us apart."

She laid her cheek on his shoulder as he stroked his hands up and down her back. When her breath heated the skin on his neck, he felt a tumult of emotion tear through him like a tornado on the loose. He wanted this woman in every way. He wanted her smile in the morning over coffee, her conversation, her spiritual depths and her intellectual pursuits. He wanted her body wrapped around his, warm thighs and heavy breasts. And yet he couldn't deny the ache inside at the memory of her husband. He couldn't release his own need for forgiveness. He didn't want to push her, didn't want to betray his friend, but how could he make himself hold back?

"Todd won't ever see Abby open presents on Christmas morning," Mara said in a choked voice. "Sometimes it hurts so much."

He kissed the tear that slid down her cheek. He'd made her cry. No wonder she had hated him. She blamed him for the loss of Todd, her husband and Abby's father, and she was faced with that grief every day of her life.

Brock pondered the guilty happiness he felt that Mara had come willingly into his arms. Standing on the roadside, she had wanted him as honestly as if there had been no barriers between them. And Brock knew if Todd were still alive, he would never have known the taste of Mara's lips and the feel of her breasts.

"It seems wrong to be anything but sad," she said. "When I let you hold me, it's so good . . . and then I hate myself for liking it."

"Sometimes I feel that, too." He cupped her face in his hands and tilted it toward the soft light of the candles. "But I can't help what I want, Mara."

"I'm afraid to let myself even think what I want."

"You want to be whole. You don't want to be a half-empty widow anymore. There's more to you than being a full-time mommy, too. You've got a mind and a body that are waking up after months of numbness. You're churning with new thoughts. You're ready to get on with your life."

"Getting back to work on the fort project has done me good," she acknowledged. "And I know Todd would be glad I'm trying to save it."

"Your body is ready to be complete again, too, Mara. You lost your husband, but you didn't lose your own needs."

Her gray-green eyes searched his. "Come here, Brock." She took his hand and walked ahead of him toward the fire. "I have something to say to you." She knelt on the great woven rug, took off her damp shoes and set them on the hearth. When he had sat down beside her, she gazed at the gold rings on her finger until her vision blurred.

"You know a lot about me," she said in a low voice. "Sometimes you seem to understand things I'm only beginning to figure out. But there's one thing about me you don't know."

Mesmerized by her again, he tugged the scrap of silver tinsel from her ponytail and let the heavy mass of hair fall to her shoulders. "I'm listening, Mara."

"What you don't understand is that I'm a forever kind of person." She shivered as his fingers threaded through the damp strands of her hair. "You're right that I have a mind and a body. But please don't forget I also have a heart. I never fool around with my heart."

She looked at him for affirmation. When he said nothing, she continued. "When I was a young girl—after my parents had been killed in a car wreck—I once lived with a foster family who took me to church every Sunday. I was young, but I understood what I needed. I turned over my heart, my body, my mind, my whole life to God. Things haven't been easy, but my faith in Him has never wavered. Nine years ago, I gave my heart to Todd, too. I wanted to give him my body, but I waited four years to sleep with that man. That wasn't easy, either, and there were times I was sure I was the last virgin in America."

She glanced at Brock, but he wasn't laughing at her. His hands had dropped to his thighs, and he waited for her to continue.

"On my wedding night, I made love with Todd for the first time." She slowly turned the two rings on her finger. "I never betrayed that bond. Maybe I never will. Two months ago, I gave my heart to a newborn baby. My body nurtured her for nine months. It still does. It doesn't matter what happens in the years to come. No matter how Abby may hurt me, no matter what paths she chooses in life, no matter how hard things get, I'll never stop loving my daughter."

Mara shut her eyes for a moment. When Brock remained silent, she let out a breath. "What I'm trying to tell you is . . . I don't give myself lightly to anyone."

"It's all or nothing, is it?" he asked. "Mara, I think I did know that about you."

She studied the fire. He sat unspeaking in the stillness of the great room and tried to read the message behind her words. He had never doubted Mara would be loyal and faithful in whatever she did. She was no airheaded runaround. For years Brock had observed the passion that had driven this woman. Her zest, even more than her golden hair, gray-green eyes and tempting body, had beckoned him from the moment he'd met her.

He reached out and rubbed his hand over her wet sock. Picking up her foot, he laid it on his thigh and began to stroke. He knew what Mara was telling him. She hadn't given herself to her faith and to her husband without expecting something back. Mara committed herself only to those who were willing to commit in return.

Now she was asking herself whether she could give her heart to Brock. And she was asking how ready Brock was to give himself completely to her.

As he ran his thumbs and fingers over the muscles in her foot, he considered the question. He had married her. That showed a certain level of commitment, didn't it? But they had based their marriage on financial terms, nothing more.

Was he willing to turn over his whole life, his dreams, his future to Mara? Mind, body, heart. She talked so freely of giving her heart away. He wasn't even sure he knew what had become of his heart in the years he'd spent wandering, lost. Did he even have one to give?

"I guess this means you won't be hitting the singles bars," he said with a smile.

She glanced up at him. "I seriously doubt it."

"Whew." He brushed at his forehead in a mock gesture of relief.

"Brock, don't tease about this. I'm serious."

"Always serious." He drew her damp sock from one foot and then the other. "I like these snowmen, by the way."

"Thank you. Sandy thoughtfully brought them to everyone's attention. I was momentarily the laughingstock of the party."

He winced. "There's nothing more prickly than a jealous woman. I guess Sandy figured out where I stand with you."

Mara watched him rub her bare toes between his fingers. A liquid warmth spread through her body and melted into her knees. "Where do you stand with me, Brock?"

"As close as I can get." He looked into her eyes. "You know, something occurs to me, Mara. You tell me you gave your heart to God and to Todd and to Abby. Have you considered what each of them might think of this thing going on between you and me?"

"Constantly. Every time I imagine how Todd would feel if he knew I had kissed you, I get this terrible, guilty sensation. It's like I'm being unfaithful to him."

"I know. This evening after I saw you in the kitchen, I went into my room and turned his picture around to face the wall."

"Oh, Brock, are we wrong to feel attracted to each other?"

"Attracted? I'd call it a little stronger than that." He rolled each of her toes between his thumb and forefinger. "I don't know whether it's wrong or right. I just know that even though I would never betray my friend's memory, Todd isn't around anymore. He's gone, Mara. We've both got to get used to that. And when you think about it, Todd had about the most generous heart the good Lord ever created. Would he expect you to live the rest of your life grieving over him?''

''I don't know.''

''I think you do.'' He studied her. ''Who would Todd rather see come together than the two people he loved the most in this world?''

''Maybe...still...''

''Then there's God. Now, I don't claim to know a lot about religious matters, but it doesn't take a preacher to figure out that life moves according to a plan that's bigger than any of us. Things happen for a purpose. I do believe that. You've put a lot of stake in God, Mara. You reckon He would leave you high and dry? I mean, you lost your husband—do you think this God you gave your heart to would want you to be unhappy forever?''

''God doesn't want me miserable. But I'm not sure you qualify as the right person to—''

''And what about Abby?'' he cut in. ''Do you want your daughter to grow up without a man in her life? Don't you want her to have someone to look up to and count on?''

Mara held her breath. Brock's brown eyes were deep and beckoning in the firelight. ''What are you saying?''

He slid his hand around the back of her neck and pulled her toward him. Their lips met in a soft, tender kiss. His fingers slipped up through her hair as her breasts crested against his chest. She laid her hands on his thighs, aware of tight fabric over hardened muscle beneath her fingertips. All her moral reservations and careful considerations became dandelion seeds in the wind of desire that blew through her.

As his mouth moved on hers, their lips hungry and their tongues searching, she blossomed inside. Sparks shot down her arms. Tingles flowed to the tips of her breasts. Her thighs melted into warm, pulsing liquid. He was right. She couldn't deny her body. Everything in her wanted this man.

As he held her, she clutched his arms. Her fingers worked over the mounds of solid muscle and memorized the breadth of his shoulders. She let her lips play up and down the side of his neck, her tongue tasting his heated skin and lapping at his earlobe. When his breath filtered against her ear, something inside her broke loose.

"Brock," she moaned. "Oh, Brock."

His palm formed around her breast, suntanned skin against red knit. She was so swollen with the need to nurse her baby that just the touch of his fingers opened every dam inside her. Moisture seeped into her bra and between her thighs. Her back ached and her pulse hammered through her chest.

"Mara, I'm trying my damnedest to wait for you, woman." His voice was raspy. "I'll hold you all night and every night for the next ten years without touching you if that's what you want. But it's killing me."

"Don't talk, Brock. Don't make me think."

"Then come here and kiss me."

She did, and with her kiss she released the pent-up desires she had held so carefully in check. Her hunger now threatened to devour her. She slid her fingers through his hair and let her lips explore his whole face, his neck, his hands.

When he laid her across the rug, she slipped heedlessly against him. Oh, but the feel of his body was intoxicating—the whole length of him pressing into her. Their toes touched, their arms tangled and their mouths met again and again in sweet, heady seduction. He lifted her sweater and molded his hands around her breasts.

"I want to know your naked body, Mara," he murmured against her ear. "Every day and night for the past three weeks, I thought about you. I told myself I had put you away in a safe place, but it was a lie. You were right there, dancing through my dreams with your yellow hair and your silky skin . . . and these long legs."

"I've tried so hard to . . . to hate you. To resent you."

He leaned over her in the firelight. "Don't hate me, Mara."

"I can't."

"I want to satisfy you." His eyes traced over the curves and hollows of her body. He could hardly believe she was lying there beneath him, her arms wrapped around his waist and her sweater raised to reveal the swell of her breasts. If he pushed her, he could have her. Maybe not her heart...but he could have her body. And...he wanted her body.

But he had begun to want more. He groaned inwardly at the torment of resisting.

"Mara," he whispered, lowering himself on her just enough to capture the feeling he would make last until they could truly be one flesh. "Do you know how difficult this is?"

"Yes," she said, squeezing her fists tight against the driving need inside. "I want you, Brock."

At her confession, his heart slammed against his ribs. She did want him. He could see it in the heavy-lidded look in her eyes. But would she hate him after she'd had time to think? Would she feel trapped? Would she think he had manipulated her, used her?

"Mara," he said her name again as he rolled onto his side and took her in his lap. "I don't want you to wonder tomorrow if I qualify in God's book of approved men. And I don't want you to wake up and think you betrayed Todd. Don't you see? I want your heart, too."

She touched the side of his face in wonder at the transformation in him. Had this been the man who walked over people to get his way? Was this the self-centered bull, the thoughtless playboy she remembered? Though her body begged for release, her heart softened and began to welcome him.

"Besides," he said gently, "I think I hear a little girl who's hungry for her midnight snack."

Mara turned her attention to the intercom. Faintly, she could hear the soft snuffling of a waking baby. The little whimpers quickly grew in volume.

"I'd better go," Mara said.

Brock ran his hands down her arms, unwilling to release her. "Mind if I come along?"

She kissed his cheek. "Might as well. Someone once told me Abby needs a man in her life."

He grinned. "So does her mom."

Mara slipped out of his arms and started toward the hall. "I know," she said softly.

Chapter 15

After leaving Mara and Abby snoozing in the nursery, Brock returned to his room and discovered the stack of mail Rosa Maria had placed on his desk while he'd been gone. Letters, magazines and bills lay in a neat pile. Nothing of interest caught his eye until he spotted the seal of the United States Bureau of Land Management.

He slit the envelope and scanned the single sheet of paper inside. The Bureau had decided to terminate Todd's contract. A terse message from the project director, Dr. Stephen Long, stated the services of Rosemond Restoration were no longer required at Fort Selden and the other historic forts in southern New Mexico.

Frowning, Brock read the rest of the letter. He knew it had been addressed to him because of his contact with Dr. Long around the time of his marriage to Mara. Under financial stress and worried about her pregnancy, she hadn't balked at his offer to handle contract negotiations on behalf of Todd's company.

But the contents of this letter told him Mara must have written the Bureau to communicate her plan to run the business herself. Dr. Long responded that he could not accept her request to work on the reconstruction, and that her doing so would invalidate the contract that had been made with her late husband.

Frustrated by what he saw as a lack of vision, Brock sat at his desk and turned the contents of the letter over in his mind. Finally he made the decision to keep the news to himself until he could work out a solution. Instinct told him Mara would be angry if he didn't discuss the letter with her right away, but he didn't want to risk throwing anything in the path of their growing intimacy.

If Mara knew her request had been turned down, she again might start feeling cornered—trapped by the circumstances in her life. He couldn't let her withdraw. Not now.

Brock awoke on Christmas morning to a blanket of snow thicker and whiter than a newly washed wool fleece. He lay alone in his huge bed and stared out the window for a long time, thinking about the previous evening—the party, the trip home, the letter from the BLM. He grimaced at the last thought.

Was he betraying Mara by not telling her about the letter? No. He had always been the kind of man who fixed things himself. He repaired broken chairs and wobbly tables. He mended fences and nailed shingles on barns. Once already he had stepped into Mara's life to fix a bad situation. He could do it again . . . as his gift to her.

Brock settled back on his pillow, arms behind his head. Right after the new year began, he would call the BLM and settle the matter. He would see to it that the Bureau held up the contract, and he would preserve and build on the goodwill growing between Mara and himself. He would force himself to hold his physical desire for her in check. Like a teenager on a first date, he would be careful only to slip his arm around her shoulders or take her hand or give her a chaste kiss on the cheek. It would be rough, but he could do it.

"Brock?"

He turned toward the soft voice to find Mara outlined in his open doorway, the white nightgown he had given her in the hospital drifting at her toes. For a moment he considered tossing out his noble plan and taking her straight into his bed. She was gorgeous—blond hair hanging at her shoulders, gray-green eyes soft and warm, lips pink and willing.

Then he noticed the baby cradled in her arms. "Hey there," he said gently. "How are my two Christmas angels this morning?"

She smiled. "I just nursed Abby, and she's so drowsy I almost took her back to bed. But I'd put her in the velvet dress you gave her when she was born, and I couldn't wait to take her to the tree. Can you come?"

"Sure."

Mara swallowed as Brock threw back his bedding. He wore only a pair of light blue cotton boxer shorts. As he stood into a muscle-flexing stretch, a shiver traveled straight to the pit of her stomach. All bronzed skin, dark chest hair and lean sinew, the man wore his body with the unconscious grace of a panther. He raked a hand through his hair and rubbed the back of his neck. Snagging a cranberry robe from a hook near his bathroom, he gave a careless yawn.

"I wonder what Santa Claus brought me," he said.

"What did you ask him for?" Mara wondered aloud as they walked down the long hall to the great room.

"Dangerous question, Mrs. Barnett."

Mara tried to control her flush by concentrating on settling herself in front of the tree and situating Abby in her arms. She knew what Brock wanted. It was the same thing she wanted. But every time she had stirred during the past restless night, she had lectured herself on the importance of putting rational plans and goals ahead of her desire to make love with Brock Barnett.

"Here you are," she said, placing her gift on his lap. "I made this while you were away."

As she held Abby, he unwrapped the enormous afghan she had crocheted for him in shades of New Mexico—the purple mauve of a mountain sunset, the sage green of the prickly pear cactus, the dusty brown of the high desert. Brock ran his hand over the careful stitches that undulated across the coverlet like rolling hills. It was spectacular, and big enough to cover his king-size bed.

"It's beautiful," he said in a low voice. "Thank you, Mara."

Again she smiled that breathtaking smile as he handed her the presents he had prepared. Though he had given them a lot of thought, they seemed paltry in retrospect.

First she opened her own gift, a small box he had made in his workshop. He had used woods from his ranch—mesquite, cedar and pine—sandwiched to reveal their different hues of brown. The box had a hinged lid and a small, brass clasp.

"I thought you might like to keep jewelry in it," he said. "I'm afraid it's not big enough to hold much."

Mara stared at the box so long, Brock thought maybe his gift had offended her. Was it too small? Too crudely made? Should he have bought her something in Santa Fe? Then he saw the tear fall onto the hand that held the little box. It was her left hand.

Silently, she placed the gift in her lap and turned her hand first one way and then the other, front and back. Without saying a word, she slipped off the engagement ring and then the wedding ring Todd had given her. She put them both inside the box, shut the lid and fastened the clasp.

A wash of chills ran down Brock's spine as she set the box aside. Mara had worn those rings every minute of every day since he had married her. She'd worn them through labor and delivery. She'd worn them washing dishes and playing in the snow.

Unable to look at him, Mara began opening the second gift. Another box. This one was for Abby. Brock shifted uncomfortably as she tore away the wrapping paper to find the little Popsicle stick chest Todd had given him so many years before. Stuck on with white school glue, the fragile shells clung to the bare wood.

"I thought Abby would want something from her father for Christmas," Brock explained. "And I left my rock collection inside, too."

"Her father," Mara choked out. Suddenly the word meant more than she had ever realized. Todd was the man who had given Abby life—her father in the traditional sense. But Brock...whose boyish rock collection included bits of obsidian and a chunk of quartz...he was the man who could give Abby a future. He was the man who could teach Abby the names of the stones, how to ride a horse, how to build a fence. He could coach her soccer team, take her out for ice cream, teach her to drive a car, buy her velvet Christmas dresses, give her away at her wedding. Brock might be Abby's father, too, if Mara could let him.

"Brock, the box is...it's..." Tears rolling down her cheeks, she shook her head and hugged Abby tightly.

"Mara, I'm here." Brock went to her and wrapped his arms around her.

"I know," she whispered. "I know."

When she lifted her face, he looked into her eyes and saw his wife. Her lips were warm and moist as his mouth tenderly claimed her. She slipped her arms around his neck and gave herself to his words of promise. Before either had time to consider the consequences, they were holding and caressing each other. With the baby nestled between them, they drifted in the pleasure of the present moment.

But when Abby began to whimper, Brock remembered his promise to hold back, to give Mara time to consider what she wanted to do. He lifted his head, battled back the drive to possess her and turned away.

"Here's something from Pierre," he said, grabbing the nearest present to keep his empty hands from Mara. "I guarantee this'll be for the kitchen. He always gives me something like a pastry crimper or a noodle maker."

Mara brushed her damp cheek and tried to concentrate. "I didn't know you liked to make noodles."

He grinned as he shook his head. "Pierre likes to make noodles."

But when he unwrapped the large square box, it wasn't a kitchen tool at all. It was a heavy, leather-bound family Bible. In silence, Brock turned the first gold-edged page. The family tree had been inscribed in beautiful black calligraphy.

"Abigail Rosemond Barnett." He read the central inscription complete with Abby's birthdate. Then he read the words beneath the baby's name. "Mara Rosemond Barnett ... Mother."

When he stopped reading, Mara leaned against his shoulder. "Brock Davis Barnett," she said softly. "Father."

Brock had never known the kind of peace and comfort the following days held. Kept away from his work by the snowstorm that had covered the plains, Brock spent his hours with Mara and Abby. Together Mara and he bathed and diapered, rocked and cuddled the growing baby girl. Abby blossomed in the attention.

She wasn't the only one who felt nurtured and secure. Brock reveled in the magic of quiet time spent with Mara. Their hours of cooking in the kitchen or watching the snow fall outside the window were a tonic to him. If the years of his lonely childhood had built a wall around him, Mara's presence gently removed brick after brick.

On impulse, they decided to host a New Year's Eve party to introduce some of their friends to each other. Mara phoned Sherry and two of the teachers she had worked with at the academy. Brock invited Joe, Travis, Stephanie and a couple of others from the Las Cruces crowd. Everyone was encouraged to stay the night at the ranch house rather than drive back to the city on the dark, snowy highway. Brock dismissed Pierre and the housekeepers to spend the holiday with their families.

While preparing hors d'oeuvres the afternoon of the party, Brock couldn't keep his eyes off Mara. Dressed in jeans, a blue T-shirt and a pair of white sneakers, she was the essence of the young woman he'd met with Todd years before. She laughed and teased him, her eyes sparkling in fun as she hurried around the kitchen clinking pots and stirring saucepans.

"We should have asked Pierre to do all this, you know," she said, her fingers deep in a bowl of mushroom stuffing. "I'll bet *he* knows how to use shoestring carrots to tie asparagus in neat little bundles."

Brock gave her a mock scowl. "I still don't see what was wrong with my idea. Red string licorice and green asparagus—it even goes with the holiday season."

Mara laughed. "I suppose you'd have us put this stuffing into chocolate cupcakes?"

"Easier than pulling the damn stems off these little mushrooms."

She giggled at the sight of his large fingers working to remove the tiny, soft stems. "Those caps are starting to look more like pancakes, Brock."

"Oh, yeah?" He held up a small brown mushroom, its delicate edges hopelessly split. "Wait'll I put the stuffing in."

"You'd better do it right, or else," she said, starting across the room.

He caught her around the waist and swung her toward him. "Says who?"

"Says me."

"Woman, I'd do just about anything you asked me to," he said, his voice husky. Her lips tilted toward his, and he brushed a kiss across her mouth. As though once again a dam had broken between them, she responded so fast, so eagerly, he couldn't control his reaction. Before he knew it, he had pulled her fully into his arms. It was delicious, the feel of her body and the sensuous dampness of her mouth.

If they hadn't been expecting company, he would have carried her off to bed and damned the consequences. As it was, he knew Sherry was due any minute to help them get ready. Reluctantly he let Mara go almost as fast as he had grabbed her. She stood before him, flushed and breathless, and it was all he could do to keep from taking her in his arms again. Before he could reach for her, Mara whirled on her heel, announced she had to nurse Abby and change clothes for the party, and half ran out of the kitchen.

Busying himself with stuffing the mushrooms and arranging slices of cold meats on a silver tray, Brock spent the next half hour trying to push images of Mara out of his mind. It was impossible. In the split second when her lips had touched his, he had become aroused and as randy as a young bull. It was all fine and dandy to think through actions, to tread carefully, to avoid mistakes. But how long could this go on? He wanted Mara. All of her. As he wedged a rolled slice of beef between two rolls of ham, he frowned. This waiting was getting damned intolerable.

"Did you remember to buy the champagne, Brock?" Mara asked as she reentered the kitchen. "I didn't see it in the refrigerator."

He glanced up, and once again he was thrown a curve by the sight of this woman who had miraculously come into his life. Dressed in a short black skirt and a glittery gold spaghetti-strap top, Mara had left her blond hair hanging long and swishy. Her legs were sheathed in sheer black stockings and velvet high heels. The faint fragrance of a spicy perfume drifted across the room. He grabbed the back of a kitchen chair for support.

"Brock?" she said. "Did you hear me? I asked about the champagne."

"It's chilling," he replied. "In the lounge refrigerator."

"I hope we have enough of these sausage balls." She pulled open the oven door and bent to look inside. The hem of her skirt slid up her thighs. Brock gave up holding on to the chair and sat down in it.

"And these sausages," she said, turning to the crockery pot filled with tiny barbecued links. Brock studied her backside, boldly ogling every luscious curve and hollow. "If the sausages don't stay hot, they won't be any good."

"I'm hot," he muttered.

Mara swung around. "What?"

"Nothing."

She smiled. "Brock, would you light the candles in the dining room, please?"

He'd have crawled across the White Sands desert if she'd asked.

Brock went through the rest of the evening like a zombie on automatic pilot. Guests arrived. He poured champagne, listened to jokes, made polite conversation. All he could think about was Mara.

She drifted through the clusters of visitors, her gold blouse casting shimmery spangles that seemed to mingle with the champagne bubbles. His brain swirled like a mirrored ball at a discotheque. Mara's hair sifted and draped around her shoulders. Her long legs mesmerized him with every step.

If Brock hadn't told himself a thousand times he was genetically incapable of it, he would have been sure he had fallen in love with her. But love? Brock Barnett? No, he didn't have it in him.

Did he?

Mara spent most of the evening apart from Brock as she tended to the guests. He felt he was in a Christmas Eve party rerun. Mara talked a long time with her friend Sherry. She introduced Sherry to Stephanie, and they seemed to hit it off. Mara moved constantly in and out of the kitchen, carrying trays of hors d'oeuvres or filling bowls with nuts. As midnight approached, she slipped through the partiers to Brock's side, a shy smile tilting the corners of her pink lips.

"Having fun?" she whispered.

"Now I am." He ran his hand down her bare shoulder.

"Ten, nine, eight, seven, six." As everyone joined in the countdown, he folded her into his arms.

"Five, four, three, two." He turned her toward him and cradled her head in his hands, tilting her chin upward.

"One...Happy New Year!"

As cheers went up and confetti drifted down, he kissed her lips. Her arms slid around his shoulders, her hands molded his neck, her fingers wove through his hair. If he could have pulled away, he might have tried. He didn't have a prayer. Her mouth was sweet and wet, and when her tongue stroked against his lower lip, his body exploded with raging hunger.

Throbbing, he cupped the small of her back and pressed her hips against his. She shivered in delight. Her breasts pushed against his chest, and he was sure he could feel her nipples tighten beneath the layers of sequins on her blouse. Deepening the kiss, he explored her mouth. Their tongues touched, caressed, stroked. He struggled for control as his arousal hardened, demanded release.

"Mara," he murmured against her lips, "I've got to have you. I mean it."

Her response was the mew of a hungry kitten.

Around them corks popped and champagne flowed. Cheers turned to laughter. Music rose in volume. Someone brushed past them. Brock was lost in Mara's lips, in the image of other lips, damp lips, ready to take him inside and ease the ache.

And then there was a strange hush.

"Mara?" Brock recognized Sherry's voice.

Catching her breath, Mara pulled away from him. "Oh...is...is anyone going to pour...uh...the champagne? Well, I guess so."

"Mara?" Sherry repeated dully.

Brock looked around the room and quickly figured out that he and Mara had unknowingly become the center of attention with their New Year's kiss. Just as the silence was about to become awkward, Brock's friend Joe lifted his champagne glass and shouted, "To the newlyweds!"

"To the newlyweds," the other guests echoed, laughing.

"Did you get some champagne, Sherry?" Mara asked quickly. "I'll see what's left in the refrigerator."

Turning away from Brock without a backward look, she hurried across the room on pencil-stiff legs. She had never been so embarrassed in her life, she realized as she fled into the kitchen and threw open a cabinet door in the pretense of searching for a glass. She had been devouring Brock like a teenager at a high-school party. His hands had been all over her. Sherry had seen. Everyone had seen.

"Mara?" Sherry seemed to be able to say nothing else.

"What?" Mara exclaimed, slamming the cabinet door. "Do you have something to say?"

"I just... well, Mara... I mean, you and Brock..."

"Look, Sherry, I'm going to check on Abby. It's past time for her to wake up. Say good night to everyone for me, will you?"

Without waiting for Sherry to agree to the request, Mara left the kitchen and made her way down the long, dimly lit hall. Oh, she was a fool for the man's kisses. And she'd made an absolute idiot of herself in front of her friends.

She had been so careful to see that no one thought the marriage was anything but a business arrangement. She had been so careful to assure herself it was nothing more. But how could anyone deny what they had just seen? How could she deny it herself?

Sure enough, Abby was wailing in the nursery. The intercom that broadcast the baby's hungry cries had been drowned out by the loud music and cheering. Flooded with guilt, Mara picked up the hot, damp bundle and cuddled her for a moment until Abby's shrieks softened to piteous sobs of relief.

Mara quickly changed the sopping diaper and pulled a fresh nightgown over the baby's head. She half fell into the rocking chair and lifted her shimmery blouse. In moments, Abby's contented suckling reminded her that other things in the world were much more important than an impulsive, wayward kiss in front of friends.

All the same, as Mara put her drowsy baby back into the crib twenty minutes later, she couldn't deny that her body still shivered with the memory of Brock's mouth crushed against hers. Should she go back to the party and find him? Maybe it would be appropriate simply to let everyone know that things had changed between her and Brock. Maybe she should smile confidently and tell them that she...that he...

That they what? She didn't know what to say. As she walked to the door of her own bedroom, Mara gave up the hope of explaining herself. She didn't know what she meant to Brock Barnett, and she was afraid to admit what he had come to mean to her.

But when she walked into her room, she realized she was going to have to come up with something. Sherry sat in the chair by Mara's bed, her shoes kicked to the floor and her feet curled under her. Her eyes were soft with concern as she rested her chin on her hand.

"Is Abby okay?" she asked.

"She was ravenous. So, is the party over?" Mara hoped her voice sounded light. "I thought Abby was going to nurse forever. I bet everyone's gone to bed, haven't they?"

"What's going on, Mar?" Sherry caught Mara's hand as she passed. "Come on, it's me here. What's up with you and Brock? That was no brotherly peck on the cheek I saw a few minutes ago."

"Well . . . on New Year's Eve . . ." Abandoning the lame excuse, Mara walked to her closet and pulled her blouse up over her head. "You don't have to know every detail of my life."

"I'm not asking for details. I just want to make sure you're okay."

"I'm fine." Mara hung her blouse on a padded hanger. "Really, I'm fine."

"Are you in love with him?"

"Sheesh!" Mara swung around, half tempted to laugh at the audacity of the question. "Sherry, I told you things are fine."

"You're on the rebound, you know. You miss Todd, and you're vulnerable."

"So, when did you get a doctorate in psychology, Sher?" Mara padded across the room in her stocking feet. Her slip whispered around her knees. "You don't know what's going on here."

"Do you?"

"Yes, I do."

"What?"

"I . . . admire Brock."

"Oh, please."

"I do. He's good at his work. He cares about the ranch. He's a carpenter, too. I bet you didn't know that."

"I'm impressed."

Mara plopped down on her bed. "Okay, maybe things have heated up between us a little."

"What I witnessed in the living room was an inferno."

"It was a kiss."

"It was sex on foot."

"Oh, Sherry, go to bed. Your room's down the hall."

Sherry crossed her arms and stuck out her chin in a look that Mara had learned when they were little girls. Her blue eyes sparkled with determination as she stared at Mara.

"Spill it," she commanded.

Mara let out a deep breath and flopped back on the bed. "You drive me crazy. Okay... I'll admit I don't really understand what's happening. One minute I was sure I had done the right thing to marry Brock and take care of the future for Abby. The next minute I was in his arms—"

"The next minute?"

"It took a few weeks."

"The last time I visited you out here at the ranch, we went over all of Brock Barnett's flaws, remember? He's cocky, arrogant, self-centered, irreligious, perfectionistic, stubborn—"

"Loyal, hardworking, funny, strong, high-minded—"

"Oh, no! Mara, you *are* in love with him!"

"Todd loved him. I'm just seeing the things Todd appreciated all those years. Brock really is a very good person."

"He's pure trouble." Sherry moaned and sank down in her chair. "Mara, how can you suddenly forget about all those women he's carted around for years? The man is a bona fide playboy."

Mara stared at the ceiling of her room. "I'm not sure about that anymore, Sher. He seems very serious about things."

"Things? You're not a thing. Abby's not a thing. Have you thought about how your daughter might be affected by this?"

"Of course I have. You should see Brock with Abby. He's wonderful. He takes her everywhere. He changes her diapers and bathes her. They make breakfast together nearly every morning."

Sherry groaned again.

"And he puts his feet on the table all the time these days," Mara concluded.

"You're nuts. You've gone completely bonkers over the man." Sherry leaned forward and shook her finger in Mara's face. "You're talking about his feet, Mara!"

"Oh, you don't understand. Brock is relaxed with me, don't you get it? He feels comfortable, and so do I. I like him."

Sherry's expression grew serious. "What about Todd? How comfortable do you think he'd be over the notion of you falling in love with his best friend?"

Mara studied the half inch of bare white skin on her ring finger. "Sherry, Todd is gone. He isn't coming back."

Sherry's eyes followed Mara's gaze. "You took off your rings. Mara, do you know what this means?"

"It means I'm letting go."

"It hasn't even been a year!"

"How long am I supposed to wait? All these months, I've felt numb. I've been so empty. Right now, I swear I could almost fly. Sherry, it scares me silly how good I feel."

Sherry shook her head. "I want you to be happy. If anyone does, it's me, right? The last thing I'd wish for my best friend is to spend her life in misery. But I can't help thinking you're setting yourself up for a fall. Brock is going to use you."

"That's ridiculous. What's he getting? A wife, a baby, extra bills to pay, headaches—"

"A gorgeous blond with long legs and big bazooms."

"I'm nursing a baby!"

"So what? You have boobs like watermelons. Men go gaga when big knockers come within a two-hundred-foot radius."

"You're impossible!" Mara rolled off the bed and stomped across the room. "Do you really think this is all just physical? Brock Barnett could have any woman he wanted."

"Why should he when you're right here and willing? Have you slept with him yet?"

"That's none of your business." Mara glared at her friend until Sherry looked away. "No, I haven't slept with Brock, but if I decide to, I won't ask your permission. Don't forget, he is my husband."

"Oh, Mara! Don't you see how easily he could take advantage of you?"

"Do you think I'm a jellyfish?"

"I think you're a new widow with a two-month-old baby. I think you miss your husband, and you've been scared and lonely. I think Brock Barnett is a man who may be nice enough, but he never learned about love or commitment. He's spent his entire life chasing skirts, accumulating money and heading off on wild adventures. You aren't forgetting Brock was with Todd when he fell off the cliff, are you?"

Mara shook her head. "No," she whispered.

"Does Brock admit he was responsible?"

"We haven't really talked about it."

"Of course not. Why would he want to dredge that up?"

"No, it's my fault, Sherry. Brock has tried several times to tell me what happened. I can't bring myself to hear the details, even though I know it would probably heal both of us."

"Mara, are you really getting deeply involved with this man? Are you falling in love with him?"

"I don't know what's happening, Sher. When I try to sort it out, I keep coming back to the same thing. Todd loved Brock for seventeen years. Now I understand why."

Sherry shut her eyes and let out a deep, exasperated moan. "Todd was a man. Brock is a man. They fished and hiked and camped out together. They were buddies, for heaven's sake. Pals. You're a woman, Mara. That's completely different. We're talking sex on demand, sick babies in the middle of the night, dinner on the table at six sharp, umpteen PTA meetings and ten thousand bake sales, getting old and wrinkled together, brushing his dentures every night—"

"Sherry!" Mara burst out laughing. "Now I know why you've never married."

"Darn right. And I sure as heck wouldn't get myself hooked up permanently with a man who had an eye for pretty women and a nose for adventure. If I were you,

Mara, I'd put a halt to the whole thing and find a way to make it on my own."

"You know I'm trying to find work. I told you all about that situation with the fort project Todd contracted with the Bureau of Land Management. I'm doing my best to keep Rosemond Restoration going."

"Have you found a builder who's willing to work with you?"

"Yes, and he's terrific. He really has a feel for the plans Todd drew up. He even knows some of the history and understands the ambience I want. He's worked with adobe all his life, so this is right up his alley."

"Sounds great."

"If I can convince the BLM to honor Todd's contract, I'll start working at Fort Selden right away."

"What about Abby?"

"The housekeeper's daughter, Ramona, said she'd love to watch Abby during the day. It's hard to think about leaving my daughter all those hours, but I'm anxious to do something for myself." Mara shook her head. "Believe me, Sherry, there's nothing I'd like more than to become self-reliant."

"And move out of this house so you can start living on your own."

Mara studied her friend. "I'm not sure about that part, Sherry."

Chapter 16

The first Monday of the new year, Brock picked up his cordless telephone and dialed Washington, D.C. With Mara and Abby in Las Cruces visiting the builder, Pierre puttering in the kitchen and the housekeepers busy cleaning the wings, the house was quiet. A file that included the letter tucked under his arm, Brock strolled into the dining room as he asked to speak with the director of the fort project.

When a voice came over the receiver, it was younger and crisper than Brock had expected. "Dr. Stephen Long speaking," the director said. "How may I help you?"

"This is Brock Barnett in New Mexico. I'm calling in reference to your decision to terminate the contract with the Rosemond Restoration Company."

"Ah, you must have gotten my letter."

"It's right here."

"Good. Then you know the Bureau can't agree to continue the project without Todd Rosemond at the helm of the reconstruction of the forts in New Mexico."

"And you know that Mara Rosemond Barnett now heads the company. She's expecting you to honor the contract."

"I'm aware of that." His voice hardened. "Mr. Barnett, surely you know your wife doesn't have the appropriate qualifications. We're dealing with seven sites of vital historic significance here. We can't have a history teacher and a man with a bulldozer attempting to accomplish a professional restoration."

Brock sat down in his chair and propped his feet on the dining room table. "Anything else?"

"My position was clearly stated in the letter."

"Dr. Long, when was the last time you looked at the contract you made with Rosemond Restoration?"

There was a moment of silence. "I'm looking at it right now, as a matter of fact. It's signed by Todd Rosemond."

"I see that signature." Brock propped his copy of the contract on his legs. "I also see that the two parties in the contract are the Bureau of Land Management and Rosemond Restoration Company, not you and Todd Rosemond. As I said before, Mara Rosemond Barnett now owns that company, Dr. Long. And she's completely capable of restoring those forts."

"I hardly think so."

"I definitely think so. I also think a legal battle over the situation would be needlessly costly to all concerned."

"I'm not worried about that. There's a time limit on the contract, and it's nearly up. She won't be able to put together a legal challenge before the contract runs out."

"If I were you, I wouldn't put her to the test on that."

"What are you suggesting, Mr. Barnett?"

"I'm suggesting you let Mara supervise the project."

"Look, let's be candid here. I got your wife's résumé in the mail. She's obviously educated, and maybe she did help her husband with the research and plans for the fort. That still doesn't make her a qualified restorationist. You're a successful businessman, Mr. Barnett. Would you let someone with no experience, no references and few credentials take over a position of such historical and economic importance to the State of New Mexico?"

"Sure I would. There's nothing to lose and a lot to gain. Mara is the best thing the Bureau has going right now. Read the contract. There's a clause on page three that allows you to inspect her work and terminate if it doesn't meet with your approval. Give Mara a month, then fly out here and take a look at the site. If you think she's doing a good job, that'll save you putting out for bids and starting the whole process over again. If you don't like what she's doing, shut her down."

For almost a minute, the silence on the line told Brock his suggestion was being weighed. Then Long spoke again.

"Considering your concern about the wording in the contract and since we would retain oversight, I'm willing to reconsider my evaluation of Mrs. Barnett as the director of the project. But even if I changed my mind, it wouldn't do much good."

"Why not?"

"Money. Frankly, the fort project has lost its base of support. Before BLM contracted with Rosemond, we promoted the project rather heavily. A foundation in Albuquerque decided to throw some funding our way. It was enough to give us the go-ahead with the Rosemond company for the first fort. But when Mr. Rosemond passed away and we weren't able to continue with the project immediately, the foundation pulled its backing. We have a little money set aside, but it's not enough to complete the work on even one fort."

Brock propped one foot on the other and studied his boots. "I don't believe that has to be a problem, Dr. Long," he said. "I imagine there are folks around with a little spare change who are looking for a tax write-off. You know, a lot of money was made in the New Mexico oil boom a few years back. I suspect some of that cash might be up for grabs."

Long fell silent for a long moment. "Well, I can't think of a better place for a man to put his money than into enriching the heritage of the land."

"I can't, either." Brock lifted his focus to the snow melting outside his window. "I'd better be going, Dr. Long. I've got some hungry cattle to feed."

"I'll be in touch."

"You talk things over with Mara next time. She's the boss."

"I'll do that."

Brock pressed the button on the phone and set the receiver on the table. His face softened into a smile. Mara was going to be one happy woman.

"You never used to eat lunch at the house," Mara commented the following Thursday as they sat in the dining room over plates of pasta vinaigrette. "As a matter of fact, you didn't eat supper here very often, either."

"No reason to," Brock said simply.

"Same food."

"Different company." He speared a curly noodle. "You beat out old Pierre for conversation any day, and you're a lot better looking."

Mara smiled. Brock had kept his distance since the incident at the party, and neither of them had brought up the subject of their kiss that had so shocked everyone. All the same, he had eaten every meal at the house, he had come in early in the evenings, and he had spent a lot of time with her and Abby. In spite of Sherry's dire warnings, she had enjoyed every minute with him.

"Maybe so," she conceded lightly, "but Pierre wins hands down in the kitchen."

"I don't know about that. These baguettes you made are the best I've ever tasted."

"Pierre's a good teacher." Mara fiddled with her napkin, oddly pleased at Brock's compliment. "Unfortunately, I haven't had a lesson in ages. I've spent so much time on the fort project I haven't even worked on the quilt with Ermaline."

"How are things with the builder?"

"Great. I'd like to invite Mr. Dominguez out to the house some evening for dinner. You'd enjoy talking to him. He's read all the plans, and he doesn't see any problem doing the wall reconstruction. He's an older man, and he's spent years building adobe homes. He says all the good jobs these days are going to the young men who work in steel and concrete."

"Has he been to the site?"

"Lots of times. He's a serious history buff. His family has deep roots in this area, and he loves combing through museums. He goes to Frontier Days at Fort Selden every year."

"What does he think about working on the other forts after Fort Selden is complete?"

"He's ready to retire from his construction business, and he and his wife have decided it would be fun to buy an RV and live at the different sites." She let out a deep breath. "Everything is falling perfectly into place, Brock. I just hope I don't have trouble with the Bureau of Land Management over the contract."

"I doubt you will."

"I wish I had your faith. They really dropped the ball after Todd—"

"Excuse me, Mrs. B.," Ermaline said, stepping into the dining room. "You have a phone call from a Dr. Long. Shall I ask him to call back after dinner?"

Mara frowned. She didn't know any physicians named Long. "Just take his number, and tell him I'll—"

"No," Brock interjected. "Go ahead. Take the call."

Mara shrugged as Ermaline handed her the phone. "This is Mara Barnett."

"This is Dr. Stephen Long with the Bureau of Land Management in Washington, D.C."

"Oh, yes." Mara glanced up at Brock and gestured toward the phone. "It's him," she mouthed. As Brock nodded, she returned to the conversation. "What can I do for you, Dr. Long?"

"Well, I'm hoping you can go to work for me."

"I'd be glad to."

"Next Monday I'll be flying into El Paso and then driving up to Las Cruces to begin a tour of several of the fort sites. I'd like to meet with you for an interview at that time. Would that be all right?"

"Perfect. I'll be there."

"Good. We'll also invite the state monument ranger and the head of the visitors' center at Fort Selden. They're eager to get to know you. If all goes as I expect, you can begin your work on the restoration right away."

Mara could hardly speak as a bubble of elation welled up inside her chest. "I'll bring Mr. Dominguez," she managed. "He's my builder."

"Yes, of course." Dr. Long was silent for a moment. "You do understand that this situation will be subject to my inspection and approval?"

"Certainly. But I'm sure you won't be disappointed with my work, Dr. Long."

"Well, then, I'll see you Monday afternoon about two."

As Mara placed the phone on the dining room table, she knew her hand was shaking. Never—not even when she was hired for her first teaching position—had she felt such excitement.

"I have an interview," she said in almost a whisper. "Monday."

Brock grinned. "That job is yours."

"I hope so. Oh, Brock, I want this so much. At first I felt I had to keep the company going for Todd's sake. It had been his dream all his life. But as time went on, I knew it was something I needed to do for myself. Now I want to touch those adobe walls and breathe life back into the old fort."

"You will, Mara."

She stared into his deep-set brown eyes. "Thank you, Brock."

"For what?" He shifted, suddenly uncomfortable. "I didn't do anything."

"You believe in me. That means a lot."

He studied her for a moment. "You mean a lot to me, Mara," he said, his voice low. "You and Abby. I guess you know that."

She shook her head. Wanting to hear more and at the same time wanting to flee, she sat immobilized.

"I've kept my distance like I promised," he said. "But when you kissed me on New Year's Eve, I knew that was no holiday tradition. I'm not going to push you, Mara. But there is one thing I want to know."

She wrapped her napkin around her hand. "Brock, please—"

"If you take on the fort job, are you moving out of this house?"

She twisted the napkin. "I don't know."

"Tell me."

"I don't know!" She stood up from the table. "Are you my landlord—wanting thirty days' notice?"

"Mara, you're my wife." He pushed back from the table, rose and walked around to her. "I deserve to know. Damn it, Mara, I've pussyfooted around you for weeks. I've held back from Abby."

"No, you haven't."

"No? You think all I want to do is change her diaper and give her a bath? I'd like to take her out in the pickup and show her things on the ranch. I'd like the hands to meet her. I'd like to let a few more of my friends see her. Let them see you, too, for that matter. And I'm not talking about introducing the pair of you as my best friend's wife and daughter. If I had my way, I'd stop this crazy game we're playing, Mara, and start...start..."

"Start what?" Her heart was beating so hard she was sure he could hear it. "You see? You don't know, either. What are we? Acquaintances? Friends? Housemates? Or husband and wife? Every time I think about it, I get confused and wary. You do, too. You don't know what you want. Brock, I'm walking out of this room now, and I'm asking you to please just...just..."

"I do know what I want, Mara. It's the same thing you want. You want me to follow you right out of this room. You want me to take you in my arms and hold you and kiss you until you're shivering. That's what you want. Why don't you admit it?"

"Because I'm afraid," she said softly. "Afraid I won't want you to stop until it's too late."

Dropping her crumpled napkin on her chair, she turned away from him once again and left the room.

* * *

Mara spent the rest of the afternoon preparing for her interview with Dr. Long. Earlier that morning, Abby had developed a stuffy nose that made her cranky and demanding, so Mara decided to keep her nearby in case she needed comforting. She laid the baby on a blanket on the floor so Abby could kick and play with her rattle, then she picked up a yellow legal pad and began to jot notes to herself. Surely keeping busy would help her not to think about Brock.

Wrong. She scribbled his name across the paper, then she outlined each letter in curls and zigzags. She wrote her own name—all of it—and added the Barnett with particular flourish. She printed TODD in careful capitals, but it didn't make him seem more real.

Brock was real. He was her husband and her friend. Why couldn't he be her lover, too? She tried to remember Sherry's admonitions. They rang hollow. Mara wanted everything about Brock, and he wanted her. Was that so bad?

After she wrote Abby's name on the yellow paper, Mara looked down at her baby. Tiny feet up in the air, Abby was gazing in fascination at her hand. She turned it first one way and then the other. Mara was reminded of the Christmas morning when she had taken off her wedding ring. Though her left hand was still bare, she felt very much like a married woman.

"Oh, Abby," she whispered as she stretched out on the blanket beside her daughter. "Do you want Brock to be your daddy?"

Mara stroked her fingers across a cheek so soft she almost couldn't feel the downy skin. Instinctively, Abby turned toward the touch, her mouth pursed in search of her mother's breast. Mara smiled and kissed the baby's forehead.

"All you really want is to eat and sleep and stay dry, don't you?" She dabbed at the baby's damp nose with a soft tissue. "There, is that better?"

She let Abby's tiny, curled fingers wrap around her own much larger index finger. As she wiggled her finger back and forth, Abby's hand moved in unison. "We're two peas in a pod, you and I. You're ready to nurse right when I'm so full of milk I think I might pop. You fall asleep right when I'm so tired I can't keep my eyes open. I think we're connected, little one. So tell me, what do you think of that man who likes to make breakfast with you every morning?''

Abby did her best to put Mara's finger in her mouth. Realizing it was useless, she let out a whimper of frustration. Her tiny forehead wrinkled and her skin turned bright red. As her mouth opened in the beginning of a wail, Mara chuckled and picked her up.

''All right, have it your way.'' She sat up and settled Abby on her lap. Lifting her T-shirt, she nestled the rosebud mouth at her breast. As the baby began to suckle, Mara let out a deep breath.

The decision about Brock was obviously going to have to be hers alone. She flipped the page on the legal pad and again turned her thoughts to the fort project and the coming interview with Dr. Long. The rest of the afternoon, she focused on her work and her daughter.

By suppertime, she felt sure she had put everything in perspective. Those were her priorities, after all—Abby and the restoration company. Brock was a confusing, unexpected wrinkle in the tapestry of her life. The best thing to do was to stay as far from him as possible until she could secure her job and move out on her own. From a distance, she would be able to look back at the situation and evaluate how she felt about the man. But here—in his house—she was much too close to him to see clearly.

Over the intercom, she called the kitchen and asked Pierre to send a meal to her room. She took a long bath in lavender oil while Abby slept, then she slipped into her favorite nightgown and fuzzy robe. Curled before the fire in her bedroom, she ate broiled chicken breast and julienne potatoes, and she decided she was handling a difficult experience with amazingly good sense.

But in spite of her self-assurance about Abby, the baby chose this night to stay awake for hours after what was to have been her final nursing of the evening. Mara wiped her daughter's runny nose, gave her Tylenol and worried that what she had thought was a cold might be something worse. She tried feeding the baby several times, but Abby only grew more distressed. For what seemed like an eternity, Mara rocked and rocked until she was so mesmerized she could hardly hold her eyes open. But every time she tried to get up and put the baby in the crib, Abby burst into tears again.

Worn out, Mara finally checked her bedside clock. Two in the morning. With a groan, she picked Abby up and began to walk her around and around the room. Instead of calming the baby, this only made her sob harder. Mara tried singing as she walked, then she tried dancing, then she broke down and started crying herself.

"Abby, please don't do this," she pleaded over the baby's shrieks. "I have three days to get ready for my interview. You need to rest and get well. Let's go to sleep."

As she bounced the screaming baby on her shoulder, Mara did her best to quell the frustration welling up inside her. "Abby, what's wrong with you? It's almost time for your night feeding, and you haven't slept at all."

Fear ran its icy course through her stomach. "Abby, what's the matter? Oh, honey, I wish you could talk to me. Where do you hurt?"

"Mara?"

Brock's voice from the doorway stopped Mara's restless pacing. She looked up to find him standing just inside the room. His bare chest and boxers were half covered by a thin cotton robe.

"Is she sick?"

"I don't know," Mara choked out. "It's okay. I can manage."

"Let me hold her."

"No, we're fine."

He walked toward her. "Mara, let me have the baby. You're dead on your feet."

"Brock, I can do this without you."

"I know you can. But I'm here, so give her to me." He lifted the baby out of Mara's arms. "Hey, Abby, what's up?" he crooned. "Why are you so cranky, pumpkin?"

Mara stood in silence, her empty arms hanging at her sides as Brock settled in the rocking chair with the baby. Still wailing, Abby flung her fists at Brock's bare chest and turned her head from side to side in distress. Mara clutched her stomach.

"She was fine this afternoon," she said. "She had a little bit of a runny nose. Now... she seems so sick."

"Shall we take her into town? We could go to the emergency room."

Mara shook her head. "I don't know. I just don't know. I feel helpless."

Brock stood up again and tried walking Abby around the room. As the baby sobbed, he hummed and whistled and jiggled her up and down. Mara collapsed onto the bed and lay there, eyes barely open as she watched Brock doing his best to console Abby.

"When was the last time she ate?" he called over the crying.

"I can't remember. I gave her some Tylenol a few minutes ago, but... I've lost track of when she nursed."

"Let me check her diaper, and then you can try feeding her again."

Mara followed him with her eyes as he laid the baby in the bassinet she still kept by her bed. With expertise born of practice, he whipped off the wet diaper and slipped a dry one under the baby's bottom. In moments, he had the howling bundle in his arms again.

"Can you bring her here?" Mara asked.

He sat on the bed beside her and laid Abby in her arms. For a brief moment, Mara thought about turning aside in modesty. That lasted until Abby let out a roof-raising shriek, and Mara swiftly pulled open her nightgown, freed her breast and held Abby to it.

Suddenly, the room fell silent. In spite of her clogged nose, the baby suckled with deep, ravenous draughts. The only sound was her hungry snuffling.

Mara looked up at Brock. He had leaned back against her headboard and stretched one leg on her bed. A tired grin lifted one corner of his mouth.

"I guess she was hungry," he said.

Mara couldn't bring herself to smile in return. "I guess."

"You think she's sick?"

"I think I'll take her to the pediatrician first thing in the morning." As the baby's mouth pulled at her nipple, Mara felt the tension ease from her body. She shut her eyes, one arm wrapped around Abby and the other tucked underneath her as she lay on her side. Drowsy warmth flowed through her veins.

"We're tired," she mumbled.

Brock settled his other foot on the bed. "I'll wait till she's done and put her back to bed."

"Mmm," Mara murmured.

He let his eyes run over the pair of warm bodies on the bed beside him. One was small and pink with tiny fingers and tear-streaked cheeks. The other's cheeks were damp, too, but she was bigger and curvier, and she had a lot more hair. Her eyes were shut and her lips slightly parted as the baby beside her nestled against a pair of bare breasts that were full, round and as pale as cream.

Brock shut his eyes and dreamed of those breasts.

Chapter 17

The room was bathed in a pearly gray light when Brock opened his eyes. Abby lay nestled against him, her mouth open and her tiny fingers curled through the hair on his arm. Beside the baby slept her mother, long lashes fanning against her cheeks and golden hair spread across the white pillow.

Instantly, unexpectedly aroused by the sight of Mara's curved hip and unbuttoned nightgown, Brock rubbed a hand across his eyes as a groan rumbled through his chest. Not now, not when he'd done so well to keep his distance.

But it was more than his desire for the woman that stirred him. It was the silent, early morning hour...the tangle of clean sheets...the drowsy baby...the scent of lavender... the whisper of winter breath against the window... the promise of a crackling fire...and the woman in her robe...his desire for a wife.

Sometime in the past weeks of living with Mara, he had felt this change encompass him. Maybe it had begun the first time he cooked breakfast with Abby in his arms. Maybe it was the night he kissed Mara on the snowy roadside. No matter when it started, the change had come swiftly—almost blinding in its intensity. For the first time in his life, Brock had come to believe in family...and in himself as a successful part of a family.

Not only did he believe in it, he wanted it. His image of a mother as a cynical, embittered woman who could do nothing but flee from her unhappiness had given way to the picture of a blond madonna with her baby nestled at her breast and her warm eyes filled with love. The idea of children as unnecessary nuisances to be tolerated but never enjoyed was brushed aside by a tiny baby with pink lips and downy hair who liked nothing better than to be cuddled, hugged and adored. The concept of a house as a place to do little more than sleep and change clothes evolved into the reality of home. And home became a warm, comforting haven of good food, laughter, conversation and security.

Fatherhood was no longer the province of men who didn't have anything more important to do with their lives. Nor was it an inconvenience in a real man's quest for power and wealth. Fatherhood became suddenly a place of hope, happiness, delight, surprise and dreams. Without realizing it, Brock had come to crave that role...to want fatherhood for himself as strongly as he had ever wanted anything.

Gently he scooped up the sleeping baby, rolled to one side and deposited her safely in the cocoon of the bassinet. For a moment he studied the unmoving bundle of pastel blankets and plump pink skin. A gritty lump formed in his throat as he drank in the twin arcs of her closed eyes with their wispy lashes, the bud of her nose, the perfect roundness of her cheeks. If the child had been created from his own seed, he could not have loved her more.

Yes, he loved the baby.

He couldn't let Abby go. Not ever. There was too much ahead. There were tricycles and trees to climb and drippy Popsicles on hot summer days. There were horses and picnics and swimming holes. There were breakfasts to cook—hundreds of them. There were bicycles to ride and wildflowers to gather and dollhouses to build. This baby deserved a father, a living father, who could wipe away her tears and listen to her heartaches as no one had ever done for Brock Barnett.

He reached out a finger to touch the tiny form, and a warm hand slipped over his shoulder. A soft, pliant body molded against his back. The scent of lavender drifted around him. He shut his eyes and let out a shuddering breath. Mara, his wife. And he was her husband.

Within the whirlwind of new images, the portrait of husband had changed for him, too. Husband had always been a vague term that involved financial support and contractual obligation. Now it meant deep relationship. A husband was one member of a bonded pair. A husband was friend, companion, partner... and lover.

Brock couldn't let go of this woman, either. Not ever. Turning toward her, he saw that she had come to him in her sleep, as he had always imagined a wife would come to her husband. Was she thinking of Todd? Maybe.

Running his hand down her arm, he fought the sparks of need that shot through his body. Her white nightgown gaped at the breast, and he allowed himself to study the shadow of her cleavage, to remember the sight of her ripe nipple as she placed it in her baby's mouth, to imagine touching and tasting her himself.

With a murmur, she nestled closer against him. He tried to remind himself she was thinking of her first husband. He told himself to get up and go check his cattle. Instead, he let his hand slip apart the edges of her gown. His finger trailed slowly down the crevice between her breasts. She was velvety and so tempting he couldn't resist tracing up and around the curved flesh.

"Mmm," she murmured somewhere deep in the back of her throat.

At the animal sound, his body reared up in ravenous response. He pushed closer against her, nestling his throbbing need into the comfort of her belly. With only the thin fabric of his shorts and her gown between them, he could feel her heated skin against his flesh. The thought of silken thighs and taut nipples sent a flame raging through him.

No more games. He would have the woman know which man lay beside her.

"Mara," he said in a low voice.

She stirred and ran her hand over his bare chest. Eyes still shut, she threaded her fingers through the mat of his hair and circled her fingertips around his flat nipples. Her lips parted and her tongue slipped out to dampen them.

"Mara," he growled.

"Mmm." It was almost a moan. She brushed her mouth across his scorched flesh. "Brock," she said in a breath.

She knew. Even if she was still half asleep, she knew. The realization tore through him in searing waves. He pushed aside the edge of her gown and trickled his fingers back and forth over her breast until her hips began to move against him.

"Mara."

This time her eyelashes fluttered open. Gray-green eyes gazed at him for a moment. "Brock," she whispered.

He slid his thumb over her nipple. And again. Beneath the pad of his thumb he felt the tip tighten into a round, ripe cherry. He stroked circles around it, and then he pulled slightly.

"Brock," she gasped.

"Awake?"

With an affirmative moan, she shut her eyes again. Oh, yes, she was awake. And aroused. And here he was beside her in her bed. What could she do but run her fingers over his chest and touch the side of his neck with her tongue? What could she do but sway with him as his hardened body pushed against her pelvis?

It felt so right, so perfect to lie in bed with him. She savored the caresses of this new man. His touch was so different—sensual, earthy, almost animal. Memories of other lovemaking curled into a hidden place in the back of her mind, and she felt almost virginal . . . yet at the same time drenched in wanton, flagrant desire.

When he pulled apart the placket of her gown and boldly exposed both her breasts, she shimmered with delight. "I want you, Mara," he murmured. "I've wanted you for months. Maybe for years."

His hands formed around her, lifting and reveling. The taut pink peaks of her nipples peered between his fingers. He gently squeezed and tipped and rolled them until her skin sizzled with tiny flickers of lightning. Oh, she wanted him, too.

"I have wanted you," she managed. "I do want you...need your touch...your kiss..."

When his mouth found hers, she gloried in the warm dampness of hungry lips. She let her hands explore his shoulders. Firm, round muscle rippled beneath her fingers as his own hands molded the skin of her breasts, her waist, her hips. With a sigh, she parted her lips and took him inside to toy with her tongue in sweet, languorous strokes that held rainbow promises.

When her bare breasts touched his chest, she knew she was completely lost to him, and wanted to be. Suddenly, she ached with a desire she wasn't sure she had ever known...a starvation for carnal release. The drowsy contentment of the night fled as she trailed her fingers down his flat stomach and touched the waistband of his shorts.

"Mara," he said against her ear. It was the closest to a plea she knew she would ever hear.

Obedient out of her own desire, not his, she lowered her caress, cupped him and stroked up and down. Heightening his pleasure, she slid her hands inside his shorts and took him completely. Oh, but he was magnificent, and she knew she had to feast her eyes on him. As he lay in paralyzed ecstasy, she pushed down his shorts and played him until he was trembling.

With a groan of disbelief, he dipped his head and licked at her breasts until she blossomed and melted into throbbing, liquid hunger. Any doubt evaporated inside her as he gathered her gown in his hands, raising it up her thighs, over her hips and finally freeing her completely. While she moved against him in pleasure at the touch of his hot, hard body, he formed his hands around her buttocks and pulled her tightly to him.

"Finally," he uttered.

Echoing his breathless relief, she came fully into his arms. Their mouths met again and again. Their legs tangled and toes touched. Any uncertainty Mara felt about this moment was brushed away by the caress of his hands over her body. He was magic, his fingers sensual and his tongue carnal as he plundered her.

Shivering, she lay in a dewy trance. He explored her thighs and stroked the nest of curls between them. Heedlessly wanton, she spread herself to him and he dipped his fingers into her. She was sure he would come inside her...she wanted him to...and in lovemaking before, it had always been like that.

But Brock had other ways. Caressing her mouth with his, he fingered and titillated her until her hips writhed. Sure she would cry out, she tangled her fingers in the sheets and kissed him with bruising kisses. He wouldn't stop the delectable dance, first playing her hard and certain until she rose to the peak of release, then stroking her with petal-soft trickles that took her unimaginably higher.

"Brock," she groaned. "Oh...please."

When he was sure another touch would send her over the edge, he rose over her and thrust deeply into her creamy flesh. She buried her fingers in his back as he lifted and fell on her, his shaft stroking every inch of her nest inside and out. His hands clutched her hips. His mouth drank hers.

She was sure she could bear no more...and then he bent down and took her breast in his mouth. The swift tug of her nipple severed the final restraint and her core blossomed into waves of shimmering color—purple, blue, pink, gold. Stars shot down her legs. Lightning streaked across her skin. She convulsed in ecstasy.

"Brock," she cried. "Oh, Brock, Brock."

He remained poised inside her, savoring every moment of her orgasm until his own could hold back no longer. Erupting deep in her flesh, he shuddered with pleasure... again...and again. His body trembled with the utter, soul-wrenching majesty of connubial bliss.

"Mara," he gasped. "Mara...Mara."

She wrapped her legs around his waist, wishing she could take his whole body inside hers. Her tongue lapped at the damp sheen on his neck and shoulders. His hands gripped her buttocks, massaging out every last ripple of ecstasy for both of them. And then he sagged onto her, his heaviness sinking her into the mattress as his mouth moved hungrily over hers.

"Mara," he murmured again, his lips touching hers as he spoke the word. "Mara...my wife."

She lifted her eyes to the ceiling and blinked back misty happiness.

"It's honeymoon time at the Barnett house," Brock announced into the phone he had taken from Mara's bedside table. His eyes devoured her as she sat curled on the bed, her naked body cradling her baby as the little one suckled contentedly.

"Take today and the rest of the weekend off, Pierre," he continued. "And tell Ermaline and Rosa Maria, too. I don't want to see hide nor hair of any of you for three days, got that?"

"*S'il vous plaît,* what about your work? What about the cattle?" The chef's voice was stilted, echoing his disbelief at his employer's declaration. "Surely the men on the ranch will wonder where you are, no?"

"I'll call them and explain."

"Well...if you think it is best."

Brock could hear Pierre's wife in the background as she uttered exclamations of delight. "Honeymoon? *Très bien!* They are together now, Pierre. Leave them! Put down the telephone!"

"Whist, Yvonne!" he growled at her. Then he returned to his amused employer. "What about your dinner tonight?" Pierre asked. "Perhaps you will change your mind concerning this three-day honeymoon, no? Perhaps you will become hungry."

Brock slid his hand up Mara's bare thigh, thinking how hungry he was right at the moment. "Nope," he said. "We can take care of things around the house."

Pierre fell silent for a few seconds before speaking up again. "Perhaps this happiness *en famille* will mean you do not wish to dine *à la française* any longer. Perhaps five-star cuisine and a chef trained with the very finest on the Continent will no longer be necessary for the Barnett household. What do you think? Will everything change now?"

Brock leaned over and kissed Mara's knee. She tousled her fingers through his hair. Things had definitely changed, but not the way his chef thought. "Don't worry, Pierre. Mara's going to start working at Fort Selden next week. She won't have time to cook."

"No?" Pierre's voice brightened. "Perhaps no time to clean house, either?"

"I imagine she'll be busy with other things." He hoped he could keep Mara so happy, so delirious with *amour* she wouldn't have time even to run a finger across a dusty table. "And tell Ramona she's on full-time duty with the baby starting Monday."

"Oh, *très bien!* Full-time is good. Give our love to the *chère enfant*. Please tell your lovely wife not to worry, all will be taken care of to perfection. *Au revoir!*"

Brock was smiling as he set down the receiver. He scooted next to Mara on the bed and tucked her against him as she continued to nurse her baby. Abby's eyelids were so heavy she could barely hold them open. All the same, her gaze was transfixed on her mother's face.

"Is everything okay with Pierre?" Mara asked.

"Très bien." He traced her face with the side of his finger. "Is everything okay with Mara?"

"It's hard to think about leaving Abby all day long. I'll have to wean her."

Brock studied the now familiar sight of Mara holding her daughter to her breast. He reached down and took one of the baby's round pink toes between his thumb and finger. As he rolled the tiny digit, he thought about what must have gone into her decision. "If you worked part-time, you could keep nursing, couldn't you? Are you sure you want to work full days at the fort?"

"Yes," she said, her voice almost a whisper. "It's time. I have to get my life back on track, and I know Ramona is wonderful with Abby. Still... it's not easy."

"Mara, you know you don't have to do this for the money. My promise to provide for you is good, no matter what."

"It's not that."

"Are you doing it for Todd, then?"

She lifted her eyes and clearly read the message in his. "No, it's not for Todd. I want to do this for me."

Brock couldn't suppress the elation he felt at her words. Maybe Mara finally had begun to see her first husband as a memory to treasure, but a memory nonetheless. If she felt Todd was a part of the past, that left the present and the future open to Brock. Would she let him fill it?

Seated behind Mara, he watched her lean over the edge of the bed and nestle her sleeping baby in the bassinet. Her smooth, bare hips and lean thighs beckoned. As his body responded, he stroked his hands down her spine and around the curve of her buttocks. He trailed his fingertips up and down the backs of her legs, focusing on the sensitive skin behind her knees.

She looked over her shoulder at him and a coy smile lifted her lips. "Did I hear you tell Pierre this was a honeymoon?"

"That's what I said."

As he continued to stroke her legs and hips, she slid chest-down onto her pillow and hugged it against her breasts. "Does that mean what happened between us this morning wasn't an accident?"

"Can the same accident happen twice in one day?"

"Mmm," she purred as his fingers explored the warmth between her legs. "I hope so."

He could hardly believe she lay so comfortably open to him, her body languorous on the bed as he caressed her. This morning he could almost believe there had never been any barrier between them. Their loving had been spontaneous, intense, perfect. It would be again.

Stretching out on top of her, his knees to either side of her hips, he slid his hands beneath her breasts. She shivered as he plied her nipples, still sensitive and wet from the baby's mouth. Behind her, she could feel his arousal pressing hard and urgent against her bottom. The image of the man—dark, magnificent and virile—stirred her until she could do nothing but sway her hips in a dance of seductive invitation.

When she lifted onto her knees and spread her thighs, he let out a deep growl. "Mara...what you do to me..."

"Do it to me, Brock," she urged. Her body felt as though it were glowing with a red-hot halo of flame. As he entered her, she whimpered in ecstatic disbelief at the sensation. It was as though he were tearing her in two with deep, sure strokes that massaged the very essence of her being. His hands cupped her breasts, his fingers plucking at her nipples until they throbbed.

"I swear," he murmured in a husky voice, "I swear I've never felt this way. Never."

She shut her eyes, reveling in the threshold of release that was fast approaching. Never. No, she had never felt this way, either, and that realization almost frightened her. This man was raw and earthy, a masterful demon who had taken charge of her body and mind. He would play it until she sold him her soul, and gladly.

"Yes, Brock," she begged as his hand left her breast, traveled down her stomach and slid in magic circles between her thighs. "Yes, yes, ohh...Brock, ohh..."

"Mara!" His explosive release caught her by surprise. He clutched and rocked her as every ounce of that masterful power drove into her.

Suddenly, in a blinding crescendo, her body sang with his. Wave after wave of ecstasy spilled through her. They sank onto the mattress, rolling with pleasure. His mouth found the back of her neck, dampened her skin and sent tingles up her spine. She gripped his knees, reveling in hard bone, sinew, the crispness of his coarse hair.

"Mara, I can't believe this," he murmured. "I never thought...never knew it could feel this way."

"I'm alive again." Her voice was filled with wonder. "It's you...you...who brought me back."

She turned in his arms and pressed herself tightly against him. How could this have happened? How could she feel this way about a man, any man other than Todd? And how could lovemaking possibly be this wonderful, this deliciously hedonistic?

"Mara," Brock whispered against her ear. "Look at me."

She shook her head. "I'm afraid to."

"Why?"

"I'm too happy. This has to be a dream. I'm scared if I open my eyes, you might vanish."

"Hey, lady." He lifted her chin and kissed her eyelids. "I'm not going anywhere. What about you?"

She looked into his brown eyes and a wash of emotion poured through her. She loved him. She loved Brock Barnett...differently, but just as deeply as she had loved her first husband.

"I'm not going anywhere, either," she whispered.

And she didn't. For three days Mara's world consisted of her bedroom and the kitchen. Between nursing and playing with Abby, she and Brock explored every nuance of physical ecstasy. Mara was sure she had somehow slipped across the perimeter between heaven and earth and was walking down streets paved with gold.

Brock was absolutely the most sexual man she had ever met. But his body was no demanding machine. He somehow sensed the rhythms of her desire and played them to perfection. One time he would touch and toy with her in a slow dance that left her nerves thrumming on the edge of cataclysm. Another time he would tease her in a game of playful tag until she felt she was chasing him, almost begging him to end the delicious torment. And another time he would enter her with the forceful pride of a stallion, his touch so ruthlessly carnal she ached from the pleasure of their union.

They spent hours sleeping, talking, laughing, eating. Oh, they ate. Late Sunday evening, while stretched out naked by the fire in her bedroom, a plate of home-baked chocolate chip cookies beside her, Mara worried aloud that she was gaining back all the weight she had lost after Abby's birth. Brock laughed, handed her a cookie and told her he'd want her no matter what she weighed.

"I wanted you when you were nine months pregnant and your stomach stuck out to here," he reminded her. "I want you right now, even with cookie crumbs on your chin. And I'll want you when your hair has turned white and your skin is wrinkled and soft."

Mara stared at his face and absorbed the honesty in his deep brown eyes. But how could this be the carefree, insincere, uncommitted Brock she had always known? "Are you sure you'll want me? Even when I'm old?"

"You and nobody else." He brushed the crumbs from her chin. "I hope you believe that."

She rolled over onto her back and studied the heavy beams in her bedroom ceiling. The past three days had been a sensory blur. She had thought about nothing but satisfying sexual and physical urges. Even Abby, who seemed to relish the extra attention of two doting adults, took second place to Mara's craving for Brock. It was as though he had become her entire world, and there was nothing but the present moment. She had relegated the past to memory. And the future...

"Brock, what's going to happen to us?" she whispered. "Job interviews, work, the fort, the ranch, church, friends. The outside world is going to start turning again tomorrow."

"And we're going to get back on. Together. I want everyone to know the business arrangement we made is off. This is personal now—a marriage created in heaven, not on earth."

"What will people think? I haven't even been widowed for a year. And you were Todd's best friend."

"Do you care?"

She shut her eyes as he trailed a finger over the tip of her breast. "Not really."

"I don't give a damn what anyone thinks. This is between us."

"If we don't let other people tear us apart, the only thing that can separate us is our fears."

"What are you afraid of, Mara?"

She clutched at her thoughts as they attempted to flee beneath the overwhelming rush of sensation that his touch evoked. "I'm afraid you don't really know me," she said, her words no more than a shallow breath. "And I'm afraid I don't know you."

He bent over her and traced the pink circle of her nipple with his tongue. "I know you, Mara. I know you inside and out. I know you better than anyone could . . . we're two of a kind. That means you know me, too. You know who I am, what I do, what I want. You understand how I think. You know me, Mara—you're the only woman I've wanted to know me."

She slipped her arms around his broad shoulders as his heavy body lowered hers onto the crocheted afghan she had given him. When his familiar scent drifted around her and his hands stroked her in places no longer secret, she shivered with a mixture of delight and fear.

"I do know you," she murmured, dangerously, hopelessly lost in him again.

Chapter 18

Mara's interview with Dr. Stephen Long of the Bureau of Land Management could not have gone better. She instinctively liked him, and his memories of Todd added to the storehouse she was saving to share with Abby one day. On site that Monday afternoon, he approved her position as director of the restoration project.

A trip to the pediatrician later that day affirmed that Abby was healthy and strong, growing like a weed, developing perfectly. Mara had decided to wean her daughter, and the doctor taught her the procedure she would need to follow. Armed with infant formula, a huge supply of bottles, more diapers than Abby could wear in a month and enough motherly reminders to fill two volumes, Ramona waved goodbye to Mara at the front door that Tuesday morning.

Brock rode with her to the end of the driveway, where he kissed her so passionately she was tempted to be late on her first day at work. But she let him off and watched him saunter across a pasture toward the barn, his blue jeans and denim shirt in sharp contrast to his black hair and black boots.

She loved him. That was the clearest thing in Mara's mind as she drove toward Fort Selden. She loved Brock, and she wanted to live as his wife for the rest of her life. But did he love her? He had never said those words—and maybe he didn't feel them.

Again she wondered how well she knew the man. In spite of their intense lovemaking, he had said very little about his hopes for their future. He spoke of Abby growing up in the ranch house, but he didn't ask for Mara's opinion on the matter. And even though he had told Mara he wanted everyone to know their marriage was on different terms now, he had said nothing about their separate bedrooms. He had given her no ring, no words of love and no blueprint for their restructured relationship.

And she knew Brock Barnett was a blueprint kind of man.

But there was little time for worry as she plunged into her first day of work as a restorationist. Dressed in khaki slacks and layers of warm sweaters, she had pulled her hair up into a tight ponytail and laced heavy boots on her feet. Seated in the open air with the melting adobe walls surrounding her, she held her first meeting with Mr. Dominguez, the State Park personnel and the fort supervisor.

Even in its dilapidated state, Fort Selden welcomed more than 11,000 tourists a year. Three full-time rangers offered tours to local organizations and groups of schoolchildren. Once a year, the fort's Frontier Days provided black powder shooting, farrier demonstrations, square dancing, races and other competitions, hayrides and a nineteenth-century fashion show. In summer, living history demonstrations were scheduled each hour during the afternoon on Saturdays and Sundays. In the midst of all this activity, Mara would have to conduct her restoration work so as to disturb the events as little as possible.

The plans Todd had drawn up called for the work crew to shore up and preserve in their present condition most of the single-story adobe structures in the complex. But the two-story administration building, the hospital and the prison were to be completely rebuilt according to the original blueprints. This meant Mara would need to haul in adobe bricks from a Las Cruces manufacturer and hire a crew of skilled carpenters, bricklayers, electricians and even plumbers. Mr. Dominguez would supervise.

Within the first three days, she had ordered and received her first shipment of bricks—heavy, brown twelve-by-eighteen inch slabs of mud mixed with straw. The blocks looked more like giant bars of chocolate candy than building supplies. Adobe, she quickly learned, was actually easy to use in building. Though the blocks were heavy and awkward, they mortared well, dried fast and were simple to design with. The ease with which adobe went up, Mara discovered, contributed to the ease with which it came down. Under less than ideal conditions, and without regular maintenance, adobe walls could disintegrate rapidly—as the fort evidenced.

Though she had no experience in construction, Mara absorbed Mr. Dominguez's enthusiasm about building with adobe. Whole walls could be erected and windows cut out later. A pronged tool scraped down the side of a wall provided a trench in which to lay electrical wiring or plumbing. A quick slap of mortar over the top of the trench and the wires were safely sealed away. There was no framing, no insulation, no Sheetrock. Best of all, the structures were cool in summer and toasty warm in winter.

Late her first Friday afternoon, Mara stood at the edge of the site with her crew to survey their work. Every muscle in her body ached from the heavy labor. Her clothing was splattered with mud and her boots were caked an inch thick. Though she had managed to wean Abby almost completely to the bottle, her breasts still sometimes ached. She was physically more tired than she'd ever been, but Mara knew she had been victorious.

She and Mr. Dominguez worked together like cogs in a smoothly oiled machine. He respected her opinions and her position as director, and she respected his enormous experience. Their hastily assembled crew had proven themselves loyal and eager to succeed in the interesting task. Even the rangers, who had been concerned about the workers' interruption of their routine, had decided to incorporate the re-construction into their daily guided tours. They urged visitors to return often to "see what will happen as Fort Selden grows." And Mara was delighted to explain her plans to the groups of excited students.

"I think we might be able to finish the administration building in two months," Mr. Dominguez said. "But you better order some more adobe. The last thing this old, tired body wants to do is build wooden forms and pour them bricks myself. You never knew hard work till you tried mixing mud and straw, I'm telling you."

"I'll do it right now," Mara agreed. "I'll place a call from the visitors' center. If we keep the bricks protected from the rain, it can't hurt to have extra supplies sitting around."

"Not if we don't make them an eyesore."

"True. Dr. Long is coming back to inspect the site in a couple of weeks. That'll be our ultimate test. If we don't pass muster, we're out of work."

Mr. Dominguez glanced at the other workers who had gathered for the meeting. "Keep your noses clean, boys, and do what Mrs. Barnett tells you. This has been a good week, but we're just getting started. Next week the work really be-gins." He took off his battered hat and rubbed a handker-chief over his balding scalp. "Let's go home before we get some more tourists who want to parade through the work site."

"Great idea," Mara agreed. "I'm beat."

"Oh, no, now look. Here comes a truck."

Mara started to groan, then stopped short. "Wait a min-ute, that's . . . that's Brock!" Mara slapped Mr. Dominguez on the back. "That's my husband. And he's got Abby!"

She took off toward the pickup, her blond ponytail bouncing behind her. As Brock's long legs emerged from the front door, her heart soared. The past few days had been so different from the weekend before. Supper had been their only meal together, and the hours of talking and touching were condensed into a few minutes each night. Mara had mourned the loss of their ecstasy, and she was anticipating a weekend of nothing but family—her, Brock and Abby.

"Hey, beautiful!" He waved as he lifted the baby from her car seat. "Thought we'd drive out and take a look at what you were up to."

"Come meet my crew. Mr. Dominguez and the others are just about to head for home."

Mara took Abby in her arms and gave her a kiss as Brock planted a kiss of his own on Mara's forehead. "I miss you," he murmured.

"Not for long," she returned with a wink. She called out a greeting to the elderly builder who was lumbering toward them. In moments, he was cuddling Abby and shaking hands with Brock. The others in the crew, most of them work-roughened men, each had to gander at the baby, and two insisted on taking a turn at holding and bouncing her in their arms.

"You've got to see what we're working on," Mara said, lacing her fingers through Brock's free hand as he cradled Abby with the other. "This has been such an amazing week. It's like Todd knew exactly what needed to be done to bring the administration building back to life. He was a genius, Brock, he really was."

"I never doubted it." As he walked beside Mara, he couldn't take his eyes off her. He had never seen her so gorgeous—not even lying naked in the firelight. Her attractiveness was not diminished by muddy clothes and blistered fingers, nor did it have anything to do with gleaming hair and supple thighs. Mara's beauty came from the light in her gray-green eyes and the glow on her cheeks. As she spoke, her breath misted in the crisp air and her laughter pulled at his heart.

He would do anything…anything…to keep this woman. He coveted her excitement, her laughter, her intelligence. He wanted to hear every thought that crossed her mind. He wanted to wipe away every tear that fell from her eyes. The strength of emotion tore through him, twisting with a force he had never experienced. He could think of no other word for it than one. Love. And the power of it scared the hell out of him.

She walked him around the site, pointing out the locations of buildings that were now no more than velvety brown walls, half melted by rain and wind. "This central area is the parade ground...that's the hospital and there's the post store," she explained. "The fort was originally built to house one company of infantry and another company of cavalry and its sixty horses. After 1879, the commanding officer received word to begin dismantling usable materials for shipping to Fort Bliss in El Paso, and the post was abandoned."

"Was it ever rebuilt?" Brock asked, trying to concentrate on Mara's tour.

"All the buildings were destroyed and left absolutely worthless. But in 1880 the fort was reactivated and reconstructed. This time, though, it could only accommodate one company. During that building phase, Captain Arthur MacArthur came to the post with his family, which included six-year-old Douglas."

"The Douglas MacArthur who became a general?"

"You got it." Mara rewarded him with a grin. "It's another reason we want tourists to visit the site. This fort is one of the cradles of U.S. history."

Brock studied the crumbled walls. "I wonder if some of the underprivileged children in Las Cruces could be brought out here. Give them a sense of their roots, you know? In fact, if you could connect all the forts with a network that would make them easily accessible, you could bring children from all over the state to see this part of their history."

"Kids like Todd was," Mara continued, seizing on the idea. "He didn't really have much of a chance, given his background. He overcame that with sheer determination. Not every child has Todd's innate willpower, but every child deserves a taste of the past."

Brock nodded. "Let somebody see the past, and they might want to make something of their future."

Buoyed by the notion Brock had proposed, Mara made a mental note to explore the possibility as they strolled around the grounds. "The administration building is our first project," she told him. "It's complicated because we have to make sure the structure is strong enough to support a second floor. Adobe buildings are usually only on one level.''

"Like my old trading post."

"That's right. This is so tricky, but you should see how Mr. Dominguez goes at it. He's amazing." She tapped the roll of blueprints she was carrying. "And Todd has every detail drawn in, right down to the floorboards and nails. The plans are perfectly in tune with this structure, Brock. They show exactly where everything has to go. Todd's got such a sense of historical authenticity. He is just brilliant."

"Was," Brock said.

Mara glanced up in surprise.

"Todd *was* brilliant," he repeated firmly.

She stared at him. "I know. But it's like I can sense what he was doing here. I feel like I hear his voice talking, explaining things to me. We worked so hard together over these plans, and I know his thinking when I look at them. I understand what he intends with every line."

"Intended."

"Brock—"

"What he intended, Mara. Past tense."

Her fingers tightened on the blueprints. "Brock . . ."

"Mara, what are you doing? Are you forgetting?"

"No, but you don't have to be so blunt."

"You don't have to keep on talking like he's right here."

"Brock, I'm trying to tell you—"

"Mrs. Barnett," Mr. Dominguez's voice cut across her words. "We got an unexpected visitor here." He touched her arm and leaned close. "It's that Dr. Long fellow."

"Dr. Long?" Mara's heart jolted. "Oh, my gosh."

Without pausing to conclude their discussion, she whirled away from Brock, smoothed down her hair and set off across the open parade ground toward the waiting vehicle. Dr. Long wasn't due back for a couple of weeks. Did she have everything in order? Would he be annoyed with something she'd left undone? Less than a week on-site! She'd hardly had time to get her feet wet. And what about Brock . . . and Abby?

She swung around again, focusing on the tall man holding the baby in his arms. "I'll be right back," she called out.

"We'll be at the ranch house." His voice was clipped.

"Wait, Brock." She watched him turn away. Facing the newly arrived car, she muttered to herself. "Great ... just great."

There was no time to reason with Brock. Her stomach in a knot, she did her best to paste a calm smile on her face as she heard the sound of his pickup pulling away from the fort. Had she hurt him so deeply with her mention of Todd? Didn't he understand she would always love her first husband—but she had no illusions about the fact that he was gone? Didn't he understand how much he—Brock—had come to mean to her?

"Mrs. Barnett!" Dr. Long greeted her warmly, his hand extended.

"This is a surprise," she managed, dusting off her palms on her thighs before shaking his hand. She wished she'd at least had time to brush her hair and wash the mud off her face. "I didn't expect you back so soon."

"I was up north checking on the other forts. Since my flight leaves from El Paso, I thought I'd drop in on you to see how things were going."

"Oh, how thoughtful." She could have throttled him. "Things are going very well. Mr. Dominguez is doing a terrific job with his crew, and we already have our first shipment of adobe. In fact, we began laying it this morning."

"Mind if I take a look?"

"I'd be happy to show you around." Mara glanced at the cloud of dust rising from the road as Brock's pickup vanished in the distance. She felt sick inside. How could they have argued over something so small? But was it small? Obviously, Brock cared a great deal how she felt about Todd. After all this time ... after their lovemaking ... he should have known what he meant to her.

"My goodness, you have been busy," Dr. Long commented, oblivious to her consternation. "I don't believe I've ever seen so many adobe bricks."

"The company we're using is extremely productive, and we're fortunate they're located in Las Cruces. They supply adobe materials as far north as Albuquerque and Santa Fe."

"So, you think you'll have enough here?"

"This will get us off to a good start. I was planning to call in another order in a few minutes."

Dr. Long nodded as Mara walked him around the site, pointing out different aspects of the work. "Mr. Dominguez and I think we may be able to finish the administration building in two months. The other structures shouldn't take nearly as long."

They strolled across the parade ground to the ruins of the jail. "Have you thought about what it will mean to your family, Mara, when you start on the other sites? Those forts are certainly not within driving distance of your husband's ranch."

She toed a clod of dirt. "I'm focusing on this project right now, Dr. Long. It's difficult to look beyond it at the moment."

"But you have a new baby. And what about your husband? What does Brock think?"

"We haven't discussed it in any detail."

"Your husband mentioned he owns a small plane he could make available to you if you wanted to commute."

Mara glanced up. "He did?"

"Yes, and I think he's very supportive of your endeavors."

"You spoke to Brock?"

"About two weeks ago we discussed the future of the restoration company. I assumed he shared that with you."

"No." Mara frowned. She knew that around the time of their marriage, Brock had been in contact with the department. Had he also been talking with them during the weeks she was pitching her proposal?

"Now, this jail will be an interesting tourist draw," Dr. Long said, changing the subject abruptly. "People love to look at jails, prisons, courtrooms, crime sites and battlegrounds. Bring the people in and you suddenly have funds, legislative support, all kinds of good things. Do you have any historical documentation of the jail's use?''

"I'm working on it. I'd like to create artifact displays inside each restored building.''

"Great idea. That would complement what's already in the visitors' center.'' He walked beside her around the walls of the old jail. "You know, Fort Craig has three warehouses—each bigger and deeper than an Olympic swimming pool. There was once a bakery, a guardhouse, officers' quarters. And that fort was encircled by an earthen wall. Do you suppose we could rebuild that wall, Mara?''

"As I said, I'm taking one project at a time. Fort Selden is the best preserved of all the sites, and look at the shape it's in. I have detailed blueprints for each of the forts, of course, but I guess everything depends on whether there's money to restore them all.''

Dr. Long gave her an odd look. "The funding looks very strong at this point.''

"That's good to know.'' She brushed back a wisp of hair that had come loose from her ponytail. "As I work on this project, I'll continue to pull together what I'll need for the next one. Mr. Dominguez is willing to move to each site, and I'll speak with my husband about his airplane.''

"Good. I'm pleased with the start you've made here, Mara. It looks like Brock was right. You do have what it takes to run this company.''

A little frown tugging at her lips, Mara walked him back to his car. "I take it you've spoken with my husband several times?''

"Yes. He's a fine man. Totally supportive of you and this work.'' He pulled open the car door. "I'll be back in a couple of months to check on things, but don't hesitate to give me a call if you run into any snags. I'll do what I can to smooth your way through the red tape.''

"Thank you, Dr. Long. I do appreciate that.''

He started to sit down, then straightened again. "Oh, and thank Brock again for me, would you? The donation from the Barnett Foundation put us back on track. When other corporations got wind of it, the funding bottleneck opened up." He gave her a warm smile. "And I know Brock is pleased with the good work you're doing—we all are."

Mara's mouth went dry. "Thank you," she mouthed, but no sound emerged.

Dr. Long gave her a thumbs-up as he settled into his car and pulled the door shut. "Two months!" he said. "See you then."

Mara watched him pull away. As his car bounced down the dirt road, a film of dust settled onto her hair, her shoulders, her boots.

Chapter 19

"Donation," Mara muttered under her breath as she drove down the dirt road away from Fort Selden. "Buy off is more like it."

She shifted gears, turned onto the highway and glared at the yellow line that streaked beneath her car wheels. "He's got a plane you can use," she said in Dr. Long's ingratiating voice. "Oh, he does, does he? How come he never mentioned that to me? And since when have you two become best buddies?"

She tugged the band from her ponytail and shook her hair loose around her shoulders. An airplane? Not that using one was such a bad idea. But what else did the wealthy Brock Barnett have up his sleeve? Had he mapped out her whole future with the Bureau of Land Management?

She could almost hear him talking on his beloved cordless phone. "I'm a wealthy man. I'll donate all the money you need to keep the project going, and you give the little woman a job. How does that sound, Dr. Long?"

"Sounds illegal to me," Mara said out loud. "Illegal and unethical and...and manipulative...and controlling... and obnoxious!"

Oh, she could just wring his neck! After all this time, how could he have failed to tell her he owned an airplane? What else hadn't he told her about himself? That he owned an island? Or a yacht? Maybe he really hated babies. Maybe he had girlfriends in every city in America. Maybe he was just biding his time, operating undercover with his old methods, until he grew tired of playing the loyal husband game.

Was the man she had lived with for almost three months just pretending to be common and down-to-earth—someone who had learned to enjoy the same things she liked? Or was he really the cocky, domineering, selfish stranger she had thought in the beginning?

How dare he pull strings to get her that job?

Half choking on repressed, angry tears, Mara pulled the car up the driveway of the ranch house. As she pressed the garage door opener, she watched his pickup come into view, the infant chair comfortably buckled onto the front seat beside the driver. Abby adored Brock.

Oh, Abby! Where was her baby? All Mara wanted to do at this moment was hold her daughter tight and escape from the tangled mess of her life.

She parked the car Brock had given her to use and shut her eyes for a moment. His car...his house...his money. She had sold out to him, just as Sherry had warned. She had trusted him in spite of her better judgment. Worse, she had slept with the man—and not just once. Umpteen times.

Slamming her palms onto the steering wheel, Mara threw open the car door. How could her body betray her? He was deceitful, egotistic, bullheaded....

"Mara." His hands on his hips, Brock was standing just inside the kitchen door as she entered the house. A tower of black hair, piercing eyes and dusty blue denim, he looked downright menacing. "I want to talk about Todd."

She threw her purse on the counter. "Where's Abby?"

"In the nursery. She fell asleep in the car, and I just put her to bed." He moved toward her, his dark eyes locked on hers. "So, what's this about Todd?"

"What's this about you owning an airplane?" She lifted her chin. "Can you tell me that?"

"I have a plane in Las Cruces. You didn't know that?"

"And you and Dr. Long have it all worked out that I'm supposed to commute to the other forts."

"If you want to. I've offered the plane."

"You offered it to Dr. Long."

"I'm offering it to you. If it would make things easier, I'll hire a pilot, and you can use the plane to get to work and back."

Mara clamped her mouth shut. This wasn't how he was supposed to be acting. "You might have told me."

"What's mine is yours, Mara," he said. "I thought that's how marriage worked. Give-and-take."

"Like you give Dr. Long a lot of money so he'll take me on? Is that the kind of give-and-take you're talking about?"

"What?"

"Oh, stop playing games with me, Brock. Dr. Long told me you donated money to keep the fort project afloat. That's why he hired me. You pulled all the right strings."

"Bull." He glared at her. "You got that job on your own merits. And you'll keep it or lose it based on how you manage the business."

"Or, you could just give another sizable donation to Dr. Long."

"I didn't give anything to Dr. Long. Barnett Petroleum has a foundation that supports lots of causes. The money does some good. The company gets a tax write-off."

"Yes, and aren't *you* Barnett Petroleum, Brock?"

"I didn't give that money to influence the department. Dr. Long told me he might be interested in working with you, but there was no money. After Todd died, the funding evaporated. The fort project was defunct. I wanted that money donated for one reason—to keep Todd's dream alive."

She stared into his eyes, aching to believe him. "Don't lie to me, Brock."

"I'm not lying, damn it." His eyes narrowed. "Do you think I'd do something illegal?"

"I don't know. I'm not sure I even know you at all."

"The hell you don't. You know everything about me."

"Like that airplane you own?"

"You want to see my portfolio? Fine. I'll call my lawyer tomorrow morning, and we'll look it over. There's an airplane in Las Cruces, an apartment complex in Albuquerque, a vacation house and two racehorses in Ruidoso, a small plastics company in El Paso, a boat in the Gulf of Mexico and another one in San Diego. I'm part owner of an Indy car team. I've got interests in a white-water excursion company in Wyoming and a mountaineering outfitter in Washington state. I own a hot-air balloon, a hang glider, a dune buggy, a parachute—"

"Stop!" She covered her ears. "I don't care. You can have whatever you want."

"I want you." He stepped toward her. "I want you, Mara. You're all I want. I'd chuck everything if I could get you to trust me. Trust me? I can't even get you to forgive me. I gave that money to the fort project so Todd's dream could come true. But you won't accept the things I've tried to do to atone for his death. You still haven't forgiven me, have you?"

"Brock, I—"

"No, you still talk about Todd as though he's alive. You tell me you can hear his voice and see the two of you doing things together. You're still holding on to him, aren't you? You're still in love with him, aren't you?"

"I'll always love Todd, but—"

"That's what I thought. And you'll never forgive me for what happened on those cliffs. If you can't forgive and forget, Mara, how can we ever escape the past and build ourselves a future?"

His eyes were red-rimmed, his jaw clenched with suppressed emotion. Suddenly she wanted nothing more than to feel his arms around her. Nothing mattered but this man and the love she felt for him.

"It's you, too," she said, her voice almost a whisper. "You haven't let go of the past, and you can't forgive yourself. What future does that leave us, Brock?"

Shaking his head, he backed away from her and swung around. He grabbed his hat from the rack by the door and threw his coat over one shoulder. As he pulled open the door, she called out.

"Brock, where are you going?"

"Climbing," he growled.

Mara watched through the kitchen window as Brock loaded the back of his pickup with climbing gear. Ropes, more ropes. Gloves. Rock shoes. Belt. Harness.

She chewed on her bottom lip. She should stop him. She should run right outside and throw her arms around him and somehow find a way to work everything out.

No, she should let him go. If he wanted to climb up the side of a cliff, let him break his damn neck. She hated climbing! She hated all his crazy recklessness. She hated his money and his stubbornness and his devil-may-care selfishness.

But as his pickup pulled out of the driveway and started down the road, Mara realized that wasn't true at all. She didn't hate him. She loved him. She loved his smile, the sound of his voice, his intelligence, his kindness. She loved the way he put his feet on the table when he relaxed. The way he held Abby against his bare chest. The way he laughed. The way he loved her.

And that was all there was to it, she admitted, dropping into a chair by the window. Sex. She just wanted him for the sex. He was so good, the mere thought of the man left her damp and aching. Sherry had been right on the money about that one. Mara was simply a lonely widow on the rebound, and Brock would give her what she wanted until he got bored with it.

Mara stood again and studied the plume of dust that rose high against the setting sun. Let him go. Let him climb away, from her, far away until he was back in his world of race cars, parachutes and hang gliders. She had a daughter, a job, responsibilities. Any woman with an ounce of sense would move out of the house, rent an apartment, get as far from Brock Barnett as possible.

With a jolt, Mara realized her childhood dream had come true. She could use her job as a stepping-stone to freedom.

For the first time in her life, she could live on her own—fully capable and independent.

In fact, she would call Sherry right now. They could go apartment hunting in the morning. By Sunday night, she could have everything moved out of Brock's house and be living on her own.

She walked into the great room and picked up the phone. A quick succession of buttons, two rings, and her best friend's voice came on the line.

"Hello?"

Mara tried to speak. *Tell me I'm a fool to love Brock. Tell me I'm crazy to want him. Tell me he's no good. Tell me I'll regret it for the rest of my life.*

"Hello?" Sherry said again. "Well, I'll be doggone."

As the phone went dead in her ear, Mara stared blindly at the side table. She placed the receiver on the smooth wood and thought of the man whose hands had sawed, nailed, planed, sanded and oiled it. Brock. Oh, Brock!

As her eyes focused again, two little boxes sharpened into view. One was sleek and polished on the outside, perfectly created and so handsome it made her sigh. The other was lovingly, tenderly made of Popsicle sticks.

Brock and Todd.

Mara picked up the Popsicle stick box and held it for a moment. She could almost see Todd's freckled fingers carefully gluing the little sticks in place. His tongue would be firmly tucked between his teeth, and his red-blond hair would spill over his forehead as he concentrated on the job.

Mara blinked back tears. She would always love her teddy-bear Todd. He was the man she had married, promised her future to and lived with for five years. He was the man who had given Abby life. Was it wrong to mourn him? Was it wrong to hold his memory inside her heart?

"No," Mara said out loud. It wasn't wrong.

She ran her fingers over the uneven surface of the little box. Then she lifted the lid. Inside lay a jumble of stones. Brock's rock collection. Some of them obviously had been purchased at a curio shop, machine-polished chunks with dots of glue and paper still attached where they had been pried from their cardboard mounting. Others must have been found in the New Mexico landscape—rose quartz, obsidian, granite, mica.

Mara dug through the stones, lifting each one and holding it to the fading light. Included among them was a piece of hardened rubber tire and a pebble of gravel from the driveway. When she came across a shard of broken glass from a soda bottle, she had to smile. No doubt the little boy Brock thought he had found a diamond.

Then she picked up the smooth box he had made her for Christmas that year. She lifted the lid and gazed at the wedding rings she had put inside it. They were small and rather plain, but she had always loved them. Now her fingers were as bare as Brock's promises on their wedding day.

Did he love her? Did he plan to spend the rest of his life faithful to her? She didn't know. And what about his accusation that she had never forgiven him? Well, *had* she forgiven Brock for asking Todd to climb those cliffs with him? Had she forgiven Todd for dying?

Most important, Mara thought as she shut the lid on her rings, had she forgiven herself and let go of the root of bitterness in her heart? She brushed her hand across her damp cheek.

Her options stood out as clearly as the two little boxes on the table. She could keep loving and living with the memory of the Popsicle stick, teddy-bear Todd, and she could view Brock as the slick manipulator who couldn't commit and didn't have the capacity to love or make a successful marriage. With those underpinnings to strengthen her, she could take her daughter away from this house, use her job to support the two of them, create a life of her own. The voice of sanity and reason instructed her firmly that this should be her decision.

If not, she could take the greatest risk of her life. She could go after Brock and hand over to him her love, her heart, her future—and her daughter's future. She could choose to put Todd's memory away in his Popsicle stick box, always loving him but always letting him go. And she could choose to see Brock as the man who cradled her baby, who put his money where his heart was, who told her again and again how much he wanted her.

Maybe he didn't love her. Maybe he didn't know how to love. But all the same, she could choose to give her heart to the man who believed broken glass was diamonds.

Mara stared at the telephone. Then at the two boxes.

Chapter 20

The moon gleamed like a silver Christmas ornament cushioned in the dusky blue velvet of gathering night. Stars spangled the winter sky, twinkling in the crisp air. Along the road, dry yucca stems rattled as a jackrabbit tore at a clump of brown grass. A barn owl winged across the open plain, its shadow black against the gray ground beneath it.

Mara steered her car down the bumpy road and hoped the rumble of the engine would put Abby back to sleep. She had thought about leaving the baby with Ramona, then decided against it. This was a family matter.

As she drove toward the dilapidated trading post, she realized her stomach was churning. Had Brock gone to his old climbing place? Or had he chosen somewhere new, somewhere unfamiliar? What if he was halfway up the cliffs? What if he had fallen?

Dear God! She chewed on her bottom lip, praying earnestly in the silence of the car. Don't let him fall. Don't let him die. I love him. Abby loves him . . . Abby needs him. I need him more.

Oh, please, please. She swallowed hard as her headlights picked out the smooth brown edges of the former store.

With sweaty palms, she steered the car into the open area behind the old building. As she cut the engine, she looked out her window. The cliffs towered above, so high they seemed to touch the moon.

Brock, she breathed as she scanned the vertical face. Please, Brock. Blue denim...black hair...blue denim. Where was he? God, please show me where he is!

She glanced at her sleeping baby, then she pushed open the car door. Tilting back her head, she searched every crevice, every outcrop, every slab of flat stone. Her eyes followed the rise and fall of each shadow, each glistening mound. There! A dark form clung to the side of the cliff, legs outstretched. Mara sucked in a breath. Brock!

No, it was a tree with bare limbs and exposed roots that had grown in a nook of the rock.

Her hands knotted as she peered into the growing darkness. Where was he? Oh, Brock! She let her focus drop lower and lower, terrified that she would find his crumpled, broken body sprawled at the bottom. She couldn't look. Couldn't.

"Brock..."

He was standing at the base of the cliff, his head bent and his expression one of such sadness and loss Mara thought her heart might break.

"Brock," she said more loudly.

When he heard her and lifted his head, the tension in his face eased. He straightened, stepped away from the cliff wall and simply said, "You came."

"I couldn't let you go, Brock."

"Mara...I don't want to go up that cliff."

"That's not what I meant." She walked toward him. "I can't let you go, Brock. I don't want to lose you."

"Mara."

As they came together, he pulled her into his arms and held her tightly, so tightly he knew she could hardly breathe. He rocked her back and forth, unable to speak, unable to think beyond the miracle that she had come to him.

"I love you, Mara," he said, his voice rough. "I love you. Everything I've done, every damn fool thing I've said is because I love you. And I don't know how to let you know."

"Say it, Brock. Say the words again. Say them every day, a hundred times a day."

"I love you, Mara."

"Oh, I love you, Brock."

He lifted her off her feet and turned her around and around. "Lord, I feel crazy! I feel free. I'm a man who just got out of prison, Mara. I can say it and mean it and count on it. I love you. I love you."

She laughed through her tears. "Don't let me go!"

"Never. But I would have, Mara. I'd have done anything for you. I gave that money to honor Todd and take care of the people he loved. If I could keep his dream alive, I knew it would be within your reach. I wanted you to stop feeling chained to me and my damn money." He shook his head. "Instead, I made you think I'd bought you the job."

"It's okay, Brock. I understand now."

"I don't have the power to make you stay with me, Mara. I can only hope you want to. I hoped...and I prayed. But tonight I was sure I'd lost you."

She laid her cheek on his broad shoulder and tightened her arms around his chest. The feel of his body was so solid and good, she wished she could hold him this way forever.

"I want to stay with you, Brock," she murmured. "I don't ever want to go."

He swallowed at the gritty knot in his throat. "What about Todd?"

"What about him?"

"He's Abby's father."

"Todd gave Abby life. He gave her that red-gold sheen to her hair and that funny smile on her lips. But Todd isn't the father she knows. Only one man can be that to her." Mara looked up at him. "You're Abby's father, Brock."

He lifted his eyes to the stars in disbelief at the joy welling up inside his chest. "I'd do anything for that little girl."

"I know."

"I love her, Mara, and I don't know how it happened. Look at me—I'm not equipped to do a decent job of parenting. I don't have the training. But I'll tell you, I'd give my life for her."

"I'm not worried about your qualifications for the job, Brock," Mara murmured. "You're a natural."

"You reckon?"

She ran her hand down the side of his face, reveling in the rough brush of his whiskered jaw. "No doubt."

"But what about Todd?" he asked again. "Todd and you?"

Mara let out a shaky breath. "I've been so afraid to let go of him. I've been afraid to let go of my anger, my hurt, my grief. Somehow it seemed like if I kept all that, Todd wouldn't ever really leave. I could keep him real and alive. But he's gone, Brock." She looked at his face through the blurring mist in her eyes. "I want to let him go."

"I'll never forget him," he said, "but I want to let him go, too."

"Tell me what happened. Tell me about that day on the cliff."

He turned away from her and sat down on a fallen boulder. Burying his face in his hands, he fought the pain. For so long he'd been wanting to talk. Could he do it now, when telling Mara might push her away again?

Only when he felt her slip to his side and settle on the ground at his feet could he speak. "It was getting dark because we'd been climbing all day. We made the decision to down-climb the cliff without ropes. Rappelling can take a lot of time because you have to secure the equipment or it's not trustworthy, and Todd was afraid we'd have to leave something behind. He never liked to do that. Thought it was wasteful."

Mara nodded, picturing the thrifty Todd.

"We checked to see that the route was free of loose rock, and we started down. I'd been there before a few times, so I led. We started down, face out with our backs to the wall. Then the angle got steeper." Again the unavoidable memory of that day flashed in Brock's mind. He paused. "You want me to go on?"

Mara tucked her bottom lip between her teeth and nodded.

"I knew we needed to turn around and face the cliff wall, and I wanted to use a rope at that point, just to be safe. I tossed my rope to Todd. He caught the end of it. We stretched it between us, and he was trying to anchor it—"

Waiting for him to continue, Mara could feel the pain of memory wracking through his body. For the first time since Todd's death, she became the comforter. She laid her head on his thigh and kissed his knee.

He didn't speak for more than a minute. When he did, his voice was rough and broken. "He had hammered in a piton, and he put some weight on it to test it. The thing popped out, and Todd started sliding. He cried out to me. 'Brock!' I reached for him, but he tumbled past me too fast. I grabbed at his hand. I missed."

He shook his head. "I missed, Mara. I missed!"

She knew her tears were soaking through his jeans. "Where was the rope?"

"I thought he had it. I jerked at my end to bring him up tight and steady, but he'd already let go. I shouted at him, but he kept falling. He rolled and rolled, and I saw him hit his head. When he came to a stop, I was already halfway down to him. I don't know how I did it without ropes. It was like I flew, like this blur of rock rushing past me as I scrambled down, screaming at him."

"Oh, Brock."

"When I got to him, I knew it was over. I lifted his head and held it in my lap. He was gone, Mara. Just like that. Gone."

He sat weeping as she slipped into his arms and stroked his back. "It's okay, Brock."

"I should have put in the pitons myself. I should have told him to secure the rope. I've down-climbed cliffs a thousand times, and I didn't warn him! I should have caught him. I should have reached out just that much farther and caught him, Mara. Why didn't I? Why?"

"Brock, it's all right." She molded her hands around his damp face and lifted his chin. In the moonlight, she read his anguish. "It's over. It was an accident. I forgive you, Brock. You didn't even need to tell me the story. I forgave you a long time ago."

He brushed his eyes with his sleeve. "I needed to tell it."

"Brock—thank you. Todd's life was richer for having you as his friend."

He studied her. "I love you, Mara." He glanced upward, then at her. "And I don't have to climb that cliff."

As his lips met hers, she responded with all the pent-up emotion of the last hours. Peace...the feeling descended over her like a warm cape. She felt at peace with this man, at peace with herself, at peace with their future. His hands caressed her shoulders, and his fingers threaded through her hair. Wanting more of him, she kissed his neck and tasted the salt on his cheeks. He spread his legs as he sat on the rock, and she slipped between them. Together they drank in the moment of promise.

"Mara," he murmured, tilting her face into the moonlight. "I love you, you know."

"Keep telling me," she said softly. "Take me home and hold me and tell me again and again."

"I'll show you how much I love you."

They stood and started toward their vehicles. Suddenly, Brock stopped. "Oh, yeah." He unsnapped the flap of his shirt pocket and fished around in it for a moment. "I almost forgot. I've been carrying this damn thing around for a week."

Mara stiffened as he held out his hand. A circle of diamonds caught the moonlight—so shimmery she felt as though a spell had been cast over her.

"I'd like my wife to wear a ring," he said. "If she will."

"Oh, Brock." She held out her left hand. Gently, he slid the sparkling circlet over her third finger. "It's beautiful."

"I'd like a church wedding, too. It's the only way I can think of to let everyone know neither of us is up for grabs. Besides, I want to announce my promise to love you forever so the whole countryside can hear it."

"Forever, Brock?"

"As long as we both shall live." He gave her a quick kiss. "What do you say to that?"

"I say, amen," Mara answered with a laugh.

At that, he swung her off her feet and lifted her into his arms. As he started back toward the waiting vehicles, he shook his head. "First we have a baby, then a marriage, then a honeymoon, then an engagement, and last of all a wedding. We're a mixed-up pair, you know that?"

"I want the honeymoon again," she whispered. "Lots of times."

"You got it."

They were almost to the car when Mara heard the distinctive sound of Abby's restless wake-up cry. "Oh, dear," she said softly.

"You brought the baby?" His face broke into a grin.

Brock let Mara slide to the ground and opened the door to the car. She watched him edge his big shoulders into the open space. As he bent to unbuckle the crying baby, she heard him murmur.

"It's okay, honey. Don't cry anymore. Daddy's here."

* * * * *

Get Ready to be Swept Away by
Silhouette's Spring Collection

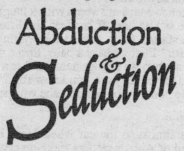

Abduction & Seduction

These passion-filled stories explore both the dangerous
desires of men and the seductive powers of women.
Written by three of our most celebrated authors, they are
sure to capture your hearts.

Diana Palmer
Brings us a spin-off of her Long, Tall Texans series

Joan Johnston
Crafts a beguiling Western romance

Rebecca Brandewyne
New York Times bestselling author
makes a smashing contemporary debut

Available in March at your favorite retail outlet.

HEARTBREAKERS

Hot on the heels of **American Heroes** comes Silhouette Intimate Moments' latest and greatest lineup of men: **Heartbreakers.** They know who they are—and *who* they want. And they're out to steal your heart.

RITA award-winning author Emilie Richards kicks off the series in March 1995 with *Duncan's Lady,* IM #625. Duncan Sinclair believed in hard facts, cold reality and his daughter's love. Then sprightly Mara MacTavish challenged his beliefs—and hardened heart—with her magical allure.

In April *New York Times* bestseller Nora Roberts sends hell-raiser Rafe MacKade home in *The Return of Rafe MacKade,* IM #631. Rafe had always gotten what he wanted—until Regan Bishop came to town. She resisted his rugged charm and seething sensuality, but it was only a matter of time....

Don't miss these first two **Heartbreakers,** from two stellar authors, found only in—

Silhouette celebrates motherhood in May with...

Debbie Macomber
Jill Marie Landis
Gina Ferris Wilkins

in

Three
Mothers
& a Cradle

Join three award-winning authors in this beautiful collection you'll treasure forever. The same antique, hand-crafted cradle connects these three heartwarming romances, which celebrate the joys and excitement of motherhood. Makes the perfect gift for yourself or a loved one!

A special celebration of love,

Only from

Silhouette®

—where passion lives.

Southern
Knights

Join Marilyn Pappano in March 1995 as her **Southern Knights** series draws to a dramatic close with *A Man Like Smith*, IM #626.

Federal prosecutor Smith Kendricks was on a manhunt. His prey: crime boss Jimmy Falcone. But when his quest for justice led to ace reporter Jolie Wade, he found himself desiring both her privileged information—and the woman herself....

Don't miss the explosive conclusion to the **Southern Knights** miniseries, only in—

INTIMATE MOMENTS®
™ *Silhouette*®

THE MEN OF MIDNIGHT

RITA award-winning author Emilie Richards launches her new miniseries, **The Men of Midnight,** in March 1995 with *Duncan's Lady,* IM #625.

Single father Duncan Sinclair believed in hard facts and cold reality, not mist and magic. But sprightly Mara MacTavish challenged his staid beliefs—and hardened heart—with her spellbinding allure, charming both Duncan and his young daughter.

Don't miss **The Men of Midnight,** tracing the friendship of Duncan, Iain and Andrew—*three men born at the stroke of twelve and destined for love beyond their wildest dreams,* only in—

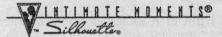

INTIMATE MOMENTS®
Silhouette®

MENM1

Men and women hungering for passion to soothe their lonely souls. Watch for the new Intimate Moments miniseries by

Beverly Bird

It begins in March 1995 with

A MAN WITHOUT LOVE (Intimate Moments #630)
Catherine Landano was running scared—and straight into the arms of enigmatic Navaho Jericho Bedonie. Would he be her savior...or her destruction?

Continues in May...

A MAN WITHOUT A HAVEN (Intimate Moments #641)
The word *forever* was not in Mac Tshongely's vocabulary. Nevertheless, he found himself drawn to headstrong Shadow Bedonie and the promise of tomorrow that this sultry woman offered. Could home really be where the heart is?

And concludes in July 1995 with

A MAN WITHOUT A WIFE (Intimate Moments #652)
Seven years ago Ellen Lonetree had made a decision that haunted her days and nights. Now she had the chance to be reunited with the child she'd lost—if she could resist the attraction she felt for the little boy's adoptive father...and keep both of them from discovering her secret.

$\blacktriangledown$ *Silhouette*® ...where passion lives.

BBWW-1